TAINTED
BLOOD

TAINTED BLOOD

FERREL D. MOORE

2012

Tainted Blood is published by White Cat Publications, LLC.
Copyright © 2011 Ferrel D. Moore

Cover art copyright © 2011 Sergey Kalinin
Rear cover art copyright © 2011 James and Jane Baxter
Cover design copyright © 2011 Melanie Hooyenga
Interior design copyright © 2011 Natasha Fondren

Edited by Charles P. Zaglanis

FIRST EDITION
10 9 8 7 6 5 4 3 2 1
ISBN 978-0-9846920-0-2
Published in January 2012
Printed in the U.S.A.

Published by White Cat Publications, LLC.
33080 Industrial Road, Suite 101
Livonia, MI 48150

www.whitecatpublications.com

Acknowledgments

Tainted Blood could not have been written without the love and support of my family and friends or the tireless efforts of my editor, Charles P. Zaglanis.

It is dedicated to Ninja Grandmaster Robert Law and Michel Farivar, M.D. The Grandmaster taught me to think for myself and to act on what I learned. Michel Farivar, M.D., who will one day take on the mantle of Grandmaster Law's ancient art, showed me the grace and respect to allow me to come to grip with the struggles of my life on my own terms. I have found no better friends or teachers than they in my life.

CHAPTER ONE

Sveta made a mistake when she signed on with Hauck. Now she just had to live through whatever was coming and get out alive.

Evgeny was posted with a sniper rifle and a spotter somewhere in the vicinity to cover the extraction. They never knew where Hauck positioned him on any given mission. He was always watching over them, as invisible as Hauck himself. Motionless in the cold, scanning with a Trijicon ACOG scope while Yuri's electronic spotters fed him information.

Yuri was their eyes and ears. He was posted two blocks off Fort Street in a white delivery van jammed full of electronics; his face would be moving from monitor to monitor like a hunter scanning the woods. Bodin, Yuri's bodyguard, squatted on a steel bench near the van's double back doors, clutching his SIG 550 assault rifle, his eyes concentrated on what lay outside the vehicle. Yuri and his computers were the heart of the operation; both were too valuable to leave unguarded. Sveta knew that in the monitor's pale radiance his eyes would gleam like liquid mercury. Tonight, their silvery brightness would shine with images of burned out vacant houses in Detroit that looked like Warsaw after the bombings.

"What do you see?" asked Hauck.

His voice in her electronic ear bud was as clear as if he were standing next to her.

"Hooker giving head in the doorway where that Mexican restaurant was," said Yuri. "Couple of bags blowing down the sidewalk."

"Any traffic?"

Sveta winced at Hauck's tone, and pressed closer against the back wall of a garage one block away from the target house. Waiting for Crue and Chenko to show up. Trying to steady her nerves. Calming breaths weren't cutting it. She had a bad feeling about tonight. The air was cold and moist and smelled faintly like a smoker's car; the peculiar odor made her impatient. Something nagging at her thoughts. She wondered what was taking Crue and his repulsive partner so long.

According to their best information, Drogol was the only person living in the four block area of abandoned houses. Most people seemed to avoid the area subconsciously. Earlier recons failed to turn up even a homeless person. Evgeny reported back to Hauck that the only living creatures he could find moving among the broken glass and crumbled bricks were the "fucking rats."

Hauck never took things for granted. He'd lost Drogol once many years ago, he'd told them, and wasn't going to let him get away again. One last recon before they moved in. Sveta was glad it was Crue leading the sweep. She trusted him. He was one of the team. Slabs of muscle assembled into a six foot four frame. Twin Makarov PM pistols always with him. Three time winner of the IPA Kirov shooting championship. Someone who had proved himself trustworthy under fire.

Chenko, however, was another matter. A thin faced Muscovite with corrosive breath brought in by Hauck to take the old man known as Drogol back to Russia after they captured him. Why Chenko was chosen to do this, no one questioned. That was one of the things that bothered her. He reeked of Russian Mafia or Russian Police. Maybe both. Sveta wanted to ask Hauck straight out who Chenko really worked for, but she knew better.

Hauck gave instructions, not answers.

All she did know, if they were told the truth, was that thirty years ago, Drogol killed fourteen men and wounded Hauck while escaping from a high security prison outside of Moscow. Hauck was the KGB agent in charge of Drogol's case file. He was held responsible. A price was placed on the spymaster's head and he'd been on the run ever since. When they captured Drogol tonight and turned him over to Chenko, that price would finally be eliminated. He could retire without looking over his shoulder. He could come in from the cold.

That was the plan, anyway. That was what he'd told them and why he was paying them. What worried Sveta was what he hadn't told them.

"All clear," Crue's voice came through her headset.

Overhead, restless clouds pushed and growled at each other as Sveta looked up and down the alley, her irritation building. If Crue didn't hurry up and finish, they'd be working in the rain.

Sveta saw Crue and Chenko emerge from the shadows on the opposite side of the alley, their bodies like luminescent ghosts in her night vision goggles. Crue's green-white form towered over Chenko.

"Let's move," said Sveta.

Unease gripped her stomach as she stalked silently forward, like she'd reached the top of a dangerous roller coaster and was about to plunge over the downward side. Chenko couldn't be trusted; she'd known that as soon as she met him. He wasn't one of them. He dressed like a convict on parole and Sveta felt his eyes on her even when her back was to him.

And there were the mercury filled bullets. Why were they using them and why did Hauck shut down anyone who questioned their use? Who was this old man they were hunting and why was Hauck insisting they use mercury bullets on him if he gave them trouble? He was, according to Hauck, fifty years old when he escaped Ryazan. He would be nearly eighty now. Why were they going after an eighty year old man with mercury bullets?

Something was very, very wrong. The others might not sense it because they'd been with Hauck a long time. She was the new hire, called in at the last minute when he decided he was one short for this mission after a car crash took out one of his regulars. With the kind of money he paid, she didn't ask the questions she should have. She hadn't left the GRU on the best of terms and needed the cover Hauck could provide. If only she didn't have the sense that Hauck was lying to them.

Her father, a general in Soviet Army intelligence, once warned her that at least once in their career every operative had to choose between loyalty and life. "If your organization has betrayed you," he told her, "choose life."

They moved slowly, keeping to the edges of the alley. Sveta to one side, Crue and Chenko on the other. Sveta pulled her Stechkin APS free from its holster.

The wind suddenly whipped down the alley like a kid running from cops, ducking in and out of shadows and jumping fences. Yuri gave the team the forecasted weather details down to the minute before they left, including the good news of a thick cloud cover to hide their activities. Sveta's gaze swept the alley before them. Overhead, the sky looked as if it'd been painted over like the windows of a Moscow interrogation room.

"Twenty feet from the backyard," Sveta reported.

"Keep it low, keep it soft," Hauck's seductive voice whispered in her earphone. "No more talking."

Prick, Sveta thought.

She'd never seen his face. Humphrey Bogart and Hugh Jackman were her current fantasy favorites. But Hauck stayed out of sight, always in the background. Invisible. Brilliant. Handsome and with a sense of élan about him. A man of wealth and discernment. Or, a fat, sweaty old spy who smoked cigarettes one after the other and wore cheap aftershave. Sveta preferred the former but feared the latter. She'd never met a good-looking spy.

What he was, though, was a persuasive digital phantom who ordered them about like a chessmaster pushing pawns.

*****

Crue sprayed the hinges of the back gate. The chemical glowed like radioactive waste in the night vision goggles. After a few seconds, he gently pushed it open and Sveta slid in. Crue grinned at her for good luck.

Trees and bushes choked the yard. The house, one light on in a wide second floor window, was quiet. It was three a.m. and thin ethereal puffs of fog floated in and out of the tree branches. Ground fog hovered over the yard. Sveta knew that wherever he was, Evgeny was not happy. Fog was not a sniper's best friend.

Before moving forward, Sveta considered the lighted double window. *Drogol probably fell asleep reading in bed*, she thought.

The night air was cold even for late October, and Sveta told herself that was why she felt the back of her neck prickle. Three operatives against an eighty year old man. There was no reason to be afraid.

But her intuition still told her this was a much more dangerous mission than she'd been led to believe.

They were halfway across the yard when Sveta held up her hand for Crue and Chenko to stop. The upstairs light was now off. She pointed at it with her left hand. Crue nodded.

Sveta motioned them to fan out.

Before they could obey her orders, glass exploded high overhead.

Sveta looked up to see something massive hurtle from the second story window frame as a blood-freezing howl shook the night. She jumped to her right, hit the ground and rolled back to her feet as something crashed through the bushes and slammed into the ground. A pulsating green-white glow rose from within the shrubbery in front of her. Eight—maybe ten feet tall—with eyes white as LED's. Sveta felt her chest constrict. What she was seeing was not possible.

From her left she heard a short burst of shots and knew without turning it was Crue letting loose. Sveta felt cold terror flood through her as she raised her own pistol to fire. But the thing moved so quickly all she saw was a blur of angry light across her night vision goggles.

"What the hell is that?" Yuri shouted in her ear.

"Bodin, move in," said Hauck. "Now. They need backup."

Sveta reacquired the target but saw it lift a body up between the two of them, blocking her shot. Chenko screamed and tried to break free as Crue fired off another burst. The creature snapped its jaws and bit through Chenko's neck. Sveta fired straight at the beast's head.

"Evgeny," she heard Hauck say, "have you got a target?"

"No."

"Why not?" demanded Hauck.

"Too bright, too big. Can't tell it from them."

"It's fucking huge," Yuri yelled into her ear.

"Move, Bodin," snapped Hauck.

Crue ran toward it, not away. His image was a man-sized blur firing as he walked straight at the thing.

Sveta saw the shape of its head—like a giant demon wolf. She shot it three times in the throat. The beast slapped one hand over its windpipe and roared like a jet engine. Three bullets in the throat, and it was still standing. It swung its head between her and Crue. She fired again to distract it from Crue, but it went for him anyway.

"Get back," Hauck shouted.

Too late.

A blur of white claws and Sveta saw Crue's' ripped neck spray blood like green white rain into the night. Six more bullets to the back of its head while it shredded Crue, ripping off his bulletproof vest and ammo belts; biting off one arm.

Sveta knew it was time to get out. She ran toward the gate but heard the beast ripping up the ground behind her, smashing through trees and bushes like they weren't there. She veered left through a tangle of trees, ejecting one clip and slamming another in place as she bobbed and weaved past low-hanging branches. Her heart pounded with each step. She didn't look back, but she could feel the thing behind her, closing fast.

It shrieked and she heard it hit the ground.

Evgeny to the rescue. Somewhere on a rooftop his scope found the monster.

She ran to a tall plank fence and a found a spot where the boards were loose. She pivoted to one side and broke them in half with a kick, then spun back, pistol extended. The thing was on its feet again and looking right at her.

Suddenly Bodin appeared like a ghost behind the beast, firing round after round. Sveta tried to tell him to run, but nothing could be heard over the sounds of the enraged creature. She fired, but it was already on Bodin. His screams were the last thing she heard as she squeezed through the hole in the fence.

CHAPTER TWO

Sveta crouched low as she ran through the bushes at the back of the house. Couldn't hear anything behind her. She didn't know where Evgeny or the others were and she didn't care. Crue, Chenko and Bodin were dead. Yuri and Hauck were shouting into her ear buds. She ripped them free and tossed them into the dark.

Got to keep moving. Her intuition was right and she had to act now. She had to make a clean break.

Hauck must have known about the beast. He sent them right into a deathtrap. To survive, she needed to focus on staying alive. Life over loyalty.

She ran through the adjacent yards as fast as she could. The alley was dark and she spun left without so much as glancing either way. She and Crue took out all of the alley pole lights with air guns the night before. Evgeny had night vision, but she thought he would be concentrating on the yards, thinking she would avoid the alley. As soon as they found out she'd deserted the team, she would be a legitimate target. If they could catch her.

Sveta moved quietly as she could, but concentrated on running fast and hard while the situation was confused. With no good options to choose from, she picked direction and kept going. One course and keep to it until she could boost a car and escape.

Drogol was Hauck's primary target, she thought. She was now a secondary objective and not worth the trouble if they could take the old man instead. But that was his problem. She had to focus on survival. Besides, if she managed to escape, they would come for her later. No one left Hauck and stayed alive for long, but Sveta would be the exception to that rule.

She adjusted her night vision goggles before she got to a fence and quickly scanned for a dog. Nothing. Up and over the twisted chain link and moving across the yard swinging her head from side to side. She crouched low and listened.

Still nothing. She relaxed, turned around and was surprised to see a young woman standing near the edge of the yard looking straight at her. In Sveta's night vision goggles, the woman's face was pale green.

"Hurry," whispered the young woman, urgently motioning toward Sveta with her hands. "Follow me. There is no time."

Sveta raised the Stechkin APS again and pointed it straight at her.

"Quickly," said the young woman. "Put away the gun. I have a car. Drogol sent me to help you. We've got to get moving or we'll both be dead."

The choice was whether or not to shoot her. One shot to take her down and then keep moving. The right move or not? Whose side was this girl really on?

It was a gut call. She would sort it out later. Sveta quit thinking and followed, wondering instead who she feared most—Evgeny or the wolf or the FSB? Hauck. She feared Hauck most of all.

"Where's your car?" she asked.

Without turning, the girl whispered back, "Two blocks down toward Fort Street. But there's a streetlight and we'll have to walk in the open for a short way."

"No. You bring the car," said Sveta. "Then pull into this driveway like you're changing directions. Wait. Unscrew the overhead dome light first. Then open the door as soon as you stop in the driveway. I'll get in, and then we can take off. I'll stay low. With any luck, one of them won't shoot you."

The girl stared back at her, thick hair tossing about in a sudden gust of wind. Dressed in a long dark coat with wide eyes pale bright in the night vision. Then she nodded, turned and began walking away. Her footsteps clicked like a timer.

Sveta glanced around into the back of the yard, looking for movement, for the form of someone or something. Nothing. Nothing but a backyard. A scream cut the night a short distance away followed by a single shot. Then silence. Not even a siren. She moved a few steps forward and pressed herself against the side of the house in case a light came on, but none did. In Detroit, as in so many ruined cities she had been in, people stayed inside and pretended they didn't hear.

The Stechkin felt heavy in her hand.

Headlights suddenly lit the street. Sveta took in a sharp breath of cold air as she ducked behind the porch, turned off her night vision, flipped the goggles up and raised her weapon. Suddenly the car pulled into the driveway, came to a quick stop and the woman driving it flicked the lights off but left the engine running.

"Hurry," she urged. "Get in the car. He can no longer control the beast."

Sveta hesitated only a second. It was suicide to stay. She took another deep breath, then crouched and raced to the car. The passenger side door flew open and after a quick glance inside to see that the young woman alone, she got in.

"Go," she said, keeping the Stechkin raised and scanning the dark yards to either side.

The girl backed out of the driveway, threw the car into drive and hit the accelerator.

"Slow down," ordered Sveta.

But parked just ahead no more than a block away, she saw Yuri's white van. Before she could react something large and black ran across the street and smashed head on into it. The van rocked up and over and crashed onto its side. She saw the windshield split and sections of shattered glass spill onto the pavement.

"Go," Sveta shouted.

The girl jammed the gas pedal all the way to the floor.

Sveta jerked back, but quickly pulled forward, nearly jamming her nose into the glass. She saw the animal leap onto the van and rip the driver's side door off its hinges, throwing it onto the street. It bounced high in front of them—she thought it was going to crash down on the hood of their car—but the girl twisted the wheel to the left. The door crumpled and bounced again, missing them by a few feet, spraying pieces of glass like a showerhead spraying water. They flew past it as Sveta looked back over her shoulder to see a struggling man pulled out by a dark blur and thrown into the air like a discarded toy.

"What was that?" said Sveta.

She turned to face the girl, who hunched over the steering wheel and sped away as though being chased by the devil himself.

"Where's Drogol?" she asked.

"He'll find us," said the girl. "You can't hide from Drogol."

Sveta was too pumped with adrenalin to notice the bloodstain on the girl's coat.

*****

"Chenko," repeated Hauck. "What's happening?"

The scar that ran across the left side of his throat came alive with heat. He pressed his palm over it, tried to concentrate, and said again, "What is going on?"

The old man in the kitchen hadn't moved. He sat drinking tea with the light off watching Hauck. They had spoken only a few words all night. Hauck knew why he was present. The woman with the cigarette stained teeth had sent him. If Hauck didn't produce Drogol, then the old man would deliver her Hauck's head packed in ice. Hauck pushed the thought aside.

The man was an old school Soviet named Andrei. His voice was like sandpaper dragged across cement. Hauck understood why he did not like talking. Also, this man was unimpressed by conversation. His years locked away in a Siberian Gulag had seen to that. Hauck didn't need to glance back toward the kitchen to know that the bulky old man with the shaved head and the broken face was still there, still watching. One hand on his teacup, the other on his pistol.

Crue, Chenko and Bodin down. Another on the run, thought Hauck. The operation was out of control.

He changed channels and spoke again.

"Evgeny, Yuri. I've got backup personnel on the way. This is like Ryazan all over again. Evgeny, move into position and cover their approach. Forget Sveta. We'll deal with her later. Drogol is everything. Yuri, is she still on the grid?"

"Absolutely."

"Where?"

"Looks like a block and a half away, but moving."

"Moving where?"

"Away."

"Evgeny, let her go. Repeat, let her go. She is unimportant now. Yuri, both bugs are live with good signal strength?"

"Absolutely."

"Excellent. Evgeny, take position to cover the back door. Rodin and Shestapolov should be at the front of the house now. Yuri?"

"They're there and heading around back."

"Shestapolov. Pull up short and let Sveta leave. She's bugged and findable and unimportant just now. We need Drogol. He's the target. Understand?"

"Understood," came back Shestapolov's thick voice.

"Evgeny?"

"In place."

"Yuri, pull in Leonid and have him trail Sveta. No contact and tell him if she makes him I'll shoot him myself."

"Got it."

Hauck paced back and forth in front of the monitors.

"Shestapolov—you and Rodin move in and take that thing down. Use the Rail Gun if you have to."

Behind him, he felt cold disdain emanating from the man at the kitchen table. It was as though someone had opened a freezer door.

They had four tiny video cameras posted around Drogol's neighborhood. Hauck looked at the images from two of them placed side by side on the monitors, and saw Shestapolov and Rodin move in, their high tech weaponry held in front of them like wards.

In the eerie image of the night vision cameras, details sometimes blurred. He leaned forward frowning, his head inches from the screen. There was movement behind him. He heard a chair scraped over linoleum and the brush of a heavy man past a table. He felt the man's bulk press close behind him to peer over his shoulder at the screen, as though drawn by dark intuition.

Their attention was initially fixed on the back of the house, but the sound of bestial rage and blurred movement caught their eye from a camera on the driveway side. It glowed like a phosphor smear in motion.

"Evgeny, coming around the side of the house. Do you see it?"

"Tracking."

It was big, much bigger than a man and shot forward like a predator going in for the kill. Even though he was several blocks away, Hauck had to fight the urge to reach for his gun. It was up and moving so fast it left one screen and shot onto the other as quickly as Hauck could turn his head.

"Shestapolov," shouted Hauck. "To your right."

Shestapolov and Rodin turned simultaneously, pivoting on their heels and bringing their weapons around. A fury of bright movement was on them before they could fire. Hauck heard a vicious, triumphant snarl that flooded him with fear. Light swirls smeared with something dark spiraled across the screens. A cry from Rodin that sounded like *Mother*, but must have been something else.

"Evgeny?" called Hauck.

Above the snarls and snapping and howls, he heard the snap of arcing electricity and Shestapolov's terrified cursing; either Shestapolov or Rodin was down, and the other tried to sprint across the yard, but then the beast was on him, dragging him toward the fence line faster than Hauck could believe.

"Evgeny," he called again.

"On the move," came the terse reply.

A fat finger jutted into view before the monitor. One of the back windows of the house was glowing. Smears of furious light bled into the night. A quick, sharp blast rocked the speakers and Hauck stepped back against the immovable figure of his watcher. The man snorted and pushed him away, but bent over suddenly as he did so as though in pain. Hauck ignored him and stared at the monitor. Flames and sparks shot out the windows, turning the house into a fireworks display.

"Yuri, shut down the grid."

"Already in play."

"Evgeny, can you see it?"

"It's gone. Lost it."

"Get back to the house. Throw the bodies inside if you can and then disappear."

The sudden pressure in the middle of his back caused Hauck to reach for his gun, but the man behind him was quicker and slapped him on the back of the head, knocking him forward.

"You do not move."

Hauck felt the impact of a fist between his shoulder blades. He fell onto a monitor, gasping, grabbing it to keep from falling. It was difficult to breathe; it felt like his back was broken. His gun was yanked away from him so hard the Velcro adhered holster was ripped away with it.

"You are finished now. You have lost him. She has no need of you for nothing anymore."

A fit of coughing racked Hauck's chest as he turned over and rested on one elbow, facing the man. He wiped away blood from his split lip and stared.

"You do need something from me, still," he said, rising painfully.

"Tell me little spy—what do I need from you?"

Suddenly, the man doubled over in pain. Hauck leaned back on the desk full of monitors to catch his breath and watched him struggle. Choking noises and moaning as the man pressed his hand to his side. When he fell over, he hit the ground like a piano dropped from the ceiling.

"Hauck," came Evgeny's voice.

Hauck leaned down, retrieving his gun and that of the big man.

"I'll tell you what I have that you still need," he whispered near the writhing man's ear. "I have the antidote for the poison in those tea bags."

"Hauck," repeated Evgeny more urgently.

"Here," said Hauck.

"Too hot to get inside the house, but I tossed the bodies onto the back landing. Door was wide open from the blast."

"What caused the explosion?"

"I don't know."

"Go back to the van and get Yuri out of there," said Hauck.

He looked down at the man on the floor and stomped down on his head with his boot heel.

"Yuri?" he said into the mic.

"Here."

"What about Leonid?"

"He's keeping close behind Sveta, but out of sight."

"Good."

Things had gone horribly wrong, but Sveta survived. His confidence in her was not misplaced. That was what counted. He had other plans in play now. Plans within plans. Drogol would find her and then he would find and kill Drogol.

"You want him to stay back or bring her in?"

Hauck laughed.

"Tell him to stay back. She'd kill him before he got his gun out of his holster."

The connection with Yuri went dead when the beast slammed into Yuri's van.

CHAPTER THREE

What did you mean about him not being able to control the beast? And who is 'him'?" asked Sveta.

No answer.

"Are you all right?"

The car weaved back and forth. They were slowing down. The young woman's face looked pale and when she turned to answer Sveta, her eyes wouldn't stay focused. She let go of the wheel and toppled over onto Sveta's shoulder. The car began to slow more quickly.

A sudden, panicked instinct caused Sveta to turn and look behind them. Although they were several blocks away from where the beast knocked over the van, she thought she saw something racing after them down the middle of the street.

"Wake up," she said frantically.

The woman didn't answer.

"Shit."

The thing chasing them grew impossibly larger as it came bounding down the street straight at their car. Sveta pushed the young woman's limp form over against the driver's side door and scrambled across the shift lever to sit on her lap. The steering wheel was too close, and for a moment she struggled to find its release lever. She wanted desperately to turn around again and see how close the beast was, but fought to keep her cool and her nerves steady.

Her feeling of vulnerability grew as she maneuvered to release the steering wheel lever. An image of the beast knocking over the van flashed in her mind just as the lever clicked and she slammed the steering wheel up to its highest position. She settled onto the woman's lap, kicked her right leg to one side and found the gas pedal. As she slammed it, she risked a glance at the rearview mirror.

What she saw caused her to press her full weight downward on the gas pedal.

They flew past an intersection, ignoring the red light. A brown Ford almost crashed into the passenger side door, but a squeal of brakes and a spin sideways prevented them from being t-boned. The speedometer read 45 miles per hour as Sveta's head moved from side to side looking for cross-street traffic or police cruisers. A glance at the rearview mirror showed that the beast was gaining. It was all darkness with two glints of silver for eyes.

A sign just ahead pointed the way to the I-75 ramp. The woman beneath her coughed and spasmed and her leg jerked, knocking Sveta's foot off the pedal. The wheel spun wildly left as Sveta tried to get her foot back onto the gas. The car swerved and slowed, and, without even looking at the rearview mirror, Sveta knew that whatever chased them was gaining.

She wrestled herself to the right as she got control of the wheel and shoved the woman's leg toward the door. Frantically, she slid her foot around and got it caught beneath the gas pedal. A stray glance in the mirror caused her to frantically slide her foot out again and slam it down on the accelerator. The thing behind her swiped at the car and she heard the sound of claws scraping down the trunk edge.

Bright lights suddenly flooded the car from the passenger side window and Sveta hung onto the steering wheel as though it were a lifeline. Truck tires squealed and the hiss of pneumatic brakes sounded like an air horn. She heard an impact somewhere near the back of the trunk, saw the beast thrown up and away as she swerved without slowing down to avoid a pothole big as a car tire. The woman groaned beneath her while Sveta squirmed to stay in control of the vehicle. She jammed her foot on the gas pedal as she cursed all four cylinder cars everywhere.

The freeway entrance came into view on the right. Sveta heard a siren blare somewhere in the distance. She turned the car so hard it lifted on two wheels as she hit the ramp. It fell back down with a jolting crash and she fell to one side, her foot sliding off the gas pedal. Panicked, she looked back quickly in the rear view mirror and saw nothing behind them but pavement littered with trash. She found the gas pedal again with the ball of her foot and pressed down hard until they merged onto southbound I-75.

She kept to the seventy mile an hour speed limit to avoid attracting attention, but her heart was still pounding fifteen minutes later when she saw first a Ford plant and then a giant truck stop just off the West Road exit. With a flick of her wrist the blinker flashed and she looked in the rearview mirror as she got on the freeway.

The exit looped around carrying her over a bridge that took them eastbound. The truck stop loomed like Hollywood, and she followed the long drive in to park at the far edge of the giant lot. It was better than a rest stop, with decent lighting and not too many cars. A ridge of tractor trailers hid her parking spot from plain view and any security cameras that would be monitored in the main office. All she saw over the top of the trucks was the giant revolving sign proclaiming "Good Eatin's, Hot Showers, and Soft Beds."

She parked parallel to the tractor trailers to keep an open straight away in front of her. The car idled like a lullaby and Sveta switched off the headlights. Time to think. Time to get the woman beneath her into the passenger seat or the trunk. Alive or dead, she had to go somewhere.

Every specialist planned for the moment when things went bad, the moment when they were cut loose of support on foreign ground. The objectives for those scenarios involved staying alive until they could be reunited with their team, or staying alive until their team rescued them. But the longer an agent spent in the field, the more they realized the unspoken necessity of planning for the possibility that their own team would turn on them. Spymasters like Hauck planned both ways, too. How to rescue separated agents, and how to deal with agents who, like Sveta, went rogue.

First things first. Move the woman. Then plan.

Sveta scanned the parking lot, saw nothing of concern, then opened the door, keeping the engine on and idling. The air was brisk and smelled of diesel. Truck engines purred and sent hot exhaust up their shiny vertical pipes, as drivers too cheap to sleep in the motel slept in their cabs. No one else moved about, but truckers had two-way radios, so she'd have to be quick. She slid her feet out and onto the ground, her pistol held loosely behind her back. The dome light didn't come on and Sveta was grateful she'd earlier told the woman to remove it.

"Hey," she said.

The woman didn't respond. Sveta shook her shoulder. Nothing. She removed a glove and checked for a pulse. Faint, but there. With a practiced hand, Sveta went through the woman's coat and shirt pockets, retrieved bundles of paper and threw them on the passenger seat. A purse lay on the floor, a cell phone next to it.

It hit Sveta right then. She was wearing a transponder somewhere in her assault gear. Not much time at all if she wanted to live through the night. She shoved her pistol into its holster and went to work.

Another quick check round the parking lot, and then she popped the trunk, went around back of the car, and looked inside. She found a plastic crate filled with jumper cables, a first aid kit, a can of Fix-A-Flat, and a blanket. Boxes filled with books, and two plastic bags of washer and brake fluid. She grabbed the blanket, went back and threw it in between the seats.

A clock was ticking in her head.

Hurry, hurry, hurry. Hauck and Evgeny and others would be on the way. She had a ten, maybe fifteen minute head start but she should figure only five and get back out on the road. And she was certain they knew exactly where she was.

Moving more quickly now, she opened the front passenger side door, bent down and reached over, grabbed the woman by the armpits and hauled back until she had her butt on the passenger side seat. Her legs didn't want to cooperate. Sveta tried folding them up and over the shift lever but it didn't work. If she couldn't get her over in another two minutes she would leave her on the ground and hit the road. But she tried a different approach and it saved the woman's life. She lowered the seat back, slid the girl up a bit and then managed to get her legs over and feet resting on the passenger side floor.

Sveta's first thought was to pull the seat back into place, but she changed tactics and left it right where it was. With the blanket pulled over her and her head angled just right, the woman looked like she'd pulled the seat down herself and was resting. She looked so normal that Sveta thought she knew her.

Almost.

Sveta got back into the car. She couldn't be seen doing what she had to next.

Every piece of equipment that came from the team had to go, including the gun. She hesitated a moment, then removed her bulletproof vest, her communications systems, ammunition belt, her knife and the rest and slid her pistol under the pile.

Every team member was bugged. They all knew that. It was the easiest way to rescue each other and they all knew where their bugs were. But Sveta reckoned that Hauck would have tagged another bug in her things, in case she wanted to drop off the grid. So everything given to her by Hauck had to go. Reluctantly, she took off her ankle sheath and knife, wrapped cords around them, and laid them on top of the pile.

"Very nice, very organized," said a rough voice.

Not good.

He was a bulky shadow with an extended arm. He closed the gap between himself and Sveta quickly. One of the parking lot lights stood behind him, so his face was difficult to make out save for his bulbous nose. Face round as a hubcap dented with acne like it'd been hit with buckshot. Menacing. It was the way he stood. Stupid in the way he came too close. An open black trench coat and she would bet money no vest under his sweater.

"I will take those," he told her.

She felt the end of his pistol press against her temple, but she turned her head slowly just enough to see his face. Not someone she knew. Russian accent with booze on his breath.

"I can pay you," she said.

"Shut up and give me your weapons."

Sveta grimaced, but reached one hand under the pile, placed the other on top, then lifted them toward him. Her finger found the trigger.

He held up a cell phone in his free hand, pushed a speed dial number. After a few seconds, he said, "I have her."

Whoever was on the other end shouted so loud that Sveta could almost understand what they said. She pulled the trigger, and shot him in the chest. He jerked backward and began to crumple. The suppressed round was loud enough for whoever was on the other end of the phone to hear.

Time didn't stop when she saw the shock and pain and fear trade places across his face. It was one of the mercury filled bullets, and from that distance he was dying before it left the gun. She could see enough of his features as he turned sideways to guess he had a kid and an ex-wife. Probably more than one kid. With the mercury in his system, she thought, he wasn't going to look good enough for a funeral. His ex-wife would come when they dropped him in the big hole, but she would be drunk. Somebody else would raise the kids.

It only took a few seconds, but it was what she was thinking. Happened most times when she killed someone and watched them die. Like writing their obituary to mark their death. Most of the people she killed, no one would notice they were gone.

She didn't look to see if he was still twitching, but instead let him fall then drove up even with a large blue parking lot dumpster and threw everything into it. After a quick glance at the unconscious woman, she accelerated away toward the freeway. No sense cleaning up. She had just shot a man in a truckstop parking lot. She might have got away clean after transferring the woman to the passenger side and covering her with a blanket—not likely, but possible. But after shooting a man? No. Any trucker looking out his window would have called it in. The police would be on their way soon enough and there was nothing she could do but run and find a place to go to ground. They would have a rough description of her car; she would have a few minutes head start.

As she accelerated onto the northbound ramp, she reached down and retrieved the cell phone. She dropped it between her legs and pulled the purse up on her lap as well, sorting through its contents until she found the woman's wallet, flipped it open and read the name and address. Zoe Winter. If the ID wasn't fake, then she lived on a street at the southern edge of Detroit.

Who are you, Zoe Winter, and why did you save me? And who and what is Drogol to you?

No time for thinking; she had a call to make that she really didn't want to. But both Hauck and the police were after her now, so she dialed the number from memory, and waited for her cousin Mishka to answer.

"Who is this?" came the gruff question from the other end.

"It's me," she said while watching the digital dashboard clock.

"I do not recognize this number. Is the reception good?"

"No, and it will not improve. I have a carpet that needs repaired."

"Perhaps you should find a better cell zone."

"Where?"

"Gratiot and Fourth. It's a good area."

"How will I—"

The line went dead.

Sveta thought about the time. Nine point four seconds. Well under the 30 second mark. Digital tracking was a lot quicker than it used to be. There was no way to keep up with every breakthrough. Her eyes caught a glint from the shiny black disc on the dash, right above the words "Passenger Air Bag." She felt around until she found the latch to the center arm rest, then lifted it up, and, without taking her eyes off the road, located a plastic square the size of a Blackberry and pulled it out. When she held it up to the light, she swore.

A flick of her finger on the power window control panel and the driver's side window rolled down. She tossed the portable GPS out and threw the phone after it. The disc on the passenger side was where the GPS mount fixed to while driving. Yuri could locate anyone with an active GPS if he knew the digital number. Or if he knew their cell number. If, that was, he was still alive. She shuddered as she remembered his white van being knocked on its side, the door ripped off by something or someone and a human form pulled from the wreckage and discarded as though it were a toy. With any luck, whatever it was caught hold of Hauck.

No flasher lights in her rearview, no barricades ahead. If she could make it to Mishka, she might have a chance.

She was minutes away from Detroit, driving with no guns, no weapons, and her only communication was a now discarded cell phone from a woman who might or might not work for Hauck.

A quick glance at Zoe. Shoulder length dark hair and a pretty, yet pale face. Black lipstick. Age, according to her driver's license, was twenty-six. One hand was poking out from underneath the blanket, and she saw that Zoe's fingernails were black as well. Sveta needed her to live, if only because she needed information so she herself could survive.

The Fort Street sign raced toward her and she flashed her blinker once, then hit the exit and began slowing down. Now wasn't the time to get caught. Five minutes, maybe ten, she'd be on her way to safety. Mishka was family; he would take her in. If she was lucky, she'd have at least a day before he sold her out to Hauck.

CHAPTER FOUR

Pacing the roof of an abandoned apartment building, the beast roared its fury to the night. From the building's edge, he watched his home flare in the darkness, filling the streets with angry, twisting flames and his heart with a raging desire for blood. A high wind blew across the rooftops and lashed his face. He turned into it, stretching wide his arms and snarling with fury.

Then he saw flashing red and white lights speeding toward the blaze, stoking his anger to new heights. He leaned over the edge as though about to leap from his four-story perch, but instead glared intently at the city below.

Occasional headlights burrowed through vacant neighborhoods and beyond them the skyline of Detroit towered above the ruins that ringed it. I-75 was lit by street lamps; its overpasses caged with steel fencing and barbed wire to keep street thugs from throwing trash and bricks into the path of oncoming traffic. Fluorescent flashing pinks and blues proclaimed the casinos, and at the river's edge towered the three cylinders of the General Motors building

But the beast cared for none of this. Its eyes were filled with the catastrophe of fire, sirens, blaring horns and red flashing lights.

Its mind was filled with the sound of his enemy's name.

Its heart was torn by hunger.

Its nostrils filled with the smell of the woman.

With a single step, it was on the building's parapet. It crouched, looked down, and then hurtled off the edge toward the cement sidewalk below.

*****

"We have lost communications with him, Mother," said Sasha.

She continued to sip her tea slowly, holding the tiny porcelain cup by her knotted, arthritic thumb and forefinger. Those who did not know her would assume that she didn't hear what her son had told her. After a moment's silence, she set her cup gently on the silver tray resting across the arms of her wheelchair, then reached up to pull her thick blue shawl tighter around her shoulders. Her son moved to help her, but she held up a warning hand, and finished adjusting it herself.

Behind her, off to her left shoulder, stood her counselor and body-guard, Ivan Kusnetzov, who was sometimes known as Ivan the Terrible. His white hair high and brushed back, his dimpled skin pale as though he had spent too many hours locked away in the forbidden mountain caves near the village he was raised in. Pale blue veins shone through his wax paper temples. His pale red eyes matched so closely the pink lenses of his wrap-around sunglasses it appeared he had no eyes at all. He stood, hands clasped behind his back, gazing past the old woman as though staring into the beating heart of mysteries only he could see. And as a starets of the Khylsty, monk confessors to pilgrims who pursued divine ecstasy, those mysteries were many.

Across the room, staring discreetly out the penthouse window over the brilliantly lit Atlanta nightscape, was Dr. Fyodor Pazyryk, the Iron Woman's tall and aristocratic personal physician. The doctor closed his pale gray eyes for a moment, praying that her blood pressure stayed within limits.

"Speak," she said. "Explain yourself. Tell me of your incompetence."

Sasha kept his eyes lowered and looked at her teacup as he began to speak. She allowed no one to look her in the eye. It was a rule as unbendable as titanium and inexplicable since her cataracts were get-ting so much worse.

"Mother, Drogol has escaped, Hauck lives, and Yuri is either dead or injured."

"And Chenko? What of my friend Chenko who suffered so much for me? What of him?"

Sasha trembled.

"Speak to me," she said, raising her voice. "What of my friend Chenko?"

"He is dead, Mother."

"How did he die, Sasha?"

"We don't know yet."

"We?"

"I. I don't yet know, Mother."

"So. It has come full circle. I betrayed Hauck so many years ago, and now he has betrayed me. So it is. Now we will see who will emerge the victor."

She smiled tightly, her lips like wrinkled wax. After a moment's thought she beckoned him to lean forward, signaling she wished to tell him something only family should hear. Sasha did so quickly, anxious to appease her. When he was just a few inches away, she brought her hand up as though to caress his cheek, but instead slapped him so hard across the face he fell back a step.

"Mother," protested Sasha, his hand pressed to his burning cheek.

"Chenko kept me alive in the camps," screamed his mother.

"Anna," said Dr. Pazyryk quickly, "your blood pressure."

"Shut up. I am dying and you can do nothing but feed me pills. You are as blind as I am and if I didn't need you to bring me tea and vodka I would have you shot."

"There is no doctor that can do more than I, Anna," he said, stepping away from the window. "There is no cure for what you have."

"Silence," she shouted. "There is a cure and it is now running loose in that American shithole of a city that I have refused to step foot in until now, but it seems I must go there myself."

"Mother, no. It is too dangerous. Let me go, I beg you. Let me redeem myself."

"And what will you do for Chenko?"

"What can I do for the dead, Mother?"

"You can bring me his body."

Sasha swallowed, and considered his next words carefully.

"I will do it. I will do what is necessary."

"And what is that, Sasha? What will you do? How would you proceed against Drogol?"

"I will take a team of my best men with me. Clearly we underestimated him."

He froze. His mother had not changed her expression, but he felt a shift in her emotional state as clearly as if the temperature in the penthouse had dropped.

"I mean, *I*. Clearly, *I* underestimated him."

"I must have that man alive," she hissed. "Do you understand this? I must have him alive. *Must*. And you, you are no match for him."

"Tell me what to do, Mother."

Anna Kazakova said nothing for a moment. Her skin was finely cracked porcelain, her hair thin and white, brittle and sparse because of the treatments. Eyes filmed and blue white like cold marbles; cheek bones set high and regal in her face. Even the illness could not bow her head, and her posture, despite all the hard years, was still stiff and erect.

"You and I are the last of our family," she said, and though her expression had not changed, her voice was distant. "I have only you to carry on our dynasty. Yet you are too young, Sasha, too impetuous to know and understand the meaning of peril. You think that more guns and more muscle will overcome every problem. This worries at me day and night. What am I to do with you? How can I send you against Drogol when you are too young to understand who and what he is, and the depth of peril that all who seek him face?"

"May I sit, Mother?"

She nodded her assent, and waited irritably while he pulled a chair over.

"May I speak freely, Mother?"

Again a nod.

"I am a grown man. Have I not proven worthy in every task you have set me 'til now? Have I not managed our Organizatsiya well? I have eliminated or conquered our enemies and rivals and kept our products flowing into the streets of the world's capitals. Is this not true, Mother? Have I not bribed and extorted the police of countries everywhere? Have I not found markets for our weapons and moved the money of nations about like shells in the game? Have I not killed for us with my own hands?"

Anna waved her hand dismissively.

"Why, Mother? Why is this different? Why is this *man* different? Who is he and why do you fear him?"

"I fear no one," she snapped. "Nothing and no one. Never forget that. Never."

Sasha waited impatiently. The gold and pearl clock on the room's French provincial desk showed one forty-five in the morning. The television was off. The stereo played nothing. His mother had no use for entertainment. Dr. Pazyryk idly picked up his drink from the bar and drained it discreetly, quietly. The doctor knew Anna found the sound of ice against glass particularly irritating. Sasha nodded at him approvingly.

The clock read one forty-eight in the morning. Since the suicide of his brother, these moments where she would sit thinking could stretch on for ten or fifteen minutes and were becoming more and more frequent. Now that both his brother and her friend Chenko were dead, he wondered if she would withdraw further into herself.

In the labor camps she and Chenko had suffered through after Drogol's escape, she had not been allowed to speak for days, then forced to talk for hours without stopping or be beaten with a rod by a succession of guards who thoroughly enjoyed striking women. Fifteen minutes of silence was not much for a woman who had endured so much. Such was the reason that he had requested he be allowed to sit.

Finally, she said, "Would you play chess with me, Sasha?"

"You know I despise the game."

"This, you see, is what worries me."

"Mother, will you not finally tell me about this man?"

"Did you know that when I worked at the Directorate, I had in my employ the most brilliant and ruthless man I have ever met? Many good men and women took orders from me in those days, but none as intense as that one. He was a reckless but forceful chess player like the great Mikhail Tal. He saw an opening, and he attacked. And he was handsome in a cruel sort of way. Yes, I noticed such things in those days. I was not a blind old woman back then."

"This was Drogol?" asked Sasha eagerly.

His mother shook her head.

"That man was Hauck. Drogol was—"

"Then tell me more about them, Mother. How can I help you if I do not understand your enemies?"

"Doctor," she said, "bring me something to drink."

Ivan Kusnetzov swiveled his head to focus on the doctor. When he noticed that the doctor was lost in thought and had not responded to his Mrs. Kazakova, he waved his hand peremptorily. It was never good for her to be without vodka for any length of time. On some nights, it was all that she would allow between herself and the debilitating pain that racked her body.

The doctor jerked up at the sound of Ivan's finger snap and, when he looked around and saw the man's pale terrible eyes fixed on him and his long, milky white finger pointing at the liquor cabinet, he moved to get Anna a drink. It was bad to keep Anna Kazakova waiting. It was worse to have her mad monk angry at you.

"I have decided now that we will go to Detroit," she said. "Sasha, call Chenko's brother. He will meet us there. He has the right. Ivan will handle the other arrangements."

"What other arrangements?"

"If I wanted you to know now, I would tell you now. Do not try me."

"But—"

"Enough. I will tell you everything on the plane. Be patient, Sasha. No one else in the world has heard the story you will hear tonight. Not a living soul."

Sasha considered this.

"You are too weak to go. Coming to Atlanta has been enough strain on you."

Her clouded marble eyes seemed to glare at him.

"You must do one more thing before we leave. Call Mishka in Detroit. Tell him to meet us at the airport. I have provided him a small army of soldiers and weapons to control that city since the casinos moved in. Time for him to work for his money."

"What else should I say?"

"You must tell him," she said softly, "that I am coming to hunt."

At the bar, Dr. Pazyryk almost dropped the Iron Woman's drink.

*****

Evgeny found Yuri sprawled faced down on the lawn of a burned out shell of a house, alive, but with a broken arm. Across the street, the van lay crumpled on its side. Broken window glass reflected off the pavement like a neighborhood house of mirrors.

"I have him," he said into his mic.

"Status," asked Hauck.

"Breathing and swearing but a broken arm, probably a few broken ribs. The van's ruined. Knocked on its side; looks like it was hit by a bulldozer. I saw it happening, fired three shots into the thing that crashed it."

Hauck did not bother to ask if he hit it; Yuri always hit his target.

Instead, he said, "Tell me what you saw."

"Something big, like an ape, but faster. It took off after a passing car."

When Hauck went silent; Evgeny could imagine his thoughts.

"Status?"

"Didn't even slow it down."

"Eliminate the van immediately," said Hauck.

"Understood."

"Then get the hell out of there. Proceed to the extraction point."

"Understood."

Evgeny scanned the neighborhood. No one on the street. The windows were dark. A burning house two streets over, a wild beast knocked over a van and a shooter stood firing after it, yet no one ventured out. They would be on the phones, though, he knew. He hoped that Yuri took down the communications grid before the beast hit him.

From a side pocket, he withdrew a single device, moved quickly to the van's open door and threw it in. Then, he ran back to where Yuri lay, and helped him to his feet.

"Tell me you didn't do what I just saw you do," said Yuri.

"Move," said Evgeny, "and don't look back."

They were moving through the alleys when the explosion cracked the night and bright light plumed overhead. Sirens blared closer than Evgeny liked. Even Detroit came alive sooner or later.

Chapter Five

Sveta did the math in her head. Three left turns and three right turns from the street corner Mishka had given her. Mishka loved codes. From Moscow street punk to made man and station head in the Russian Mafia and he still used the same codes, still played the same games. But it was good tradecraft. Anyone listening in to her call to Mishka on Zoe's cell phone would be six blocks away, waiting in the wrong place

The streets were nearly empty. Twice she was passed by police cars who drove by and kept on going. She held her breath and watched their taillights disappear into the night. Street people wandered in and out of shadows when she stopped at streetlights. Crumpled papers and plastic bags jumped up and raced down the road ahead of her whenever the wind blustered. Darkened storefronts were locked away behind thick metal gates and she drove by more pawn shops and liquor stores than she had seen in any other American city.

The young woman stretched out in the passenger seat did not move beneath her blanket. Sveta worried that she was dead or dying, but could do nothing without Mishka's help. She would not trade her own life for the life of someone she didn't know. Taking her to a hospital and leaving her was too risky. Driving her to Mishka was risk enough.

Her nerves were on overdrive. Too much in one night. Crue, Chenko and Bodin dead. Turning on Hauck. Drogol. The wild beast. And this Zoe that lay still as death. All connected in ways that she did not understand and had no time to think about. First she had to survive and escape and that would require guns, papers and money. As Russian Mafiya, those were things her cousin Mishka was well suited to supply.

As she approached the appointed intersection, Sveta saw a black

Humvee idling in a parking space. It looked as out of place as an Uzi in a trash heap. Russian gangsters like Mishka were notoriously unrepentant about their wealth and power. But Sveta would have preferred for them to have driven up in a slightly battered older car that would fit the neighborhood and draw less attention. Still, she had no choice and pulled her car behind theirs.

The driver and passenger doors opened at the same time, but two very different men emerged. The sight of both men coming toward her car made Sveta wish for her pistol. The driver was six feet of jet black hair and broad shoulders. He wore an unbelted trench coat and she could see by the way he walked he was armed for trouble. The thickset bald man who approached the passenger side was packed with muscle beneath his turtleneck sweater and he moved like a man used to breaking anything in his way. Sveta thought he was built like a heavyweight class Olympic weightlifter. Every nerve in her body told her to slam her car in reverse and keep going, but she knew that they could catch her in their Humvee. She knew that even before she made fifteen feet, the dark man in the trench coat would break out his automatic weapon and kill her and Zoe both.

Slender fingers bunched and knocked against her window. She hit the button and waited til the window was halfway down before asking, "Yes?"

"You have a rug in need of repair?"

Sveta motioned her chin toward Zoe.

"Turn off the car, get out with your hands where I can see them, if you please, and then follow me. We will take you to the cleaner. My partner will bring your merchandise along with him."

She did as she was told. No real choice. These two were not from Hauck.

"Backseat," said the man, pointing toward the Humvee.

He had the eyes of a man waiting for a chance to hurt you. They were deep set and dark and dull with indifference. He walked with her, a safe distance back, always a free hand near the slung stock shotgun hanging beneath his coat. Far enough back to swing it up, enough time to splatter her if he didn't like her moves.

Sveta got into the backseat of the Humvee. He closed the door behind her—there was no door handle for her to pull it closed herself.

The passenger side door opened and Zoe, blanket and all was placed inside by the muscleman. He arranged her like a mannequin, and as he did so, Sveta saw the ragged scar that cut down the left side of his face. He stared back at her for a second, then smiled and closed the door.

The Humvee began to roll forward while Sveta contemplated the thick glass wall that separated her from the two men. She and Zoe were prisoners behind tinted glass and armor plating. The muscleman turned to face her again. This time he didn't smile.

She heard the whir of an invisible motor, and a black cover slid down and blocked the two men from view.

*****

They drove for half an hour or so. Sveta had no way of knowing for sure, because she could not see out of the Humvee's windows. Zoe didn't move. Her skin seemed dangerously pale; there was nothing for Sveta to do but hope she could hang on until Mishka provided a doctor.

But she finally had time to think.

Hauck had involved another group to bring in Drogol—that much was clear by Chenko's presence. Whether it was Russian Security or Russian Mafiya was not yet clear. But he had no use for his new partner and appeared to have been working at cross-purposes to them all along. Whoever they were wanted Drogol alive, while Hauck must have wanted him dead. That would explain the mercury bullets.

What she did not understand was why this man was so important that Hauck wanted him dead. No question because of the mercury bullets. The other side wanted Drogol alive. But she didn't know why.

What if he had been infected as part of a secret biological research program? Thirty years later he was still walking around, and the world had not changed as a result of it. Was he some sort of a biological time bomb? Sveta knew that she was thinking crazy conspiracy thoughts, but kept her mind open to the possibilities.

Could he be a political asset or liability to someone high up? She doubted this, too. Kremlin cold war secrets from over thirty years ago were ancient history. Yeltsin was dead and Gorbachev did book tours. The new generations of Russians and Westerners alike wanted to forget the past.

One thing she knew was that Hauck could still hunger for revenge after thirty plus years. After what happened in that prison under his watch, Sveta was surprised he hadn't shown up in person to shoot Drogol.

But the biggest thing on her mind was the beast that knocked over Yuri's van, then came after her and Zoe as they drove away. What was the creature?

She tried to remember exactly what the monster looked like and couldn't. It moved with incredible speed and had enough weight and power to knock over the white van, rip off the door, and drag poor Yuri out. It ran on four legs as it slammed into the van, she was sure of that, but she sure she had seen it move just as easily on two. And it kept up with the car and pulled up close enough to rake the trunk as she drove at forty miles an hour.

The Humvee pulled to a stop. She heard a motor kick in and the squealing protest of metal, and then the vehicle pulled forward a bit more and stopped. Doors opened and closed. They had arrived.

*****

"Sveta," Mishka exclaimed, "how good to see you again."

The bright warehouse lights blinded her momentarily. The thick smell of oil and solvents hit her before her sight cleared.

A circle of perhaps ten or twelve hard looking men fanned around her as she stepped out. Mishka stood at their center, his rich, black cashmere coat and crème colored scarf setting him apart from the others the way an executive stood out from the hired help. He was tall and handsome in a brutal sort of way, with a full head of black hair swept back from his narrow forehead. With a fluid motion he moved forward and embraced her so hard she lost her breath. When he stood back, his smile bright as halogen lights, he spun round and opened his arms to the assembled men.

"I give you my dear cousin, Sveta. Is she not the most beautiful creature on the face of the earth?"

No one replied.

"She has her mother's beauty and her father's boldness. Once, a major in the GRU. Can you believe this? One side of the family produces officers, and the other, my side, I must confess, produces criminals. Yet, here she is coming to me for help."

"The woman," said Sveta, "she needs medical attention."

"Of course, of course. Sergei, you and Vladim take the woman to where the doctor waits."

The crowd of men seemed to press closer to her. She could feel the tension in the air. The two men who had driven her went around to the passenger side of the Humvee and removed Zoe.

"Careful, Vladim," said the thinner man, answering the question of who was who.

"I would like to go with her," said Sveta.

"Nonsense," said Mishka.

He ran his eyes over her, and Sveta felt a cold chill go through her body. When they were teenagers there was a night when they drank too much and too much happened. Mishka's father stumbled in on them and beat Mishka so badly he was hospitalized for two days. But that was a long time ago, and the only man Sveta truly feared now was Hauck.

"She has information I need."

Mishka looked around at his assembled men and shrugged.

"Later," he said, "when the doctor has done what he can."

They were in an open bay of a warehouse that could have housed a football field. Rows of wooden crates big as cars were stacked almost to the lights. Palletized boxes, forklifts, and motorized winches on a network of rails were street legal stage props for a Mafiya front operation. Windows darkened with black paint ran along the upper edges of the walls to prevent any chance of someone looking in. Sveta didn't know what they were shipping, but it wasn't legal.

"Can we talk somewhere privately?"

"Later," said Mishka dismissively. "I have someone important to meet at the airport. You are my guest here until I return."

"There are things that I need, Mishka."

"Perhaps a woman as pretty as you should be more careful in a man's world."

When he brought his hand up to brush his thick black moustache, she saw the red flash of his ruby ring. The night before he fled to America, Mishka cut off the finger of a small city's mayor. The next morning, he mailed the man's finger to his wife, but kept the ring for himself.

"I can handle myself."

He stepped forward and ran his hand along her cheekbone. She flinched, but did not move. Thirteen to one were not good odds.

"You are more beautiful than ever," said Mishka. "But tell me, why are you here in my city?"

"Business."

Mishka lowered his hand and caressed her neck. The semicircle of men watched impassively. He was, she knew, looking for an excuse to slap her in front of his men.

"And what business brings you to my city?"

She said nothing.

"Answer me."

"Private business, Mishka, that I can speak of only to you."

"But you did not see fit to inform your dearest cousin of your arrival?"

"It is private business."

He started to turn away, but spun back again and whipped his open palm against her face. She rocked back so hard her back slapped against the Humvee. Even though she'd seen the blow coming, Sveta didn't move out of the way. He was playing the Mafiya kingpin in front of his men, and she took the hit knowing it for what it was. Blood trickled from the corner of her mouth.

"Everything that goes on in this town is my business. If you weren't family I would have Gennady cut out your tongue and make you eat it."

A swarthy man behind Mishka pulled a knife from his pocket, pushed a button that shot the blade out to its full length, then twisted and turned it, reflecting the light into Sveta's eyes.

"I'm sorry, Mishka."

"Sorry," he repeated thoughtfully, then moved forward and slapped her again, hard.

Spots of light flashed as she fell against the Humvee. Her head cracked against the glass and her fingers bent back painfully as she tried to absorb the impact.

I'm coming back for you, she thought.

"Is this what you call tough in the GRU?" Mishka sneered. "Wipe your mouth."

With a flick of his wrist a monogrammed silk handkerchief sailed over and landed at her feet. Keeping her eyes downcast, she stooped while making a show of needing the support of the Humvee's door to keep steady.

Her cousin approached, then squatted to look at her as she sat on the floor dabbing the blood away from her chin and lips.

"You need money, paper, and guns, yes? It is my thought that you have been very bad in my city, my dear cousin. Gennady has all three waiting for you in that black bag near the shipping door. You see? Good. But if what you have done here has angered the Iron Woman, if it is why I have been summoned to the airport, then that black bag will be buried with you."

He stood and called out to the man with the knife. The others still stood grouped around them, still watching with little apparent interest.

"Gennady, take a few men with you and escort my cousin to our waiting room. If she gives you trouble, you may beat her, but not fuck her. And, Gennady?"

"Yes, Mishka?"

"Chain her."

*****

Mishka settled back in the fine leather seats of his chauffeured limousine, and removed his gloves and scarf. How good it was to see his cousin again, and to observe how far she had fallen. To have her come to him like a beggar for protection—it was almost worth the beating his father had given him all those years ago.

The warehouse door rolled up slowly, exposing a night as cold, as sleek, as heartless as Gennady's switchblade. He loved this town with its torn and defaced posters nailed to any spare board or pole that was available. The trash that piled in the streets, the abandoned houses, wild dogs and street people that bought and sold each other like stolen car parts. People such as these gave him no trouble; they were used to being taken advantage of by the powerful.

From the built-in bar, he withdrew a rock glass, dropped a few ice cubes in and then poured a generous amount of vodka. The Iron Woman would be arriving soon. Mishka could use a drink.

Why she was in the United States was not something he cared to think about. His only concern was that she was not angry at him. People who angered Anna Kazakova did not live long. Did she know what he and Sasha were doing? That would be very bad. After a moment's thought, he drained his glass and poured another.

Yefim put the limousine in gear, then they pulled out onto the street and turned the corner.

*****

The moon drifted out from behind a brooding mass of twisted clouds as the limo disappeared. Across the street in an alley defined only by shadows, amber-red eyes glowed. Suddenly, a deep, angry growl scraped the night.

The door operator hit the stop button.

He was a loose faced man with thinning hair and deep-set brown eyes. He drew his pistol as he stepped forward to the door opening and peered out into the night. Three other men came running up behind him.

"What was that?" asked one.

Mishka's limousine was gone from sight. The streets appeared empty. A ghostly silence spread through the night as the men grew nervous.

"Wild dog," said another. "Had to be. Pit bull maybe or a Rott-weiler. These assholes around here breed them and fight them, and then let them loose when they don't make money. Cops don't do shit about them."

"Didn't sound like a dog," said the door operator.

"It ain't a fucking cat."

A few more men came and gathered around the open door, including a forklift driver who rolled up on his machine to see what was happening. More weapons were drawn and they gripped them tightly, sensing something indefinably dangerous lurking in the night.

Gennady returned and shouted, "What the hell is going on? Close the fucking door."

"Something's out there," said the door operator. "Didn't you hear it?"

"Hear what?"

"Like some animal."

"Well maybe," said Gennady taking out his knife, "we should catch it and skin it."

The operator hit the down button again and the door began its gradual descent. It protested and groaned.

"Somebody ought to grease that sprocket," said Gennady.

He was about to say something else when he saw a giant form burst from the darkness across the street and charge straight at them. The door inched its way down, too slow to stop the enraged darkness.

The creature hit the door operator like an explosion. It spun and slashed out in a vicious swipe, and Gennady saw the man's head rip loose from his neck in a spray of blood.

Someone fired a shot that hit it in the back and its furious roar echoed throughout the warehouse. With a flash of teeth it bit his arm off at the shoulder. Suddenly, everybody started firing and two men went down from the barrage of bullets. Smoke filled the air as blood spread over the floor. The beast roared and leapt onto another man, digging its hind claws into his abdomen. They hit the concrete in a slick of blood and screams and more shots.

The forklift driver spun his wheel and drove off madly. He kept looking over his shoulder as he tried to steer between the crates. But because his eyes were locked on the mad disaster behind him, he crashed the extended metal blades straight into an electrical control panel. A shower of sparks erupted upon impact, and the warehouse was plunged into darkness. Seconds later, the emergency backup came to life, and the darkness was penetrated by twirling red strobes of light.

Gennady dropped his knife, reaching inside his coat for a pistol. When he looked up at the open jaws of the eight foot tall wolf-beast illuminated by angry red bursts, he turned and ran toward the shipping office. Other men scattered, running in whatever direction their legs took them.

One little man scrambled up the side of stacked wooden container loads big enough to hold two cars each. He fell back once, sliding downward until his chin impaled on an upward slanted hook. Fingers dug in reflexively to hold his weight in place. He tried to scream, but his jaws wouldn't work. Pain clashed so loudly through his mind that he didn't t feel the splinters shaft beneath his nails. He began to whimper and tried to wedge his toes in between an opening in the boards as the hook in his chin ground against his jawbone. Warm liquid poured down the front of his neck, spreading across the front of his shirt He hung suspended like a fish on a hook in the scarlet glow of the strobes.

There was a momentary lull in the shots and he thought that it was over. In the silence, he still heard the wounded grinding of the warehouse door pulley system. Then, a thud as the door bottomed out and he realized he was now trapped inside with the monster. His sweaty feet began to slide out of his shoes. The hook ground deeper into his jawbone. Blind with pain, he clung frantically to the splintered wood and his hands began to feel as though they were on fire.

Then, the stack of containers began to creak and groan and move. He realized that *something* was pushing over the entire mountain of wooden crates to get at him.

CHAPTER SIX

As the VIP Boeing 737-200 winged its way through the night skies toward Detroit, the moon rode high above dense dark clouds like a wary, solitary eye contemplating their flight. In her darkened private cabin, Anna Kazakova lay on an elevated bed, attached by tubes to an intravenous stand bolted to the floor. Wires ran from her body to cardiac monitoring machines, and an oxygen harness ran from the back of her head to her nose. Sasha sat at the end of her bed in a cushioned armchair staring at her intently while she looked out through the portal at the moon.

They were alone.

Off to one side of her bed, Ivan had left a television with a video player attached to it. Dr. Pazyryk waited nervously on the far side of the door, while Ivan, having plugged in the video equipment, now stood guard outside the door and stared at the doctor until he finally turned away and made himself a vodka martini.

"What I will now tell you must be told to no one else. Do you understand?" Anna began.

"Of course, Mother."

"Of course, always 'of course, Mother,'" she said irritably. "Do you think me senile?"

"No, Mother."

"An easy answer. But after you hear what I have to tell you, you may have your doubts."

Sasha knew better than to answer her last statement. Instead, he waited for her to continue when she was ready. In the silence, he thought he could hear the flow of oxygen into her nostrils, although he knew it was not possible.

"I know," she said after a time, "that you are waiting for me to die. Don't deny it. I know that it is true. You are young and rich and handsome, and your lust for power is exceeded only by your ambition. All that you need to satisfy your desires is my death. Not a word, I said."

She stared down his protests, her rheumy eyes fixed on his as though by the sheer power of her will she could keep him quiet. The luxury cabin felt suddenly colder and he realized he was thousands of feet high in the night, his life dependent upon strangers and machines. Alone with the only parent he had ever known. He looked out an oval window and thought he saw the moon shudder.

"For that, I admire you. My own blood courses through your veins and you are as you must be. You are strong as I once was. We are a family of dark secrets, you and I, and tonight, if my strength holds, you will learn the darkest of that knowledge which I conceal from the world. Listen to the engine's power, Sasha. We fly above the clouds, although, in truth, we were never meant to leave the ground."

The look in her eyes was one that he was familiar with; it was the look of the elderly explaining their sins to those who would repeat them and truths to those who would ignore them.

She tugged at her blanket with fingers too pale and boney until she maneuvered it past the tangle of electrical wires that attached her to her monitors. Although Sasha made a move to rise and help her, one cold look pushed him back into his chair. Finally satisfied, she glanced once more out the window to stare at the moon, and then begin again.

"You know some of who I am and some of what I've done. Some things you will never know and be better off not knowing. I will tell you certain things and spare you others. Everything that I tell you comes at a price. Do you understand this? Do you? Because if you agree to hear this story, there is no going back. If the two men whom it concerns ever find out that you know, they will hunt you down and kill you."

"They can try," snorted Sasha.

"And at least one of them will eat your flesh and chew your bones."

For a moment, Sasha was speechless. He stared at his mother's dry lips as though they had malfunctioned.

"One of them is a cannibal?"

Her eyes narrowed, and she shook her head from side to side.

"No. One of these two is an animal."

At first he did not notice that he had pressed himself backward into his seat, pushing away from his mother. When he did notice, he leaned forward again and pulled himself up, straightening his back and squaring his shoulders.

"Tell me, Mother. I am not afraid. You know this secret, and they have not destroyed you."

"One would. One cannot."

"Riddles, Mother, more riddles. Tell me what you will tell me but do not play for a child."

Her eyes closed, and for a moment Sasha thought she had drifted off to sleep, but she began speaking again as though she had closed her eyes to see the past more clearly.

"Many years ago, I was an ambitious station chief in the secret police. This much you may already know. I was ruthless and beautiful and there is no more deadly combination. Can you see me like that, my boy, or can you see only your old, dying mother kept alive by medicine, machines and a drunken doctor?"

Before he could respond, her eyes popped open and arms shot forward as though to be handcuffed.

"Look at my arms," she cried. "My skin sags and my veins are thin. My bones are fragile and my blood corrupted. I was not always like this. I was beautiful once. You must understand that to understand anything. Look at my face. Look at me."

Eyes wide open. Lips pulled back to show yellowed teeth and a dry tongue. Age spots on her forehead like patches of dead grass spreading across an untended lawn. Sasha could barely stand to glance at her.

"Now you see, don't you? I have memories of beauty trapped in a body that will soon be dust. But once I was beautiful and I knew it. Men followed me like dogs. They bent to my will so they might have me."

"Mother, please."

She laughed. It was a coarse eruption of delight.

"And I had power. Power from the State to protect the State. I gave what I gave to get that power and I gave what it took to keep it. Would you like to know what I gave?"

"No, Mother."

The cabin filled with her hideous cackle.

"There were always plots against party officials. Always men fermenting plans to strike against the protectors of the proletariat. It was my mission to seize such anarchists and spies, imprison them and torture confessions and information out of them. Many did not survive. Others fared worse. Of course, many of these were merely inconvenient citizens who stood in the way of what party members wanted, but the exercise of absolute power is necessary to those who would keep it.

"I received information one night about a certain man who was said to be plotting against an official of high authority. It was my duty to have him arrested and to oversee his interrogation. He lived among the underground peoples. Do you know this phrase, Sasha?"

He knew the underground people were those who hid in the shadows of Soviet life. The gypsies and Freemasons, the black marketers and criminals. They were known as such because beneath the cities of Moscow were endless sewers and tunnels, secret places on no maps and communities of people who, as Beria once said, were harder to find than spies and more difficult to exterminate than rats.

"Yes, I know of them."

"Good. He lived among them, this one known as Drogol. Down in the filthy stink that ran beneath the streets of our city. We heard of him first in an interrogation of a petty criminal who had raped the daughter of an apparatchik. Men under persuasion, men under torture, will offer anything and anyone up to stop the pain. This man had nothing for us but stories about a man who raved that he was Russia's rightful ruler. A crazy man, our informant said, with wild eyes and the devil's way with women. But this was hardly worth the descent into darkness to him. So we filed a report, as we filed reports for everything in those days."

"But you heard of him again?" asked Sasha eagerly.

"Yes. We heard of him again. This time in connection with a murder near the edge of Blagoveshenskiy Cathedral."

"And?"

"We brought him in."

"He does not sound so formidable."

His mother managed to prop herself up on her elbows momentarily. Her face lit with animation.

"He killed twenty-six men before we captured him. Twenty-six armed men. We had to cordon off twelve blocks above and below ground. We poured diesel fuel down the tunnels and set them on fire.

Armed men at all sewer and street exits. Over a hundred of the under-ground people died in the smoke and flames. No one knew they lived to begin with except others of their type, so we were able to contain what happened by blaming it on a gas leak. No one believed us, but in those days no one would dare challenge us. Even the capitalist spies kept their distance from the situation. I was well known to them and feared as well. I locked down the city so tightly that no one would dare to question me. I had the highest permissions. And, I did it. When the fires underground grew too intense, Drogol rose to the surface."

"And you took him?"

"Fah. We took him by shooting him with tranquilizers and catch-ing him in an animal net made of metal alloy fibers, then dropping a titanium cage over him."

This did not make sense to Sasha. So much force for one man? Although he did not wish it to seem that he doubted her, he had to ask the question.

"Why so much force for only one man?"

"See for yourself," said his mother. "Play the disc on the television. This video was transferred from the original tapes by Dimitri himself. By the way, do you know why the great genius Dimitri works so tire-lessly for me? No? It is because his brother was one of the guards you are about to watch die at Drogol's prison. In this copy, he has for me removed all sounds. I have heard the screams and begging too often. I do not wish to hear them anymore. If you have use of a copy with sound, I will tell Dimitri to make one for you."

This was the moment he was waiting for, the moment when he could finally see the source of his mother's fears. And she was afraid, no matter what she told others. When he inserted the disc into the machine it was as though he were inserting a key into a locked door behind which lay unimaginable wealth guarded by a terrible curse. He pushed the Play button, and then returned to his chair. He knew that his mother would not look at the video again. Instead she would watch him watching her past unfold.

Gray and white speckles flooded the screen like an electronic snow storm, and then a grainy black and white picture replaced them. Cement walls and shadows. Metal desks and grim men in uniform filling out paperwork, cleaning their pistols while two of them played chess. Young men. Maybe one in his thirties who seemed to be in charge of the shift. Thick black belts and buttons reflected light awkwardly back at the camera.

The men jumped to their feet suddenly and snapped to attention. Seconds later, a much younger version of Sasha's mother stepped onto the screen. Even in the grainy black and white video he could see that she was right. When she was younger, Anna Kazakova had been a very beautiful woman. Sasha fought the urge to turn and stare at her, so that he might compare the so very attractive woman on the screen with the matriarch with the loose and spotted skin who lay near him. The fact that they were one and the same woman made his skin crawl.

He saw the way the men at the prison avoided her eyes. He could almost smell their fear by watching the tiny twitches at the edge of their mouths. She was speaking to the sergeant, berating him coolly for something. This man could no doubt have broken her neck with a twist of his hands he looked so powerfully built. But he feared her. Sasha knew this reaction.

One of the men went to a metal door and unlocked it. The video temporarily ended.

The screen returned to show Anna and two guards on the other side of the door; clearly this was taken by another camera. The three of them walked down a long hallway lit by only two weak bulbs. Further down the hall, they stopped. One of the men withdrew a ring of keys, unlocked a door, and then stood to one side as his mother entered. He then locked the door behind them.

Time passed. Sasha could not tell how long. The men stood one to either side of the door.

Eventually, one them turned as though summoned, and unlocked the door again. His mother was escorted back down the hall.

There was a new man waiting for her in the office. Sasha leaned forward and stared at the screen.

"Hauck," said his mother in a voice just barely above a whisper.

Even in the soundless black and white video, the man's natural authority and intelligence showed through in his sharp features and his wide forehead. He was tall and well built; his uniform fit him like a glove. When he looked at one of the people in the room, he locked on them as though they were the only other person in the world. The guards stayed back from him, as though for their own safety. When he spoke, he gestured fiercely.

Sasha's mother was the only person in the room who did not appear intimidated. They seemed to be discussing something that angered Hauck so much that he could barely contain his temper. But she did not appear the least concerned. She raised her hand once for him to be silent, then exited like a Tsarista.

The video went blank again. Once again, Sasha had no way of knowing how much time had passed.

It came back, and the first thing that he noticed was that Hauck held a phone receiver to his ear. He was tapping the phone cradle with one finger as though there was a problem with the connection. He seemed to grow more and more agitated. The guards around him looked nervous, and one worked at the buttons for a bank of blank video monitoring screens.

This is it, thought Sasha. *This is where it all begins.*

The lights flickered in the guard room. All the men except Hauck looked up to the ceiling to see what was wrong. Hauck pulled his sidearm and he screamed a furious command. Sasha would ask the great Dimitri to restore all sound for him, if only so that he could hear that one command.

One of the men looked at the same door that Sasha's mother had taken to interrogate Drogol in his cell; this guard, a bulky flat faced man who looked like a Ukrainian of mixed blood, went to that door, unlocked it, and began to turn the handle. He held his gun close to his chest and tilted his head as though he heard a noise.

Hauck saw what the guard was doing and held up a hand of warning as he screamed. Too late. The door cracked open. Hauck brought up his pistol, but another guard reacted without thinking and yanked Hauck's arm away. Sasha saw the pistol buck and fire, and in his mind he could hear the shot, hear the bullet banging off of iron and cracking concrete.

With his face distorted by rage, Hauck came back around and took aim again just as the metal door pushed all the way open *from the other side.*

Sasha forgot about his mother and where he was. He forgot where they were going and why. He saw only the hair covered beast that ducked under the door sill, roared back as Hauck's first bullet hit it, then raised its clawed hands and sprang into the guardroom like Judgment Day.

Hauck moved to get out of the way as the beast snapped at his throat, but it flung a big metal desk after him and Hauck flew back like he had been hit by a train and disappeared beneath it. The monster seemed to change form as it moved, as though one moment it was a man and the next moment it was a wild beast. Its image rippled as it changed.

A spray of black blood splashed across the camera lens, but through its thin smear Sasha saw men ripped apart and their innards torn loose. Their mouths formed silent screams, and Sasha—who had himself both seen and delivered brutal death—began to sweat. The creature moved so quickly that it was over in a matter of moments.

Then the feeding began.

When it became clear that the video had run out, Sasha turned the machine off and, after a few moments of staring at his hands, looked up and turned to his mother.

"What was that thing? Where did it come from? How did it get into a secure prison?"

"So many questions. So long ago. First, I must have something to drink."

She touched a button on the speaker console bolted to the side of her bed.

"Ivan," she said in a detached voice, "have the doctor bring me something to drink. And bring something for Sasha."

"I need nothing, Mother, except to know what happened in that video. What was that thing?"

He extended his index finger toward the screen like a pointing rod.

"Let me answer your questions in reverse. Ah. Wait. Here is the doctor with my drink."

Sasha paid no attention to either man. His desire for answers was like a fire burning him up from the inside. When Dr. Pazyryk interrupted his mother's answers by arranging a tray table on the bed railing and then swinging it around in front of her, Sasha felt like pushing him out of the way.

"How did the beast get into the prison? That, at least, is simple. We let it in ourselves. Where it came from originally is difficult to say, although Drogol himself told me its origins. I just did not believe him. I was too young and stupid."

"Then tell me this—what was it?"

The first smile that Sasha could remember seeing in many years crossed his mother's face. Her teeth were yellow with nicotine stain, and she showed iron from years of Soviet dentistry, but still she smiled.

"It is not exactly for certain what that thing is. All I know is that it is still out there, and I want it captured. But Drogol is the key to everything, Sasha, and we must take hold of him again."

"But what about that creature?"

"What is important, what is the single most important thing, is that we draw Drogol out of his lair. The creature cannot be avoided."

"I don't understand. How will we accomplish this? He is in Detroit, not Moscow. We cannot burn the streets of Detroit to get at him."

"Who would notice? But no, I have a better plan. And remember, I have captured him once already when others failed."

Sasha relaxed a little. The thing on the screen had been terrifying, but his mother was right, she had taken him once before and she could figure out how to do it again.

"And what is your plan?"

His fear was fading. They were, after all, Red Mafiya, and it, whatever it was, was only a beast.

"We need bait. Something that Drogol and the beast want so badly that they cannot resist our trap."

"But what can we use as bait, Mother? That was no ordinary animal."

Ivan stepped over to him, but he tried to waive the man away.

"No, Ivan. I cannot drink now."

His mother nodded as though he had made a good choice, but Ivan did not leave. Sasha looked up in annoyance and saw the man smiling for the first time since he had known him, and then Ivan the Terrible stuck the two metal probes of a stun gun against the skin of his neck.

His back arched violently and he began to spasm uncontrollably. Ivan held him down in the chair as he shuddered into a final collapse. His eyes stayed open as lay there, aware but confused, conscious but unable to speak. Terror and chaos overpowered his thoughts. It was difficult to tell how long he lay there, staring up at Ivan's impassive face. Eventually, the starets stepped away. Sasha could not feel his arms or legs.

"Move his chair over toward my bed so that I can see him," he heard his mother say.

"Anna, let me look at him first," said Dr. Pazyryk.

"Fah" she said, "Bring him to me."

Sasha had never been so terrified in his life. His mind did not seem able to communicate with his body. Tremors raged through his muscles like electrical storms. Nausea seized him as he saw Ivan's face again and was lifted up to see his mother, who propped herself up on her elbows again. Her visage was grim. Sasha felt sick. The sudden smell of his own urine made him sicker still.

"You asked what I would use as bait. *You* will be my bait. You who act so devoted and loyal. You who are so respectful. You. Yes, you will be my bait. You who conspire with my lieutenants. Did you really think I didn't know? I have done all that you have done long before you were born. Like all children, you fantasize that your parents do not know your thoughts. If you studied chess, you would not make such mistakes.

"How do you think the beast got in, you wonder? More importantly, Sasha, how did it get out? You do not study chess so you do not think analytically. Think. Think, boy, for what else can you do now that your body will not obey you?

"Ahh, so now you see? I betrayed Hauck. I betrayed the Directorate and I betrayed my country. I fell in love, Sasha. Yes, with Drogol. And yes, I had been sleeping with Hauck. He was a handsome, brilliant young man. Much younger than I, but I was permitted because of my position. But Drogol had power. Power over anyone who met him. He was the most sexual, charismatic man I have ever come into contact with, and I would have done anything for him.

"Can you believe that I fell in love with him right in his own cell? That we first had sex against the stone walls of his prison?

"I became his willing tool. I smuggled him keys and codes and told him everything about the layout of the prison. I became a woman I never dreamed I would be, a woman at the mercy of a man I did not know but needed more than anything in life. Are those tears leaking from your eyes, Sasha? Don't worry; I will have him back again. You will be the bait that returns him to me, to us. He and his beast will not be able to resist coming to save you.

"Yes, Son, that beast, that *thing* as you called it—it is your father."

Tears continued to flow from Sasha's eyes.

"Ivan," said his mother. "I'm done with him; we understand each other now. Take him to the storage compartment and lock him in the cage. We don't know if he will change as we grow closer to his father."

*****

Dr. Pazyryk adjusted Anna's Kazakova's intravenous stand while Ivan took Sasha to the storage compartment to lock him away. The ride was smooth, with a few inconsequential bouts of turbulence, but the doctor was taking no chances. They were on the approach now to Detroit. He knew what would become of him if anything happened to Anna.

The old woman lay sound asleep on her bed, blanket pulled up to her chin, and pillow fluffed beneath her pallid skin and thin hair. An almost peaceful smile graced her lined face as she slept. He checked the oxygen flow again, considered for less than a second the idea of strangling her in her sleep, and then left the room to pour himself yet another drink.

How did he end up in this situation?

One simple mistake all those years ago. Showing up drunk for surgery on an important party member. A slip of the scalpel. One simple slip. Maybe two. An incompetent nursing staff. But he was the surgeon. He was responsible. He was going to be sent to prison for the rest of his life. Or to the Gulag. Or he would be shot and possibly a combination of all three.

There were witnesses. Too many. And a very angry and powerful family. He had considered suicide. It was inconceivable that he, an educated, trained surgeon could survive in a work camp. But Anna Kazakova had sent someone to fix the situation. She had sent Ivan to offer him a position as her private physician and protection from the authorities. Anna Kazakova had the power to save him.

Now, she owned him.

But if he could find a way to save Sasha, perhaps the young man might be grateful enough to set him free. That was a possibility. It might work. He reached behind the bar and uncapped the next-in-line bottle of vodka as he thought about it.

Bullshit.

The son of Anna and Drogol would not move aside a stone to set Jesus Christ himself free.

And there was the fact that he had lied when he told the old woman that Sasha was the son of herself and Drogol. He was, in fact, Hauck's son. It was a simple matter to switch the DNA results following Hauck's instructions. The arctic coldness of the man's directions still chilled the doctor. He had relegated his own son to captivity and probable death—all to get his hands on Drogol before the old woman.

He reached in his coat pocket and felt for his keys. Inside the door opener clipped to his key ring was a small encoded communication device that connected to his cell phone so he could send simple text messages to the only ally he had. But if Anna found out that he was spying on her for Hauck, he would no longer have fingers to type text messages.

CHAPTER SEVEN

Hauck slammed his fists against the steering wheel in frustration. What had gone wrong?

The bullets filled with mercury-silver amalgam should have killed the beast. According to all the legends, according to all the lore, the amalgam should have stopped him dead. What was he missing? What was this thing?

He drove a Ford F350 pickup truck, was dressed in a flannel shirt and jeans and his thick black and gray hair sprouted out around the edges of a Detroit Tigers baseball cap. A Styrofoam cup of lukewarm Dunkin Doughnuts coffee wiggled in his dashboard cup holder. Immersed beneath the surface was a small cube of gel explosive with enough power to flatten a city block.

He stopped carefully for a red light and took a deep breath to calm himself. Anger was not enough. Logic and analysis were what would win for him as they always had. But he needed more facts. This beast seemed to defy both myth and logic.

A white van pulled up beside him to his right. Its engine idled so loudly that he could hear it even with his windows up. Hauck looked straight ahead. The light stayed red as cross street traffic drove past him heading west toward the I-75 entrance ramp. He cut his eyes to the right slightly and saw the van driver look away quickly. In the passenger side rearview mirror he saw the back doors of the van burst open and a man dressed all in black hit the ground and ran up between the idling vehicles.

Shit.

Carjacking.

He drew his Bulgarian made 9 mm and depressed the power window switch to lower the passenger's side window. In the dim light he saw the man swinging his shotgun to his shoulder as he approached.

Hauck sneered slightly as he brought his pistol up quicker than the man's shotgun. He depressed the gas pedal hard. The truck jumped forward as he missed one oncoming car and swung the wheel to the right. He fired off three sound-suppressed rounds into the van's windshield, deliberately missing the driver by nearly a foot. Glass shattered and collapsed onto the driver.

Risking a quick look behind him, he saw the man with the shotgun lower the barrel. He was standing out in the open with a weapon and if a cop car or citizen with a cell phone saw him, he was going down. After a moment's frozen thought, the thug made a run for the back of the van to jump back in, but the tires spun and shrieked as the driver sped away, heading the opposite direction from Hauck and leaving the would be assailant by himself, a man with a shotgun and no excuse.

Keep moving, thought Hauck. *Keep moving.*

No time for petty crime.

He drove past a row of wounded houses, window frames boarded like wooden eye patches on sightless eyes, then turned away and thought hard.

The girl was the key. She provided the first clue that Drogol was in the United States in the first place. From there, Zoe had insinuated herself into Drogol's confidence. He had to find her quickly. But she had gone missing, and Hauck's communication network was damaged with Yuri down. And he couldn't even contact the minder he had planted with her as a friend.

Too much was going wrong in one night.

Sveta was on the run. Something had spooked her. Zoe was missing. And Anna Kazakova knew by now that he had betrayed her. It was a necessary risk on her part to get what she wanted. She would be bringing in reinforcements, probably including her son Sasha. It was going to get crowded on the streets of Detroit, he thought.

"This is Evgeny," came the words in his ear-bud.

"Go ahead."

He wanted desperately to ask Evgeny if he had actually hit the beast with his shots, but he knew better.

"We are in place. Our friend is being looked after."

"Assessment?"

"Functional. Fractured, not broken. Cuts and bruises and maybe a concussion. He can heal on his own time. The doctor gave him medications."

"How long before he is able to get back online?"

"Ten minutes."

Hauck glanced at the clock and saw that it was quarter to three in the morning. The night around him was filled with abandoned cars and litter. Stop signs sprayed with graffiti. He braked at an intersection. This time, he was alone except for the body of a cat five or six feet in front of his truck, lit up in his headlights like a crime scene victim. A family pet or a wild animal, he wondered idly. Across the street he saw someone crouched beside a massively dented mailbox, clutching a brown bag by the neck. With so much freedom and money, what had Americans done to their country?

"Make sure he can think straight."

"Understood. Second team?"

"Have our friend or yourself contact me to reassure me that the game is still in play before we join in again. And Evgeny?"

"Yes?"

"Call me with news about our friend watching the Tarot reader. I fear he's not feeling well but want it confirmed."

"I'll take care of it."

Hauck terminated the conversation.

They employed a simple, but elegant solution for avoiding Homeland Security intercepts. Yuri ran an online multi-player role playing urban fantasy game where players from all over the world communicated via voice over internet telephony. Communications were about targets, weaponry, kidnapping and gun battles. The infrastructure and sheer numbers allowed Hauck's own communications and those of his team to blend in with the game traffic. Still, they watched what they said.

Raindrops tapped against the windshield, glistening cold drops that disappeared in a fluid swipe when he flicked the wipers on. They came harder and faster still until the sound was near deafening and the water surged and flowed past the windshield wipers as though they weren't there. After a moment, the pelting slowed and he could see more clearly. The light changed and he drove forward down a black glass street. Streetlights now haloed the wet pavement and the lights from a neon liquor store sign bled toward a storm drain in moving pools of smeared colors.

It was time to call in the Instructor.

Hauck didn't want to do it.

First there was the cost. Second, the man was difficult to work with. He was a gruff, brutal force of nature crammed into a five foot four body more muscle than anything else. Third, he was scarcely controllable in the best of times. But he was unusually well qualified to reacquire Drogol. If he would agree to take the job. He had to agree to take the job. And the Instructor was the only man Hauck knew that might survive an encounter with the beast.

Mistakes should be assessed, even analyzed, but not repeated. He had made a mistake thinking that Drogol and his beast were older and weaker. Sveta, Crue and the team should have been able to terminate an eighty year old man, even working with Anna's thug Chenko. She wanted Drogol and his beast alive. Hauck knew they both had to die.

That was my mistake, he thought. *Thinking nobody could be dangerous at that age.*

Since Hauck knew that no plan survived its first encounter with battle, he always prepared for chaos and recovery. He seeded three fully equipped command posts throughout the city. Three team levels was a heavy operational expense load to carry, but Hauck knew too much about his opponents to go in with only one team and he'd funded it mostly with Anna's money.

He drove around for another ten minutes, getting the feel of the city streets, driving over potholes big as car tires, letting his mind float as he looked for answers.

"Evgeny here," came the voice in his ear.

"Go ahead."

"Our friend passed away tonight."

"Is that so?" said Hauck irritably.

"Yes."

"Details?"

"Dead before he hit the floor. Blow to the head."

"The woman?" asked Hauck.

"He had a knife in his hand. Blood on the blade. She was gone. Car missing as well."

"I see."

"Network is live, Yuri says."

"Understood."

They clicked off.

Zoe's watcher was dead. Zoe was gone and her car along with her. And if it was Zoe's blood on the knife, then it was better for the watcher to be dead than for Hauck to get hold of him.

CHAPTER EIGHT

Sveta opened her mouth to scream for a guard, but closed it quickly without saying a word. Gunshots cracked like there was a war going on outside her cell. The screams and bestial howlings made her press her body back against the concrete. She knew before the thought formed that the beast had followed them.

Desperately she shook and pulled at her restraints; she knew she had to get away, but her wrists, ankles and neck were banded and chained to the wall. She sat on a metal shelf bolted to the back wall, manacled into place like an exhibit in a torture museum. Her back and shoulders stretched to the limit as she tried to break free.

Nothing gave way. No bolts pulled loose from the wall, no cables snapped. She was still a prisoner.

Automatic weapons fire joined in and Sveta felt her breath catch in her throat. She flashed back to Chechnya where she had been hand-cuffed to a pole in a room with three guerillas when a firefight broke out in the stairway. But in Chechnya the shots had been fired by her team coming to set her free. She knew instinctively that whatever was loose in the warehouse was not coming to save her.

For once she was glad to be locked up. She was safe behind a metal door, with riveted metal strips and an electronic key lock with thick bolts sunk deep into a lock-plate to secure it against forced entry. Whatever was happening to the men outside her room, she was glad she wasn't involved. After the beast was killed, she would have to figure out how to get free, but for now she was safer in the room than in the warehouse.

Zoe was somewhere in the building. If she was being examined by a doctor, if Mishka hadn't been lying about that, she too, might be behind a closed door. Or, his men could have taken her into the alley behind the warehouse and shot her in the back of the head. There was no way to know what happened to her. And there was nothing Sveta could do to help her until she was set loose from her chains.

More screams than shooting came from the other side of the door now. Loud crashes like equipment being thrown about. Sveta felt her heart beating faster.

Suddenly her room was plunged into darkness. She tried to remain still and was about to bite her lip to control her trembling when it crossed her mind that the beast might smell her blood.

Was that how the animal had tracked them here? By sense of smell?

If so, there was really no place to hide from it.

A concussion rocked the room as the door burst inward along its hinges. With a percussive blast the thick metal door shot at her and bounced off the wall only inches away from where she sat. It clanged to the floor and skipped once to rest on a metal desk. Pulsing red light flashed behind a dark silhouette that filled the doorway, outlining it like a demon cutout. A smell rushed into the room like a suffusing spirit—the odor of wet fur and blood.

She fought the urge to scream.

It snarled, low and guttural, like an angry earthquake.

Sveta closed her eyes to block out the horror. There was no shame in fear. She waited, listening to the slavering growl build in intensity. Her body began to shake as it howled again. With her hands chained, it was impossible to block the sound. It was so painful that she imagined blood pouring from her ears.

Suddenly angry and defiant, she opened her eyes.

The beast was gone.

*****

"I need to speak to the Instructor," Hauck said into his secure phone.

He loosened his top collar button and walked to one of the thirty-three original paintings of Detroit that hung on his walls. This one was of a dark alley somewhere near the Institute of Arts, he suspected. How peculiar that the artist left the canvas unsigned. But that was what Hauck enjoyed most about the work. It was a stark masterpiece, painted by an artist with no need of recognition.

The apartment had checked clean. Team Two had run through every square inch of the place. The walls were covered with lanthanum doped ceramics particles that defeated any attempt to eavesdrop on his conversations and obscured the room from sophisticated thermal imaging scans. Random pinpoints of the same material coated the window as well, to prevent anyone from monitoring glass vibrations. He was an extraordinarily careful man when it came to security. With today's espionage technology, a great deal more of a modern spy's life was spent looking at computers than at people. Although Hauck connected his organization with them, he never lost sight of the need to build a network of informants. He stayed alive by knowing people, not by surfing keyboards.

He punched in the requisite security codes, gone through the switches and electronic security gates to reach the Instructor, and was now talking to a woman with a French accent.

"He is busy."

"And so am I, Madame. Tell him this is the Magician. I'll call back in five minutes. If he's too busy to take the call, I'll give the money to someone else."

She started to say something, but he depressed the "off" button.

Gatekeeper, he thought, and wondered what she looked like.

He was in a loft apartment at the edge of Detroit. Three stories tall with only four neighbors in the bottom two floors. Hauck occupied the entire upper floor of the building. He came and went as he wished using the cover of an environmental photojournalist. In Detroit, the city was simply glad to have tenants. As it was in so many of the world's major cities, not many questions were asked when a potential buyer showed up with money.

Five minutes were up. Hauck punched in the number again. He went through the electronic identification sequence and got the gatekeeper again.

"He will speak to you."

"Thank you."

"But not at this number."

"Tell him it's urgent."

"He says to convey to you, monsieur, that he received an earlier call from an elderly woman who would very much like him to kill you."

"Put him on now, please."

"The minimum is five million."

"I will only discuss money with him."

"Then this is good night."

The phone went dead.

Hauck removed his Bulgarian-made Pelitza 9 millimeter from inside his coat just to feel its weight in his hands. Depending on what she looked like, Hauck wondered how it would feel to shoot the gate-keeper. Not good enough, he decided, to risk pissing off the Instructor.

Night tightened its bitter noose about the barren streets of Detroit.

Hauck put the pistol away and waited.

Fifteen minutes passed.

He punched in the number again, went through the secure switching, and waited til her voice came on the line again.

"I need to speak with him."

"It is your lucky night."

"Thank you, Madame."

Patience, Hauck reminded himself.

A full minute passed before the Instructor's gruff voice barked in his ear.

"The fuck you bothering me for? I'm retired, I told you."

"Will you come?"

"Five million."

"You will pay me when you see the target."

"Is that so? I don't pay nobody nothing. You out of your fucking mind? I don't pay nobody nothing. You call me in the middle of the night while I'm banging the missus to tell me I'll pay you?"

Ten seconds passed as Hauck considered how honest to be. He needed this man desperately. The regular teams were professionals, well trained and seasoned in their line of work, but Hauck now realized that Drogol and his beast were beyond anything they could be trained to confront.

"I think you're the only man alive who can take it out."

Pause from the other end of the line.

"It? What are we talking about here?"

With a now steady hand, Hauck poured himself a whiskey neat, lifted the glass, and sipped its warmth.

"The challenge of a lifetime, monsieur."

"Don't give me that French bullshit. Think it impresses me? Don't dick me around. Just because I taught you don't mean you can waste my time. You know what I mean. I'm a busy guy. I'm old and I want to get laid right up to the last minute. So what have you got?"

"One million dollars for you just to watch the video I am about to transmit to you."

"You're a whack job, but send the money before the picture shit. I'm not promising anything. I got to get back to the wife."

Hauck idled over to one of his computer keyboards and pressed the enter key to begin transmission of the digitally converted file. It was from his stolen copy of the video taken so many years ago at the prison. He would wire the money after the Instructor accepted the job.

"I'd watch the video first. You might find it better than sex."

"Dream on, Pancho. Give me another hour and I'll take a look."

While pocketing his phone, Hauck noticed that one of this cuffs was not buttoned.

The trouble with disguising yourself to look like an average American, he thought, was that you so seldom had the opportunity to wear cufflinks.

Chapter Nine

Sveta shook so hard she almost collapsed with relief.

She was alive.

Sweat slicked her wrists. In a frantic spasm she yanked hard, narrowing her hands to try to slide free. She pulled again. Links of chains clinked taught, but did not give. Again. Her wrists chaffed and bled but she could not break free. She was a trained soldier with all of the skills to fight back, but she could not escape from her manacles. It was her nightmare. All her training did nothing for her in that moment.

She was vulnerable, and it drove her to a fury.

Like a contortionist she twisted her body this way and back, pulling and yanking futilely. She needed a key, but her guard was no doubt dead.

A horrifying thought rushed into her mind. What if everyone was dead and the beast left? How long would it be before anyone came for her? She could die here, chained to a wall in a Mafiya warehouse. The thought filled her with despair and anger. Her mother would never know what happened to her.

An angry roar brought her back to reality. The beast was still loose in the building. It may have sensed that she could not escape and felt no need to kill her right at that moment. But it would be back.

When it was hungry.

Silence settled in. Sveta strained her ear, but could hear nothing. The pulsating red emergency lights continued to flash in the attenuated darkness, but a sudden unease filled her. Moments passed like the silent, inexorable descent of a crushing weight. What was happening?

Then came the footsteps. Heavy, evenly measured, like an executioner walking towards a gallows.

Someone was coming.

Sveta wanted to call out, to warn them, but fear clamped her throat like an urgent warning. Who? Who was coming?

Was that why she could not hear the beast? Was it lying in wait for this person, ready to lash out and kill whoever them?

She made her decision. Whoever was coming, at least they were human. Maybe, just maybe they could find they keys and set her free so she would have a fighting chance.

"Be careful," she shouted. "There's a wild animal loose in the hallways. Help me. I'm chained in her and need to get loose. Find the keys. Please. But if you don't have a gun don't take any chances. It's dangerous."

The footsteps came closer, but there was no answer.

Sveta didn't like the feeling that coursed through her body.

She lost control, shook her chains and shouted out, "I need a gun. Somebody get me a gun."

And then she hung from her chains, limp from the effort, exhausted. She stared at the floor, seeing the red lights strobe across it like warning lights. Emergency. Emergency. Danger.

The footsteps stopped at the door to her room. For a moment, she was too tired, too filled with hopelessness to look up. Then she heard a rough voice, exhausted and haggard.

"I have come for you."

She raised her head and saw a tall, dark silhouette where a short time before she had seen that of the beast.

*****

Sveta recoiled and pressed her back against the wall.

"Who are you?"

She instinctively knew his name, but she realized that was not enough. He had to say it himself.

"Drogol. I have keys," he said, and walked toward her.

It was true. His voice was deep and heavily accented. For a moment she wondered how he had gotten past the beast. Her nerves were over-loaded. She felt balanced at the edge of her sanity. Chained to a wall and terrorized by a beast. No weapon. No way to escape or defend herself. What kind of soldier was she if she could not fight?

"I found them on the floor next to what was left of your guard."

The room grew smaller as he approached. She felt her breath catch. "Don't be afraid," he said.

His eyes were a soft luminous green in the darkness, but she could already see that he was not as old as Hauck said. Sveta felt her heart pounding with fear at the unexpected sight of the man. He stepped close to her, and with a fluid motion like a conjurer producing a spray of flowers, he held the guard's keys in front of her eyes. She felt the first hope she had felt since being chained like an animal.

"Hold out your hands," he said. "Obey me, or I will leave you here."

She hesitated.

"We have to find the girl before it is too late," he hissed. "She is in danger, I feel it."

Sveta thrust her hands forward. The metal bands fell away as he twisted the key in their locks. She touched a hand to her blood-slicked, swollen left wrist and had to bite back a yelp. The strobing red light flashing through the darkness disoriented her.

Drogol squatted down and began to remove her ankle irons. She considered how a blow to the back of the head would take him out. She had trained all of her adult life for such attacks, and her chance to regain control of her situation was right that second. But she did nothing. This man held more than the key to her restraints. He held the answers to what was really going on. Sveta wanted that information very badly.

When he straightened up, he towered above her. He stood close. More than was comfortable; as though he had no sense of personal boundaries. But it was more than that. He exuded a sense of magnetic power. Sveta wondered at the fact of it. Moments ago she had considered killing him. Now, for some reason she couldn't explain, she did not think that it would have been enough to stop him.

"Where did they take her?" he asked.

His voice was thick with power. She saw before her a man who, even in the midst of this mindless terror, was completely in control of himself.

"Who?"

"The girl. Zoe. Where did they take her?"

"I don't know."

"She has little time," he said angrily. "I feel it."

For a moment, she hesitated again. Could it be Drogol who

attacked and injured her? No. If Drogol had attacked Zoe, Sveta knew that the girl would be dead. No, that couldn't be. Zoe had said that Drogol sent her.

"I don't know. They took me away before I saw what happened to her. I asked for a doctor. She was wounded. Bleeding."

Even in the red-black darkness, Sveta could see his expression harden.

"Follow me. I will find her. I must find her."

He turned heel imperiously and strode away.

Sveta struggled to keep up. Her ankles were swollen and sore, but as painful as that was, she was yet more conscious of the scent of blood and death around her. The smell of the thing was everywhere like a fog of musk. It was so strong Sveta worried whatever animal it was that left body parts ripped and torn and thrown everywhere was still lurking about, watching them, waiting to attack and devour her. Yet she hurried to keep up with Drogol, because it seemed to be *his* beast.

"*I have come for you,*" he had told her earlier.

And indeed he had.

"The animal," she called after Drogol, "what is it?"

"Stay very close to me," he said without so much as looking over his shoulder.

Sveta hurried to catch up.

*****

They moved down the dark halls quickly, Drogol stopping to listen and sniff the air at each corner they turned. At the third corner, Sveta saw a bearded head lying against a stack of files. Dark fluid pooled away from it. The blood odor mixed with the nearly overpowering stench of the beast; she held her collar in front of her face to screen out some of the smell.

"This way," he said.

Sveta wondered how he knew where he was going, but then she saw him stop once, sniff the air, and then press on with still longer, quicker steps than before. The idea that Drogol was tracking Zoe the way that a bloodhound tracked its quarry terrified her.

"Down this hall, quickly. Stay close to me."

When he stopped suddenly before a closed door marked "Mainte-nance Supplies," she almost collided with his back.

With his tilted slightly toward the ceiling, he was sniffing the air, inhaling long moments of it as though sifting through its aromas.

"What is it?" she asked.

He grabbed the doorknob, twisted it, and pushed the door open. Zoe lay crumpled on the floor near a broom and pail of mop water. Her skin was pallid gray-white. Sveta moved into the room, pushing Drogol aside, and dropped to her knees.

"Bastards," she said. "I asked for a doctor. I told them she was wounded. I hope they burn in Hell."

No pulse throbbed beneath her fingertips as she held them lightly against the side of Zoe's neck. Sveta bit her lip, holding back the desire to scream. Another death. Another incomprehensible event in an irrational night. She looked up at Drogol and shook her head.

"She's gone."

Even in the muted red darkness she could feel the anger radiating from him. What had this young woman been to him? Granddaughter? Friend? Protector?

"Move aside," he said.

His voice was strong, authoritative.

"I told you, she's dead," Sveta said.

"She is not yet gone."

Sveta backed away to let him see for himself.

"We have to leave. These men who left her here may be dead but others will return."

"Let them," he said as he sat down cross-legged and placed the dead woman's head in his lap.

"I'm sorry for your grief, but you don't understand. These men, they are Red Mafiya. Even your beast will not be able to stand up against them. They have many men and as many guns as they need. If that's not enough, they'll bring more. If they find us here, they will kill us."

Drogol's rough long hair swung to one side as he cupped Zoe's head in his hands, then bent down to kiss her forehead. Sveta thought she saw a faint glistening track move down his cheek, as though he were crying. He began to rock back and forth, then side to side.

"She's dead—we must leave the dead behind us or we will join them," she said.

Softly, and then in a rising crescendo that coursed with power, he began to chant in an old Russian dialect that Sveta didn't understand.

As he sang them, she felt a shiver shake her spine. A word here and there was clear and had not changed over the years. He drew out the word God as though it were an entreaty.

There was no time. She had to at least find a weapon.

"I'll be back," she said.

Drogol continued to chant as though he had not heard her. The small room was closing in around here, as though his chants were stealing the air. She saw the light in Drogol's eyes grow brighter, but looked away, knowing that it was an illusion brought about by stress and lack of sleep. She had to get away.

Without another word, she turned and left.

Sveta searched the hallways until she found what she was looking for, its shoulder strap wrapped around a dead man's arm. It was all there was of him, and she wondered for just a moment if it was his head that she had seen earlier. Although she'd seen worse in combat, there was something about this whole night that was too much for her nerves. Hauck. Drogol. The beast.

That was when it hit her. Hauck would somehow learn of the warehouse carnage. He would be on his way when he got word of it. Maybe he was already coming.

Without another thought, she unwound the bloody strap, then tossed the arm down the hall. She didn't like the blood. Blood drew carnivores. And what had torn through the warehouse was definitely a meat eater.

Every separate hallway had an emergency light. She moved to the nearest to inspect the AK she'd retrieved. More by feel than sight she looked for damage and found none. The magazine was more than half full. Whoever the gun's former owner was hadn't the time to get off a full clip from a weapon on full-auto.

She could feel the sticky residue of blood on the stock and trigger. Nothing about this night was going right. What started out as a precise strike turned into a an out and out war.

When she returned to the maintenance closet to tell Drogol that it was time to go, she stopped in the doorway as though an invisible hand wouldn't allow her to go any further. What she saw almost stopped her heart. Zoe was sitting up, leaning against Drogol's shoulder. Her eyes were open and she smiled weakly at Sveta.

"You see?" said Drogol. "What is in the heart of God is more important than what we believe."

Sveta could not take her eyes off the two off them. Zoe had no pulse just minutes before. None. Zoe was dead. Now she was smiling.

Unwinding to his full height with the fluidity of a cat, Drogol raised Zoe with him.

"Why do you stare?" he asked Sveta. "Whom our most glorious God chooses to heal, is healed."

CHAPTER TEN

All I got to know," said the Instructor over his secure phone, "is whether or not this is bullshit."

"Everything on that video is absolutely real," said Hauck.

"Bad piece of work, that one there. Gonna be tough to kill."

"No one has been able to accomplish that so far."

"Yeah, well, that's what you get for working with amateurs."

Hauck closed his eyes and counted to ten. Before he could begin speaking, the old man was already poking at him again.

"My wife hates you, you know."

"I'm sorry to hear that. How soon before you can be here?"

"Who says I'm coming?"

"Five million dollars."

"I don't need the money. I'll take it, though, 'cause I'm getting old and I want to live good."

"And the chance to see that thing face to face."

"It's no wonder Anna wants you dead. My wife hates you and the old bitch wants you dead. They got something in common. Go figure. And I'll be there before noon. I'll have one of my guys drive me."

"Shall I meet you?"

"I'm coming to your place, Pancho. We got to pick up a few things when I get there."

"I can arrange—"

"Don't arrange nothing."

"You'll need an address."

"Like I don't know where you live? Dream on."

Before he could answer, the Instructor clicked off.

Hauck's face was bathed a ghostly gray-blue by the light from his computer screen. His fingers flew across the keyboard as he sent a message to Yuri and then pressed the "Send" icon.

With that out of the way, he leaned back and breathed a soft sigh. The Instructor was on his way. Now all he would have to do is make sure that after the old man dealt with Drogol that he escaped with his own life. He knew the old man. Not once during their conversations had he said that he hadn't accepted Anna Kazakova's contract.

*****

At four a.m. Detroit time, Anna Kazakova's private jet touched down. It was a smooth landing, expertly managed by her pilot, a former Russian Army fighter pilot. A team of Red Mafiya soldiers pulled up in an ambulance and removed Sasha's cage and loaded it in. Ivan had given him water laced with a sedative to insure a quiet transition. The cage itself was covered by a black tarp stretched tight and roped to eyeholes at each of its four corners.

Ivan carried both Anna and her wheelchair down the stairs from the plane and deposited her on the ground without so much as breaking a sweat. Dr. Pazyryk followed dutifully behind, and then leaned over to check the old woman's breathing.

"Get away from me, I'm fine," she snapped.

The doctor jerked back as though shot.

Mishka waited a respectful distance away. He was flanked by a man on either side, with five more sober-faced men spread out behind them. His dark cashmere coat flapped in the wind like a limp flag; his thick black hair hung down near his shoulders like a fluttering curtain.

"My car," said Anna icily.

A long Hummer limousine pulled into view when Mishka raised his hand. It rolled to a slow stop beside the ambulance and idled silently. Faint gray fumes puffed out from the exhaust, and the windows reflected back the shiny black of the night haloed by the tarmac lights.

"I don't like it."

Mishka looked aghast.

"I don't understand," he said. "Is there something wrong?"

A corner of his mouth twitched, and he nervously flung back one side of his scarf over his right shoulder.

"You are a good boy, Mishka, but you are weak."

"What have I done to offend you?"

The men on either side of Mishka seemed to learn away from him. Behind him, the others remained still. The terminal behind them was a giant gray building with two bleak eye-windows on either side of a massive hangar door. Fuel trucks were parked 150 feet away near a row of pumps, but there was no one else in sight save Anna's small entourage and Mishka's grim-looking bodyguards.

"Go," she said, motioning with her hand. "Dr. Pazyryk will show you his new patient."

"Me?" questioned the doctor.

"Or else he will join his new patient."

In his semi-drunken state, Dr. Pazyryk was about to ask another question. Ivan moved sideways, and then slammed a palm against the doctor's back. He reeled forward as though hit by a train. Mishka caught him before he fell.

To cover his loss of dignity, the doctor looked down dismissively and said, "They should have salted this. What good if we safely land then kill ourselves trying to walk?

Mishka looked hard at Dr. Pazyryk, but the doctor only smiled and walked past him.

"Yes, this way, Mishka. Is that right? Is that your name? Pleased to meet you, I'm sure. Come along and I'll introduce you to my very special patient."

The doctor's words were slightly slurred, and that terrified Mishka. Intuitively he knew that the man was afraid, groping for oblivion.

"Who is ill?" he asked.

"Come, come," said Dr. Pazyryk.

His men were staring at him. Although his bodyguards looked straight ahead, Mishka could feel the eyes of the men behind him, looking for some clue as to what was going on. They had never seen anyone talk down to Mishka and live. And he did not want to join the doctor at the ambulance. He had a very bad feeling about the situation.

When Dr. Pazyryk flung open the ambulance doors, Mishka saw a large tarpaulin covering a box or crate of some size. It instantly reminded him of a coffin. The space between his shoulder blades itched. He wondered if Ivan had a weapon aimed there. It would be simple enough to shoot him, then load his body into the box and send him away to be buried under someone else's name. He turned to look behind him, but the doctor put a hand on his shoulder.

"But you haven't seen my new patient, Mishka," said the doctor. The alcohol made him feel expansive. "Perhaps you know him."

The physician reached in and lifted up an edge of the tarpaulin, revealing the cage it covered. There was someone in the cage, Mishka realized as a cold feeling flooded through him. The man was unconscious, and covered with a blanket, but his manacled wrists were clear to see. And his face was familiar. He leaned forward for a closer look, and then stopped. It was Anna's son, Sasha.

Mishka turned and strode quickly back to stand between his two personal bodyguards. He felt his other men close in behind him. The old woman had caged her own son. What was going on here? What did she know?

"What is the meaning of this?" he demanded.

He tried to make his voice forceful, full of outrage, but it cracked along the edges like an ice floe on the verge of breaking loose and floating away. Two bodyguards. Five gunmen and himself. Eight on his side. Against an old woman, a drunken doctor, Ivan and a pilot. Mustn't forget her crew. Ivan was not someone that Mishka wanted to deal with under any circumstances. But if things escalated, he would have no choice.

The doctor was back leaning against the ambulance. Mishka saw him close his eyes as though sleeping. Ivan stood to one side of the old woman, like a ceremonial statue.

"Things change very quickly sometimes, Mishka," said the old woman. "Do you know how quickly?"

"Please. You know I have been faithful to you."

"I do indeed."

Mishka did not know what to say. His mind raced ahead, wondering whether his men would stand beside him against her.

"Things change as quickly as this," she said, raising one finger as though to test the air.

Blood sprayed on Mishka's beautiful coat as the heads of first the man to his right and then the man to his left exploded. As they fell beside him, he could only stare at his ruined cashmere. A piece of scalp adhered to his lapel, and he could see by the tarmac lights that it was a mixture of black and gray and knew that it came from the head of Lubkin. His hands began to shake, but he did not bolt and run. He knew now that he was outgunned. Anna had stationed snipers throughout the airport. If he went for his own pistol, which now weighed heavily in his coat pocket, he would be killed before he could draw it out.

His remaining men drew their guns, turning this way and that, looking for someone to shoot. They looked like blind men with weapons. Neither Anna nor Ivan moved. A fine spray of rain started, but the water beaded into droplets on Ivan's forehead and ran down his protruding cheekbones.

Mishka looked down and saw that one of his bodyguard's hands had come to rest on his shoe. He shuddered and slipped his foot backward, letting the dead man's fingers fall to the ground.

"Loyalty is more important to me than blood," Anna said after another moment.

Mishka nodded. He thought of being chained and bound in a cage.

"Do you wish me to die of pneumonia?" she called toward the doctor.

"No, Anna. No, of course not."

"Then fetch my umbrella. It is raining and I am an old woman."

The doctor held a hand up to protect himself from the rain and galloped over to where Anna sat in her wheelchair. From a compartment beneath the seat, he withdrew a collapsible umbrella, pressed a button so that it sprang open like a bouquet at a magic show. He held it over her while they all stood in the rain. Only Ivan seemed not to notice the inconvenience.

"You understand me, don't you, Mishka?"

"Yes, I do, Mrs. Kazakova. I understand you."

"I have more cages, you see. More cages, more snipers, more men, and more money than you will ever dream of. I once had a son that I could trust. Someone to groom to take over what I have built. To share in it."

The urge to look down at the dead men pulled his eyes slightly downward.

"Pay attention to me," she snapped. "They are dead. Dead men only rot."

"Yes, Mrs. Kazakova," he said in a tight voice.

She gave the faintest of smiles.

"What kind of cars do I like to ride in, Mishka?"

He could feel the sniper crosshairs on his forehead.

"I thought you might like this—"

"Get me a Mercedes limousine. Ivan and the doctor and I will wait in our private lounge until the car is ready. Have your best driver drive us. We have much to do tonight and there is much to tell you."

"Yes, Mrs. Kazakova."

Quick as he could, he gave instructions to one of his men to secure a Mercedes limo for the old woman. He wasn't dead yet, and she seemed to be offering him a chance to redeem himself.

"Also, there are Russian paramilitary here in town; some are working for me, some for my enemies. You must use your sources and get me any information that will help us find them. I want to know about any new Russians in town that your agents come across."

Mishka was about to nod, but his head froze in mid-nod.

"What is it? What are you keeping from me?"

"Mrs. Kazakova, I may already have captured one such person."

"Who is that?"

"Her name is Sveta, and she was a special operative in the GRU. She came to me for help."

"And why would she do that?" asked the old woman.

"She is my cousin," he admitted.

For the first time since he had known her, Mishka saw Mrs. Kazakova smile.

"Good. Very good."

"Thank you," he said.

"You would turn in your own flesh and blood for me. You may yet indeed go far in my organization."

As he started to breathe a sigh of relief, Mishka saw an attendant close the ambulance back doors, then get into the cab. Brake lights flashed red, and the ambulance pulled away into the cold, wet night. He wondered what would happen to Sasha. It was not a long thought. Ivan pushed the old woman's wheelchair past him, followed by the doctor who patted Mishka on the back lightly and said, "You'd better come inside. This weather is bad for the health."

Resigned to his new situation, Mishka told one of his remaining men to remove the bodies and clean up the mess.

"The sun will be up soon," he told the man.

"What do we tell their families?"

"Tell them they won't be coming home."

CHAPTER ELEVEN

Sveta led the way back through the warehouse to where she had first been brought in front of Mishka. She found the Hummer and loaded the bag of weapons, clothes and money that Mishka left behind into the hatchback. Before closing the hatch, she took out a Beretta, jacked a magazine into the grip, hung the holster over her shoulder and slid the pistol into it. With the AK slung over one shoulder and a firm grip on her pistol, she felt dressed for the first time since she had killed Hauck's man at the truck stop.

It was difficult to ignore the odor and the blood slicks, but Sveta had been in combat situations before. She understood and could adapt to that. But the warehouse smelled more like a slaughterhouse. And she would be glad to be away from the hideous emergency lights that had been flashing since the moment of the beast's attack.

Drogol gently helped Zoe into the backseat of the Hummer and then slid in beside her. Sveta hopped into the driver's side, laid the AK-47 down, reached up to an overhead compartment and got the spare set of keys, then turned them in the ignition. She adjusted the rearview mirror and took a careful look at the man who had brought Zoe back to life. He leaned over toward the young woman when she looked momentarily distressed, and smiled when she felt better. It was obvious that he cared for her. For a moment she wondered if this was really the killer Hauck was tracking. The things she had seen tonight, though, brought her back to reality.

He was not a handsome man. He had large eyes, a narrow face with a prominent forehead, thick nose and strong chin. His hair was long and brushed back so that he vaguely resembled an Indian shaman except for the dark intensity that radiated from him. That sense of power and energy was as real to Sveta as his physical features. Being close to him was like being pulled along by a human magnet.

"Drive. Go where I tell you. I have a sanctuary in this evil city."

Sveta nodded and drove the Hummer forward to where a hand-sized red button was mounted on an I-beam. She rolled the window down, depressed it, and the giant warehouse door began to rise with a complaining screech. As it went up, she withdrew her pistol from her holster and tried to calm her breathing. As the warehouse door rose enough for her to see the empty street, she wondered why she was taking direction from this man.

Because I'm using him, she told herself.

"Go slowly. Turn in whatever direction is clear. First we drive to see if we are followed. Then we go to safety."

Sveta shifted to drive again, depressed the pedal and turned onto the street.

"Concentrate on driving, please. I will look for watchers."

Time to push back.

"Drogol?"

"Yes?"

"Quit giving me orders."

From the backseat she heard his bitter laugh.

"You find that funny?" she asked.

She'd seen the dashboard button. She knew Mishka. She knew this car, since it was the one she had been locked in the backseat of hours before. It was the type of car driven by only two types of people in Moscow—politicians and criminals. Mafiya vehicles were filled with all sorts of toys. With a quick look down, Sveta found the other switch she was looking for and rested her finger on it.

"There is no time for this, young woman."

"I'm not your young woman," said Sveta, and without thinking about it she pushed down on the gas pedal and drove faster.

"All women are young to me," said Drogol. "And you are a trained soldier, are you not?"

"What about it?"

"I was born to give orders, and you have trained to take them, don't you see? So, I will give them and you will take them."

Sveta met his eyes in the rearview mirror. They were cold and unyielding.

"I can't hear you," she said. "Window's in the way."

With that, she hit the auto-lock and depressed the switch for the bullet-proof partition window. The motors silently engaged and the three inch thick silicon aluminum oxynitride barrier slid up and locked into place with a solid click.

The rage in Drogol's eyes was so hot and angry she fought the urge to lean forward. Instead, she smiled. She caught sight of Zoe leaning over to catch her attention in the mirror.

Sveta saw her mouth a panicked "No." Zoe's face was a mask of horror.

Drogol's fist rammed into the bullet-proof divider so hard Sveta felt her teeth click together.

*****

"Do you have control of yourself or do I need to turn on the knockout gas piped into the backseat?"

There was no knockout gas, but he wouldn't know that.

Drogol glared at her. His eyes grew wide and his nostrils flared as her voice boomed at him through the backseat speakers. Once again he pounded his fists against the bulletproof glass. The impact sent a concussion through the car frame. Zoe cowered like a frightened child, pressing herself back into the seat as far as she could go.

"The backseat was built for containment, so don't waste your time," Sveta said. But his eyes flamed like burning plastic. As though somewhere behind his features was a boiling vessel of rage waiting to explode into full-blown insanity. It was impossible for any man to break through bulletproof glass with his fists; but Drogol was clearly not just any man.

"Last chance before I turn on the gas," she yelled.

There was no amount of money worth what she had dealt with tonight.

She was cruising the speed limit down Gratiot trying to look normal while a six foot six man was beating on the bullet-proof glass wall that separated them in her Mafiya-owned car. Better to stick to the main roads, though, since Hauck would be covering the back roads, not expecting her to drive down a main street, even one as third world as Gratiot.

"Don't," Zoe suddenly screamed over the car's speakers. "Don't do that."

Their eyes met in the rearview mirror again.

"Don't weaken his mind while he is angry. Please."

Drogol bellowed like a wild animal. His long hair whipped about his shoulders as he howled.

"Never talk about me as though I am not present," he said in a voice loud as an imperial decree to a courtyard full of peasants.

Sveta reached for the volume control and turned it back.

"Then get control of yourself," she snapped back. "I don't have time for this. I need to stay alive and the only way I can do that is by getting out of here fast. You're slowing me down with your bullshit. I have a target on my back and I need a good plan to avoid getting shot, so I'd thank you very much to quit acting like an asshole."

"I owe you nothing," he shouted. "I set you free."

"I wouldn't have been chained up in the first place if it wasn't for you."

Zoe scooted as far away from Drogol as she could. If there were door handles, Sveta had no doubt that Zoe would have opened the car door and jumped.

Where to go? What to do?

"Who are you? And I mean really and not this I'm a poor persecuted fugitive," said Sveta. "That's for starters, and what was that thing? Was that your beast?"

Drogol's composure returned like sunlight coming out again from behind a dark cloud. He studied her eyes carefully in the mirror.

"So," he said. "How very much like a soldier. You do not know who you hunt. You do not care who you hunt. You only follow orders. Point your gun this way. Pull your trigger that way. Tell me, who did you think you were hunting? Who did you think you were sent to kill?"

"I only know your name, and that a lot of people seem to die around you."

Drogol turned his head sideways to watch the night go by through the tinted glass. Traffic was thin. He seemed to withdraw inward. For the first time she noticed he wore a heavy coat with a high collar that reminded her of a priest's robes. His face was alternately highlighted and then shadowed by the passing streetlamps. They drove by abandoned storefronts placarded with sheets of worn and cracked plywood nailed over broken windows. She saw in his face a look of haunted forlornness as he stared at them.

"I have been conspired against and hunted all my life," he said, "but I have never sought the death of another. Each spark of life is from God's eternal flame, and as His children we must keep the fires of His love alive. The man you work for, the man who pays you, he has no respect for the sanctity of life and breath. He is a man who does not know how to love. He hates me because I do."

Sveta rubbed a hand across her forehead.

"That tells me exactly jack and shit."

"Years ago, he imprisoned me on the orders of his lover, a high-ranking member of the secret police. They held me captive. Do you wish to hear more?"

"What was her name?"

"Anna Kazakova."

"*The* Anna Kazakova?"

"I don't know what you mean," he said.

Sveta tried to keep focused on the road, but of all the names in the world that Sveta did not want to hear, Anna Kazakova was near the top of the list.

"Not what, *who*. The Red Mafiya Anna Kazakova. She used to be KGB, but now she is a criminal. She must be the one who was working with Hauck to find and capture you."

She saw Drogol turn toward Zoe.

"Can this be true?" he asked.

The small, hesitant voice was almost inaudible over the speakers. Sveta turned up the volume.

"I don't know, Father. I don't know."

Sveta risked a glance in the rearview again and saw Zoe close her eyes. After a few moments, her eyes still closed, she replied, "An old woman. Yes. An evil, cold heart. Everywhere she goes the nine of swords goes with her."

"What is she saying?" asked Sveta. "And how would she know Anna Kazakova?"

"Because unlike you, she is a woman with heart and sees by inner vision."

Sveta slammed on the brakes so hard the car swerved.

"That does it," she screamed, unlocking the rear doors. "Get out.

Get the hell out. I don't need this. All I want to do is get out of town before Hauck finds me."

"How dare you?" hissed Drogol. "You who have seen a miracle from God before your very eyes. You saw that through my hands He fanned the embers of this woman's soul from death to life and now you would cast us out?"

"She was injured, she was hurt, but she couldn't have been dead. I was wrong. No one comes back from the dead."

"You would deny this? Your soul, too, has returned from death to join me, and you would deny her this very miracle?"

Sveta turned in her seat to face him.

"You're crazy," she said. "You are out of your fucking mind."

"Drogol," said Zoe urgently. "Someone is coming. Someone like you."

*****

His world was soft white gauze and confusion. Voices came and went like whispered imaginings. He had no sense of time passing. It was as though he hung suspended in a filamentous aethyr; waiting, waiting for something but he did not know what or why. From somewhere in the mists, Sasha heard a soft voice say, *"Someone is coming, someone like you."*

The ambulance hit a pothole, and his cage flew up in the air and then crashed back to the van floor.

One of the four guards riding shotgun said, "Crazy bastard's dreaming. Talking to himself in a girl's voice."

CHAPTER TWELVE

The road was slick with water as Sveta turned the corner onto a street lined with blasted warehouses and abandoned storefronts shielded with crossed wire metal grills once decorated with glass and curtains. Dawn was coming, and she thought its cold light would reveal these barren neighborhoods in an uncompromising, pitiless gray light.

They had driven for fifteen minutes, winding through streets washed with hopeless pallor, driving past buildings tall and faded, like artifacts abandoned on an alien world. Sveta felt the presence of the beast grow closer, following them like a hunter tracking its prey, and she shuddered. She was exhausted. She could not afford to imagine things.

"Which one?" she asked.

"The third from the end. Up there, on your left. The one with the big roll up door. I will go inside and open it so you can drive in. We must do this quickly."

"I see it."

As the car rolled into the broken concrete driveway, Sveta again unlocked the backdoors and hit another button to pop them open. Drogol got out and went to a metal door near the overhead, pulled a key ring from one of his pockets and moments later disappeared inside.

Sveta flicked the switch to lower the bulletproof glass and swiveled in her seat to face Zoe. The young woman's hair was disheveled and she looked slightly dazed, as though she'd been hit in the head and was still recovering.

"I need to know what's going on here," she said.

"We can't talk now. He'll be back soon."

"Who is he really?"

"You wouldn't believe me if I told you."

"Don't fuck with me," said Sveta. "I need answers."

"The door is opening."

"We'll talk later. Count on it."

The sound of chains grating across a pulley confirmed that the big overhead door was, in fact, opening. Sveta turned back to see it rise halfway up, like a stage curtain rising to reveal the next scene. Inside she could just make out an open space and a back wall stacked with boxes. If she was going to bolt, all she had to do was throw the car in reverse and leave this strange and frightening man behind. But she needed answers, so she turned off the lights and drove forward, trying to keep calm as she heard the sound of the metal door coming down behind her, closing her in darkness.

She turned off the ignition.

"Come," Sveta heard Drogol say.

"Stand away from the door."

She needed time for her eyes to adjust to the light. But a moment later, an orange-yellow light flared and she saw that Drogol had lit an old fashioned oil lantern. It swayed and sent dark shadows skittering about the garage. The smell of hot engine and burned oil diffused through the room.

Sveta picked up the AK47 and her pistol, threw her bag of clothes, more weapons and money over her shoulder, and stepped out of the car. The cold, moist air caused her to shiver, but she straightened and saw Zoe getting out as well. The girl faltered slightly, but pressed a hand against the car frame to keep from falling.

"Are you all right?" she asked.

"I can make it."

But Zoe's voice was tense with pain, and trembled with weakness.

"She lost much blood," said Drogol. "Much time will be needed for her to recover fully. Come. I have medical supplies in my laboratory."

Before Sveta could question what quality of laboratory he could have in the crumbling structure, Zoe was walking toward him.

With the lantern lifted high, he opened a door and went through. Zoe followed, and Sveta, her pistol held at the ready and her AK slung over one shoulder and duffel over the other, stepped through behind them. They walked down a hallway lined with unpainted and peeling drywall across a dusty cement floor. Zoe was an eerie shadow in the bouncing lantern light. The hallway ended abruptly at a locked steel door that Sveta glimpsed over the girl's shoulder before Drogol's back obscured her view. She heard the jangle of his key ring again, and then they followed him down a steep stairway that doglegged left and left again until it was clear that they were following a path of ever descending squares.

Zoe stumbled and Sveta hurried to catch her.

"Are you well enough to walk?" asked Drogol.

"I've got her," said Sveta.

She slid beneath the girl's shoulder and, holstering her pistol, slid an arm around her waist.

"We can make it."

The descent continued and time merged with the darkness. Drogol's lantern silhouetted him with an aura of flickering orange gold, leading them deeper into the maze beneath the surface. Under the weight of her duffel slung across one shoulder and Zoe's slack body on the other, Sveta began to tire. Like a good soldier, she said nothing and pressed on. When she was near exhaustion, Drogol suddenly stopped.

He turned slowly to face them. With his lamp held high, he looked like a crypt keeper. In the rich orange light, the unpainted wall was jaundiced. Behind him was a massive steel door, gray black and forbidding as the door holding back Hell.

"Where you are about to go I have taken no one else. It has been my sanctuary for many years, my place of safety in this evil city."

With an almost irrational sense of fear pressing down on her, Sveta looked up, suddenly afraid that the beast was hurtling down upon them. But there was nothing overhead except the shaft of darkness that speared straight up towards the surface. She had lost count of how many levels they descended in their spiral descent.

"Now, my enemies are upon me once again. Always I have had to run like a criminal in the night. Each time I abandoned my experiments and took with me only the essentials of my work. Now, I am so close, so close that I will not run. I will instead stay here and you will help me so that I will be once and for all free from the curse that has plagued me all these years. I will be separated from God no more."

His voice resonated through the hallway like a dark, hypnotic song.

Somewhere overhead, Sveta imagined that cold rain still glistened the barren streets of Detroit and the homeless still shuddered beneath viaducts and in the shadows of crowded buildings without knowing that a madman made his home beneath the broken concrete of the Motor City.

*****

Drogol stepped toward the massive metal door, and when he was within a few steps, she heard a series of loud clicks as hidden bolts pulled back into the door frame.

Hidden transmitter on him and receiver concealed beneath the drywall, thought Sveta. Had to be. She didn't want to think about any alternatives.

He turned and transfixed them with a stare so intense, Sveta saw Zoe cringe.

This mysterious, frightening man held the answers to what she needed to know.

But he was nothing like Hauck had told them; there was simply no way Drogol was in his eighties. He appeared to be no older than his late forties or early fifties. There were men who were still healthy and vital as they aged, but this was a man still charged with power and possessed an almost animal magnetism. But had he ever had the physical strength and ability to wipe out a KGB prison station?

No. No one was that powerful.

And now she was wondering if there had ever been a prison, much less a prison break. Lies within lies were all that she could believe in.

Her instincts told her that somewhere within these questions were answers that just might hold enough bargaining power to buy back her freedom from Hauck and Anna Kazakova. If germ warfare had been involved, then perhaps the stakes were still high enough to be useful to her.

Drogol set down the lantern, and she saw him grab hold of a massive steel ring welded onto the door. He said something beneath his breath then pulled backward. A hiss like a dying breath escaped the opening as the door slowly gave way, and Sveta unconsciously held her breath. The door was six inches thick and must have weighed over a thousand pounds.

He spoke once again, his words a somber pronouncement in that strange tongue he'd spoken when bringing Zoe back from near death. When he picked up the lantern, Sveta began to breathe again.

As he led them through the doorway, Sveta felt, rather than saw, Zoe move closer to her.

"You will stay immediately behind me," cautioned Drogol. "There is great danger for the inattentive here. Stay close behind my guiding light."

His voice rang throughout the darkness as though they were standing in a large cavern.

But Sveta had enough. She withdrew an LED flashlight from a side pocket within her duffel bag and flicked it on. What she saw caused her jaw to drop.

"Extinguish that light," snapped Drogol.

But the shock of revelation kept her from moving.

"Turn it off. I command you."

She felt Zoe touch her cheek.

"Please," she said.

Sveta turned off the flashlight.

Drogol strode toward them. In the swaying lamplight, his intense, almost burning gaze, his wild beard and his long hair gave him the look of a wild animal.

"This is my sanctuary and my workshop and my home. You will not defile it. I searched the world to find it, worked longer than you have been alive to re-build it, and now that I am about to complete my experiments and make real what my father created I will not have you compromise it. Do you understand me?"

The confusion on Sveta's face was evident. What she had just seen bewildered her beyond what she would have thought possible. They were several stories underground, and there before her, stretching out in the middle of a cavernous laboratory, were things that just could not be. Before she turned out her flashlight she saw glassware distillation columns, globes of glass each as large as a hot air balloon, electrical towers, substations and glistening black cables, gears big as tractor trailers and rows upon rows of shiny brass and silver bells, some large as small planes and others tiny as a child. And in the midst of that wonder stood an antique train, complete with an engine, five cars and a caboose, sitting on a track that seemed to run the length of the space and then disappear at both ends into rock walls.

Drogol snapped his fingers inches before her face to get her attention.

"Do you understand me?" he repeated. "This place is my only hope of salvation. Is it not enough that I bring you here for your safety and to help me? Must you pry instead of ask? Must you spy into that which you have not been invited to see?"

"What is this place?"

"Follow me," said Drogol brusquely, "and you will learn. Time slips away and we have much of urgency to do."

Zoe gave Sveta's arm a gentle squeeze when Drogol moved past them to lead the way again down a single flight of roughhewn stairs.

Sveta allowed him to get a few steps ahead before she whispered to Zoe, "Tell me. What is this place? And who is he?"

From up ahead, she heard Drogol's stop, then walk back toward them. The lantern creaked as it swung back and forth with each step. Again his face appeared haloed in the pallid light.

"You wish to know who I am?"

"Yes," said Sveta. "I want to know who you really are and what this is all about. I want to understand why Hauck and Anna Kazakova are really after you and what that beast is."

"And why do you care, my child?"

Sveta's temper, pushed to the limit by all that happened in one night, flared again.

"I am not your child."

"You have the temperament of an arrogant child. You are self-centered and demanding."

"I am a tired, irritable woman with an automatic rifle," she said. "So don't talk down to me."

"There, you see? I am being pursued by those who seek to take me, to use me as a specimen, and then to kill me. Yet you are more interested in my name, in who I really am. What does that tell you?"

Despite her desire just to pull the AK up and fire a warning round into the darkness, she thought about it.

"I need to know what's going on," she said finally.

"You need? How important."

"Damn it, can't you just answer the question? Who the hell are you really?"

"Why do you care?"

Throughout the entire exchange, Zoe was quiet. Yet Sveta could sense the intensity in that silence. She chose her next words carefully.

"Because I want to get out of this alive. I don't think you have any idea of the type of resources your enemies have at their disposal. They can burn this city to the ground. So why are they after you?"

Drogol's face twisted with rage.

"You lie," he screamed. "You always lie."

"Watch your mouth," Sveta said quietly.

"And now you dare to say such a thing? I know your mind. It schemes and plots. You only wish to know who I am and why these people want me so that you can bargain me away like you did so many years ago."

Drogol waved his hands wildly as he spoke. Sveta curled her finger around the trigger of her AK.

"You are crazy."

"I am not crazy. I know that it was you who bargained my life away to Yusupov. Oh, have I surprised you? Did you think I did not know, that I was a poor simpleton cowed by your imperial will?"

"I have no idea what you're talking about," said Sveta, stepping back and lifting her automatic weapon

"Do you truly not remember who I am?"

"I've had enough bullshit. I ask you a question, you answer with a question. And you're bugshit crazy. I've never laid eyes on you before tonight. So why don't you just tell me who you are and why they're after you?"

"They are," said Drogol, "after my blood."

Back to square one. *Biological warfare.*

"But you're not contagious?"

"Contagious? You really are a child. Of course I'm not contagious."

"You're like their prize lab specimen gone missing."

Drogol's angry laugh roared through the empty space like dynamite going off in a cave.

"Yes," he said, with an approving smile. "I am, as you say, their prize lab specimen gone missing. Anna Kazakova wants my blood to cure her disease. Hauck wants me dead before that can happen."

"And you? What do you want?"

"I want," he said quietly, "free of this curse. I want to regain the destiny of my own soul."

"That's what you want?"

"That is only the beginning, my child. But without that beginning, I can never achieve what I truly want."

"And what exactly is that?"

He shook his head dismissively and turned away from her and began descending the stairs again.

"Who are you?" she called after him.

"A man tested by God and abandoned by love. Do you see this young woman here?"

He waved the lantern toward Zoe. In its wavering light, she seemed younger, more vulnerable despite or perhaps because of what she had undergone.

"And?"

"God so kindly sent her to me to give me the hope to go on. She is His angel given to me, a sign that although I am tested sorely by Him, I am not separated. She was sent to give my heart hope, hope that my love unrequited is not love denied."

Sveta took a step forward, leaned her head back, and looked him straight in the eye.

"Let's get going. You don't want to tell me anything, so I'm not going to bother asking anymore."

Silence hung between them for a time like a rope knotted at each end waiting to be pulled again by one or the other. Finally, he turned around and began walking away, his footsteps strong and determined.

"I am a monster who would be a man again," he said without turning back.

It hung in the air, dramatic as an oath and frightening as a curse hurled in darkness. It was the belief, the utter conviction in the man's voice that unnerved her. She considered turning and making a run for it. If she could shake the nagging fear that the beast was close behind them, she was willing to do it. But in the dead air of the descending hallways, she had caught a whiff of blood and fur.

Sveta hurried to catch up with Drogol and Zoe. For now, she was out of questions. But she had the uneasy feeling that she should have shot him back at the warehouse.

With the AK slung over one shoulder, her duffel hanging on the other, she started walking after the two of them. She knew she should have let both out of the car and kept on driving. Too many risks staying with them. She didn't know who they really were or what was really going on, and she would likely never get a straight answer out of either of them anyway. Still, the last place anyone would ever look for her is a couple of stories under the city of Detroit. And she could not shake the feeling that between her and the exit lurked the beast.

*****

Hauck checked his electronic perimeter and found it secure. Time to rest. He went to the couch, placed his pistol under a cushion, and laid his Benelli shotgun on the floor within easy reach. There was not a time within recent memory that he had ever slept without a firearm close by.

Anna Kazakova and her troops should already be in town. He had given instructions to Yuri and Evgeny; The Instructor was on his way. All that could be done had been done. Sveta was missing and so were Drogol and Zoe, but it was his analysis that they were together. Tomorrow he would see if he was right. Sveta was a smart woman, but in today's electronic world, anyone could be tracked. She would think she was safe.

She would be wrong. Sooner or later, Zoe would contact him.

CHAPTER THIRTEEN

S ir, no one is answering at the warehouse," came the driver's voice. It echoed through the speaker system in the limo; Anna Kazakova would allow no private communications between Mishka and his men. They were less than ten minutes away and Mishka immediately grew nervous. The seats formed a rectangle in the back of the car, and in the center of this was a table of highly polished rosewood. A laptop sat next to the backside of the driver's headrest.

"Maybe a cell tower is down," Mishka offered.

"Idiot," said Anna. "Send a car ahead and find out what is going on. Have your driver circle a mile distant from your warehouse until we have confirmation of its status. I am too old to drive into a trap and you would of course be the first to die if it is. You understand me, Mishka?"

"Completely, Mrs. Kazakova."

Mishka did understand.

There were three other passengers in the back portion of the car besides himself. Anna, her physician Dr. Pazyryk and Ivan her bodyguard. It was a tense drive for Mishka. He had no idea as to the extent of what Anna knew, and that terrified him. A woman who was willing to cage her own son was capable of anything.

Sitting in the front seat, next to Mishka's personal driver, was the sniper who killed the two bodyguards standing on either side of Mishka. He was an old, thick man named Nikolai with a wide head and a dark visage. It was difficult to understand he could shoot so well with his thick shoulders and bulky body. But his work told another story.

Word finally came.

"Sir," said the driver nervously. "I have news."

"Well, what is it?"

"All dead, sir."

"What?"

"All dead and both women have vanished. A vehicle is missing. A black Hummer."

"All dead." Mishka repeated.

"How?" asked Anna.

"Madame?" asked the driver.

"Were they shot, stabbed or strangled?"

"They were torn apart. Like by a wild animal. Blood everywhere."

"I see," said Anna quietly.

"I don't understand," said Mishka, wringing his hands. "Who could have done this? They were seasoned men, well-armed."

"Quit whimpering. Do you have video?"

"What?"

"Do you have security cameras?" repeated Anna.

"Yes. Yes, of course."

"Can you access it on that computer?

She pointed to the laptop on the table between them.

Mishka's face brightened.

"I can do that," he said.

"Then do it," snapped Anna.

While they drove around at a safe distance, Mishka brought up the video access system and logged in. He had to do it three times because he was so nervous he kept typing in the wrong password. When the menu finally appeared, he breathed a sigh of relief. After a few minutes, he was finally able to locate the time where he left the warehouse to go meet Anna. His finger trembled as he pressed "Play."

They all hunched forward to see the screen more clearly except Ivan. There was no sound and it was in black and white, which made it seem all the starker. No one spoke until the beast came roaring in.

"Stop that," said Anna. "Stop it there. You see that, Doctor? It lives."

"What is it? What is that thing?" asked Mishka. "It is like a giant wolf."

"Giant wolf indeed," whistled Dr. Pazyryk. "It must be eight or ten feet tall. And look at it. It's not exactly a wolf, is it? It's like some hideous amalgam of animal and machine."

The security camera had captured a straight on shot of the beast's head. Mishka could not quit staring at it. Dark droplets dripped from its jaws, and in one clawed hand, it waved an arm. Eyes bright white. Nothing he could have imagined would have prepared him for this picture. It was as though the impossible had become possible. He felt, for the first time in his life, utter horror.

"That thing," he said, "that is real? That is what killed my men?"

"Press the button again," said Anna. "We must see everything, right to the end."

Ivan leaned toward Anna and told her, "I can feel his presence in this evil place."

"And here is where you will confront him," she told him.

With a nervous glance at the two of them, Mishka clicked the "Play" button again, and the video resumed. Images of the wild beast ripping apart his men resumed. When the forklift hit the electrical panel and the emergency lights began to strobe, he clenched a fist and began to swear softly.

"Stop," said Anna.

Mishka did as he was told.

"Go forward just a little."

Again.

"See," she said. "Do you see that Ivan? It blurs. The image of the beast blurs."

"It is unstable," said Ivan. His thin white eyebrows came together and wrinkles appeared across his forehead and the corners of his eyes. He pursed his lips as he considered the implications of his own observation.

"Probably a camera malfunction," said Dr. Pazyryk.

"Fah," said Anna. "Once, maybe yes, but twice. No, there is something important happening. Ivan is right, I think, although I cannot explain it."

"What do you mean unstable?" the doctor asked Ivan.

Ivan did not answer.

Mishka spoke up, unable to contain himself.

"What kind of beast is that thing?" he asked again.

"It is a man-beast," answered Ivan solemnly. "It is a defilement of life itself."

Mishka could sense an undercurrent of madness in this man, and, for a moment, he was not sure if he feared him even more than the beast. His white, waxy skin and his peculiar eyes so pale in the muted light in the back of the limousine gave him a corpse-like appearance.

"Stop the video," said Anna suddenly.

When he stopped it, she said, "It is him. Look. We see the beast enter, and now we see the man himself leaving. The beast is gone. But see, see he has not aged, Ivan. He has not aged a day since I last saw him all those years ago"

It was true. A man whom Mishka had never seen was walking with Sveta and the woman who she had brought with her.

"But that woman," he said, "that woman there. She was badly wounded when my cousin brought her. We threw her in a room and left her for dead. She is walking again. How is this? And my cousin, we chained her to a steel plate. How did she get away? And who is that man? How did he get in?"

Anna stared at him coldly.

"That man is Drogol."

She slapped her hand on the table and looked at Ivan with fire in her eyes.

"Hauck is a demon, Ivan. Look at that woman. Not the wounded one who is now walking, but the other. Look at her face. Fah. Drogol will have no choice but to pursue her. Mishka, can you enlarge that picture?"

"I think so."

"You think? Do not think. Do it."

Moments later, Sveta's face filled the screen. She was carrying an AK47, ready to shoot anything that crossed her path. Her hard-set face was smeared with grime or blood and her hair wired away from her head like it was electrified.

"There, there, just like that," shouted Anna, jabbing her finger at the screen. "You see it, Ivan? Do you see it, Doctor?"

Ivan stroked his chin, and Mishka felt his stomach turn as the man's albino fingers slid over the congealed waxy scar that wound along his chin all the way up to his left ear. It was as though he were stroking a bloated white worm.

"She is familiar," said Ivan. "Something about her face is familiar."

"Looks a little like Alexandra, doesn't she?" said Dr. Pazyryk. "Like in that famous painting. You know—the wife of Nicholas II."

"Thank you, Doctor, for that little history lesson," said Ivan, and glared at him.

"Sorry. Sorry. Didn't mean to offend you, Ivan. Or you, Anna. Or anyone for that matter. I'm just saying it's who she looks like, that's all."

Mishka could not help but see the fear in Dr. Pazyryk's face when he addressed Ivan. This was something he would not forget.

"How can you tell who she looks like?" he asked. "Her face is smeared with something, her hair is a mess and it is not a good picture."

"A true Russian," said Anna, "would not mistake the face of the last Romanov Tsarista."

They all sat around the rectangular wooden table in the back of the seat, now lit up with the glow from the security camera video. The windows were blacked out, and although the car was spacious, Mishka began to feel claustrophobic. There was no easy way to escape this woman and her madmen.

"Forgive me, Mrs. Kazakova. What I mean to ask is what is the difference if my cousin looks like Tsarista Alexandra?"

Anna flicked her hand at him in contempt.

"You are a boy with a pretty face and guns. What do you know of these things? Hauck, who would capture this Drogol before we can seize him, is a devious thinker. He knows that this man believes he was once in love with this woman. You look shocked Mishka. Yes, I know that the Tsarista Alexandra is dead. But Drogol believes he was alive during her time. He believes that she loved him but could not show it because she was married to Czar Nicholas II."

Mishka's brain began to hurt.

"So this man, this Drogol, he is crazy? He is insane?"

"That's not important," said Anna. Her face was soft and wrinkled, but her eyes fixed on Mishka's as though she were about to bite him. "What *is* important is that we catch this very, very dangerous man you let get away by your carelessness."

"But I couldn't know. I did not even know of this man."

"All that you need to know is that I want him alive because I want, no, I *need* his living blood. If I do not get it, I will have Nikolai hang you from a meat hook with your dick in your mouth."

*****

"I will go ahead and then return. The two of you will wait here," Drogol said.

But as soon as he said his last word, he gasped in pain and doubled over. He seemed to lose his balance, but before Sveta or Zoe could grab one of his arms to catch him, he reached for the railing. For a moment, he stood shaking, and then Sveta saw him begin to blur, as though a lens had been placed between the two of them.

It was impossible.

Sveta shook her head. For a moment, for the very briefest of moments, he was transparent, and Sveta thought she could see *through* him. She thought she saw something moving inside him. No, that wasn't right. Something *forming* inside of him. But that wasn't possible. She was about to step toward him when it happened again.

Then he seemed to regain control and straightened. When he looked at Sveta, he knew that she had witnessed the moment. He glared at her as though daring her to say something.

Then, before she could object, he quenched the lantern wick and continued down the rough wooden stairs into the palpable illusion of an unending blackness. After a moment, Zoe gripped her hand, with the tentative touch of a little girl needing her mother's reassurance. Sveta free hand tightened on her AK for comfort.

She sniffed the air looking for signs of the beast, but smelled only musty air. Yet she was still tense. So many strange and violent things had already happened that she could not understand. The beast. This strange man. The miracle of seeing Zoe being revived by him with the mere touch of his hands. His odd, old-fashioned way of speaking. And now the dense, almost suffocating darkness. Standing and waiting when she was used to having a plan.

"Nervous soldiers," a GRU major had once told her, "usually shoot the wrong people."

Still, it was sometimes better than not shooting at anyone.

"Zoe?" she said.

"What?"

"Did you see that?"

"No."

"Zoe?"

"What?"

"Just seeing if you were still here."

"Where would I go?"

"Ever been here before?"

A pause.

"No."

"Is that the truth?"

Another pause.

"Only in my dreams."

"You dreamed about being here?"

"I dream a lot."

Her voice was still shaky, still weak.

Time passed. Darkness stayed.

"We're in trouble here."

"I know."

"Okay."

"Is that it?"

"I'm tired of being the one asking the questions is all," said Sveta.

The light began everywhere at once, a soft golden uprising radiating from giant glass globes positioned throughout the vast underground chamber. Sveta held her breath momentarily at the sheer beauty of it. The sound of a faint electrical humming filled the air, and twin ceramic columns the size of steeples and ringed by levels of silver discs began to spark erratically. Electric complaints crackled through the air like old bones forced to move.

"It's incredible," said Sveta.

"Magic," agreed Zoe.

"What is this place?"

"Magic is better than questions."

"Then those must be magic bells," said Sveta and pointed at eight golden bells lined up in a row on a dull black platform wide enough to hold a tractor trailer.

They were individually suspended from an overhead I-frame and each looked big as an elevator car. In the magic light show of gold and sparking arcs of searing white, they shone bright as golden stars in a technology firmament.

"He's coming back," said Zoe, and pointed to Drogol mounting the steps.

He was a priestly figure, his legs hidden beneath his long coat as though he was wearing a cassock. Because she was a mercenary, the thought crossed her mind that he might be concealing a weapon.

When he stepped onto the small platform again, Sveta realized how small it was. She stepped back but found herself stopped by the railing.

He brought his hands from behind his back and she saw to her relief that they were empty. Zoe plucked at his sleeve to get his attention. When he looked down at her, Sveta saw her grasp his hands, bring it to her lips, and gently kiss his palm. There were tears in her eyes when she raised her head and let go of his hand.

"Thank you, Father," she said.

Drogol looked at her a long time, and though it was not at all possible, she could feel his attention on the young woman like a light, electrified pressure that caused her skin to prickle. Something about the way Zoe said the word *Father* caused Sveta's heart to fill with dread.

"You have a conscience and a good heart, my girl," he said. She was about to speak, to protest, but he held up his hand and said, "I know much, but I too have a heart and you have touched it. And your sight was true. You have returned hope to my very soul."

He spoke as though he was a holy man, but this night she had seen only violence and destruction wherever he went. The way Zoe looked at him, submissive and reverent, was enough to put Sveta's nerves on edge.

"Why did you bring us here?" demanded Sveta.

Although she tried to make her voice confrontational, the awe and wonder and fear she felt at the place below them gave her voice a tentative edge.

When he turned to face her, his stare was as real as a caress. Her face felt flush, and she colored. She felt the need to draw her pistol and keep it leveled between them. She felt the need for safety.

"You wanted to know who I am, is that not so? You want to know why they hunt me like an animal."

"And you brought me all the way down here to tell me? You couldn't have told me this while we were in the car?"

"I offer you sanctuary such as you will not find in your world. Soon, I will tell you what you wish to know, but I warn you that you may neither understand nor believe what I say."

Sveta began to feel weak kneed. He had moved closer still to her, and she could smell his rich, musky sweat.

"Okay, let's go," she said brusquely.

But he only moved closer.

She felt his hand brush across her cheek.

"I have waited all my life for a sign that I should do that which we will do tonight. You are that sign. Young Zoe brought you to me. And now, as I stand so close you, I feel life roar through my body. I feel the heat of my heart catching fire again. For the first time in over a hundred years, I feel hope again."

When he turned abruptly and descended the stairs again, it was a full minute before she could pull herself together enough to follow. Before she took her first step, she switched from three round burst to full auto on her AK47.

Sveta caught up with them at the bottom of the stairs, just in time to see Drogol cry out in pain again, then grasp the railing once more for support. Zoe rushed to him, but he thrust her back with one powerful movement, sending her over the opposite railing in a tumble of arms and legs. She hit the ground hard.

The air around Drogol charged with electricity and wavering lines of dark, oily light. He began to blur within them.

"No," he screamed and doubled over.

His face was twisted with helpless rage and fear.

"Run, run to the train," he screamed.

Sveta stepped back and brought up her AK.

Drogol shouted something she could not understand, then his face distorted and his body blurred again. An impossible, howling wind leapt into the air around her, and it seemed to be blowing right out of Drogol's midsection. His words sounded as though they'd come through a voice distortion machine.

"I can't understand you," she shouted.

Her finger nervously gripped the trigger, not knowing what to expect.

"Take Zoe, run to the train. Windows barred. Bolt doors."

"What is happening?"

Drogol's body was ripped back an inch, then shoved forward by an unseen force.

"Can't control this … can't … run. Please, God, run."

She saw it again. Something black and turbulent forming within him. A horrible sound, like those she heard in her uncle's slaughter-house. Sveta turned, went to Zoe, and helped the horrified woman to her feet.

"Run," Drogol screamed again, but his voice was distant, far away, as though shouted down a dark tunnel.

Sveta swung over the railing and dropped onto a hard earthed floor.

"Get up," she said and shook Zoe so hard that the girl cried out.

"No time to think, just get moving,"

Sveta couldn't wait for Zoe to get to her feet by herself. She grabbed a handful of hair and part of a coat and yanked her up hard.

"Go, go. Get to the train."

A horrifying roar behind her, and Sveta turned and saw Drogol shaking like a marionette. She spun and ran as hard as she could after Zoe. The girl stumbled and almost went down, but Sveta grabbed her sleeve and pulled her along. They dodged electrical capacitors, bundles of coiled snake cables, and knocked over a cabinet full of glass ampoules.

A furious roar stopped her heart and she knew then that death would soon be after them.

Thirty feet more.

Sveta risked a look over her shoulder. She saw Drogol pulled to his feet as though yanked straight up by a hidden set of strings. His mouth opened. His body ballooned inward then outward and he screamed as he was yanked back into oblivion and for just an instant Sveta saw an aperture, like a tear in thin gossamer fabric, and from that opening shot out a hideous apparition of slavering teeth and claws. It hit the ground and then stood on its hind legs. She saw red eyes and fury and felt terror such as she had never imagined.

Twenty feet.

The train ahead was painted a lustrous black but covered with the dust of many years. Windows barred as though it were a prison train. Big. Iron. Safe. Behind her the cavernous laboratory echoed with rage as the beast howled. Sveta's breath came in painful gasps. A desk seemed to appear from nowhere and slam into her knee. She went down with a painful cry.

Zoe stopped and turned to help her.

"Run," shouted Sveta. "Run to the train."

Zoe hesitated, then ran straight back to her and picked her up off the ground. She slid her shoulder underneath Sveta's and helped her move.

Behind them they heard something crash and sparks shot up high into the golden glow as the monster shrieked and spat.

"Wait," Sveta said.

She turned, aimed the AK at the oncoming beast and let loose a deafening barrage of bullets that enraged it but didn't slow it down. Sveta had seen nothing like it.

"Run," yelled Sveta, and she and Zoe hobbled and bounced toward the train. They were closing the gap quickly, but the sound of pounding fury was charging up more quickly still.

CHAPTER FOURTEEN

I'm bringing it up now," said Hauck.

He'd been sleeping for forty-five minutes, trying to ignore the annoying bleeping that sounded vaguely like an underwater alarm clock. When it finally hit him that it was his phone, he sat bolt upright and snatched it off of the small table next to his couch. The room was dark except for the faint blue-green glow from his computer monitor. Hauck reached for his pistol as he flicked the phone open.

"Yuri?" he asked.

"None other, boss. Still working with only one arm. Do I get time and a half for this?"

"I'll give you double time if you tell me you called with something I can use."

Hauck scanned the living room. Looking for something incongruous. Trying to feel if something felt out of place. Realizing he hadn't lived a normal life in so many years that he'd forgotten what a normal life was like. He moved over to the kitchen and logged onto the terminal. He reached for the single-cup coffee maker and pulled it straight toward him.

"Yeah, I found something. You've got to see it yourself, though, or you won't believe it."

Hauck connected to the IP address that Yuri sent him and saw nothing but gray blur.

"There's nothing here," Hauck said, switching to speakerphone. "Just a mess of screen static."

"Authenticating," said Yuri. "Give me a bit so I can let you in."

The screen resolved to show a sweeping camera view moving down from a rooftop to the streets below. It was shot using combined wave-length gradients, so the picture was as clear as if it had been shot in broad daylight.

"Your van?" asked Hauck.

"Yeah, that's my van. Video courtesy of Evgeny's spotter. I'm slow-ing everything down now, just so you know. The beast is going to come straight on screen in just a sec. It's going to be moving real slow because of what I want you to see. I may have to tune it up as we go; are you good with that?"

"If it's worth it, I'm good with whatever we have to do."

"Oh, it's worth it," chuckled Yuri. "Son of a bitch broke my arm and got me popping pain pills and made it so I got to quit typing to swig coffee. He's going to pay."

If Yuri were not on pain pills, Hauck would have cut his pay for swearing. He did not tolerate swearing in his organization. It was a small thing, but, in his experience, an excellent point of discipline.

"I see something, like a clawed hand," said Hauck.

"That's the hairy bastard. Check the way the claws shine."

"What am I looking for?"

"They're not made of whatever claws are made of—they look like metal or something, but whatever they are, they're definitely very weird."

"This is what you got me out of bed for?" demanded Hauck.

"That's just an appetizer. Keep watching."

Hauck loaded in a coffee pouch, filled the small, stainless steel unit and pressed the button. Realizing he'd forgotten something, he quickly took a ceramic blue cup off a little metal tree and slid it under the nozzle just as the first drop of coffee fell. After a few seconds of operation, he leaned his head over to inhale the fumes. Too many hours, too little sleep.

He swiveled his head to stare at the computer screen. He had just seen something impossible.

"Yuri?"

"Wondering if you caught that. I'm saying to myself—"

"That is a bullet trail, am I correct?"

"As ever."

Hauck clenched his fists.

"Yuri, listen carefully. Did that bullet hit the beast?"

"Oh yeah. When Evgeny shoots, Evgeny scores. But now Evgeny's got a new kind of target. Keep watching, boss. Every bulled Evgeny fired hit the son of a bitch. But they didn't do shit. It's like he was firing paint balls instead of bullets. No wonder that thing kept coming and knocked me and my van straight over on our asses."

Hauck got up and moved around his apartment, wondering about what he'd just seen. It wasn't impossible. Could the beast have absorbed that many rifle rounds filled with mercury amalgam and kept on moving? This was not cinema, this was reality. Impossible. Outside, he saw the faint edgings of light gold at the horizon, and knew that night would soon be at an end.

A soft beep signaled his coffee was ready, so he walked back and put it on a coaster to cool.

"Does Evgeny know about this?"

"Nope. You're the first to know."

"You're forgetting the spotter," said Hauck.

"Spotter didn't catch it. Couldn't catch it. You can't see any of what you were looking at with the naked eye. He just takes the pictures; I enhanced them because that thing wrecked my van. Something insane about the way it went down, you know what I mean? Evgeny tells me he pounded mercury filled bullets into the thing but it kept on moving."

"Bring Evgeny up to speed on this," said Hauck. "Good work."

"There's more," said Yuri.

"Oh?"

"This is the weirdest part."

"Get on with it."

"It's like it fades in and out of the video, like it's not always there. I'm going to play it again for you. I've modified the speed and the light spectra. Watch how it blurs and shimmers. It's like it's fading in and out."

Hauck watched it again with Yuri's new settings. His stomach began to knot. What the hell was this thing? All his certainties about what they were facing dissipated like morning fog.

"You're a genius, Yuri."

"You bet I am."

"Any ideas?"

"Well, if this thing is a werewolf, boss, then Universal Pictures and Lon Chaney got it all wrong. Question is, if that's the case, how the hell are we going to kill it?"

*****

Zoe grabbed Sveta and hauled her up the train steps. She was too terrified to look over her shoulder and see how far back the beast was. The door to the car was open so she shoved Sveta straight into the car and slammed the door behind her. Her hands scrambled over the door handle looking for a lock. Finally she found a metal bar and slid it across into a half circle welded onto the door frame, then collapsed with her back against it. She gulped in air until she grew dizzy and her head spun.

The world outside the train car went silent.

"Zoe," whispered Sveta. "Are you hurt?"

"I've been better," she whispered back. "How about you?"

"Knee hurts like hell, but I'm okay. You hear anything?"

Zoe looked up and around at the inside of the car. It was plush with velvet chairs and drapes, the inside lit by a single globe at the far end where she saw to her horror another open door.

"Close that door," she said. "There's a bar to bolt it shut like the other one. Hurry."

Sveta got the message and hurried across the floor on all fours, her knee hot like it was on fire. When she made it to the far end, she nervously reached up, grabbed the door handle, and cautiously pulled it toward her. It closed with a soft click, and she immediately slid the bolt home.

"Done."

"Thank God. What is that thing?"

"Drogol's pet. I think he needs a bigger leash."

"What?"

"It's the same thing," Sveta said, "that killed all those men in the warehouse. It's been chasing us since Drogol's house. Remind me not to do that again, will you?"

Before Zoe could answer, they heard a crash loud as an explosion, and the entire car lifted up in the air and slammed down again. Sveta saw one side of the train wall cave in like it had been hit by a wrecking ball. She rose and then fell backward, hitting the floor as the whole car hit landed on its side with a horrible crunching noise. She scrambled about looking for her weapon, and finally locked her fingers around the butt of her automatic rifle.

Velvet curtains ripped loose and fluttered away to hang by one end.

Glass shattered and sprayed throughout the car. Metal bars over the windows bent back and Sveta could see light. An apparition of wiry hair and claws rushed past the window as Zoe screamed.

"Did you see that?"

Her voice was distant and confused. Sveta felt like reality was disintegrating around her.

Movement outside the window again; Sveta fired off a burst of bullets. There came a roar like another explosion and Zoe slapped her hands over her ears.

"I shot it. I hit it," shouted Sveta.

They both stared at the bulge in the train car wall. The beast's strength was unbelievable. The impact of it ramming into the side of the car had been enough to lift it off the rails. Both women scooted back against the far side of the car, moving together without thinking. Victims huddling in the face of an unnatural disaster.

Silence outside, as though the creature had given up.

"What do we do?" whispered Zoe.

"Wait."

"For what?"

"I don't know," said Sveta, "but what else can we do?"

"Can I have a gun, too?"

"Do you know how to use one?"

Zoe nodded.

"You're sure?"

"I can handle it."

"The duffle," said Sveta. "Over there. Bring it here. There's plenty of firepower in it."

Tentatively, Zoe reached toward the bag.

"You've got to crawl over to get it. Quietly. And keep your voice down. It may think we're dead."

"You think so?"

Sveta shook her head *no*.

The bag seemed a long way away, but Zoe wanted the gun very badly. She started crawling. When she finally got within distance, she grabbed a section of the shoulder strap and slowly, very slowly, slid it over to where Sveta knelt.

"You sure you hit it?" she asked as Sveta started sorting through the contents.

"Damned straight."

"You think you wounded it?"

Sveta pulled out a Beretta, checked its load, and then flicked the safety to the *off* position. She handed it to Zoe. Zoe aimed at the window where she last saw the beast, but her hands trembled.

"Be careful with that thing," cautioned Sveta. "Make sure you shoot at it instead of me."

Zoe ignored her and stared out through the broken train window.

"You wounded it, right?" she asked again.

"I don't know. I shot it, but I think I only pissed it off. No blood spray. Nothing. It just kept on moving."

Zoe was about to say something when another roar ripped through the complex. They looked at each other for a moment like two criminals wondering who the executioner would come for next. Then the train car jerked straight up in the air and spilled over sideways as she and Sveta flew about like dolls in a car crash.

Metal screeched as the train landed on its side then flipped up again and she hit her head against a seat bench. A shower of splintered wood and glass fragments fell on her like dirt shoveled into a grave. She felt the warm flow of blood in her mouth, and then darkness took away her thoughts.

CHAPTER FIFTEEN

You going to sleep all day?"

Hauck wiped the sleep out of his eyes and felt for his pistol. The security panel lights were green, meaning his perimeter was still secure. One hand held the phone while the other curled automatically around his pistol grip as his eyelids blinked like a shutter camera as he scanned the room. He checked the phone's caller ID.

"Are you in town?" he asked.

"Come see me where we got that stuff for your back."

The phone went dead.

The Instructor had arrived in Detroit.

Hauck didn't sleep well after the Ryazan prison incident. The KGB hardliners never gave up acquiring their targets. Especially one as important as Hauck. He could change his name, but eventually they would find him. The KGB could trade in its acronym for a new one, but they were the same people as before, and they never quit. So people like him were never really safe again.

Although some thought that targets were reacquired at four o'clock in the morning when a person's responses were at their least efficient, the truth was that they could seize you anytime day or night. Asleep or awake. And you never really knew when they would come for you, which is why people hunted by the secret police never, ever slept well until it was permanent.

He stood, stretched, and looked around his apartment again. Something was bothering him. Not a nuance, not a possibility, but something right in front of him that he was missing. Hauck was never nervous, but he was always careful, which was why he was still alive. Though after Drogol's escape the night before, Hauck didn't feel careful enough. Bullets that hit their target but did nothing. A raging beast that seemed to flicker in and out of reality. For perhaps the first time in his life, Hauck wondered if his intellect was up to the job.

He'd always been obsessed with tracking Drogol to ground. Kill him with silver bullets or holy water or whatever it took. It'd never occurred to him that Drogol and his beast might be immune to *everything*. If that was true, then Yuri was right. Universal Pictures and Lon Chaney *had* got it seriously wrong.

He checked in with Evgeny and Yuri. Nothing new except from the house video. Too complicated to go into over the phone, but Yuri would download a file when he was finished checking and double-checking what he had found. Then Hauck knew what was nagging at his brain even before he had his first coffee.

"Yuri," he said.

"Yeah, boss?"

"I want you to send me the name of Evgeny's spotter and every detail we have on him. Make him a heuristic target. Go deep on him, and do it fast as you can."

"He was vetted on the front end, boss," protested Yuri.

"Was he?"

"Course he was. It was a thorough probe."

"Are you sure the man you vetted is the same man who spotted for Evgeny last night?"'

Silence for a moment.

"Has to be. But you're saying what?"

"That *has to be* isn't a good enough answer," growled Hauck.

"I'm on it," said Yuri. "But what tipped you?"

"Later. I'm on my way to see someone."

"You need backup?"

"I am backup," said Hauck, and then clicked off.

Next he showered, dressed, had a quick coffee and a microwaved breakfast, then turned on his security system and took his private elevator to the underground garage. The walk from the elevator to his car was always the most difficult for him to endure. No matter how much security electronics or staff he deployed, he never quite felt secure. It was part training, part temperament, and part law of averages.

Eventually, somebody always got through. That meant in the end he had to take care of himself.

He chose a different car, a gray Ford Focus to blend in a little with the traffic. On the dashboard screen he brought up images of the surrounding buildings and streets before he initiated the overhead door opening. Five minutes later, he was satisfied that the surrounding streets looked safe. That was the problem, though, wasn't it? You could check and look, examine and analyze, but you never knew what was going to happen until you went out the door, and you eventually had to go outside. As the metal panels folded up silently into their overhead space, he wondered what it would be like to see a shoulder-fired rocket screeching toward him from across the street.

*****

It was a tired gray building washed old and white, rich with delicate concrete scrolls edging a once elegant design. In an otherwise commonplace neighborhood of liquor stores, laundromats and loud graffiti, it seemed to Hauck like an initialed cravat found lying in a second hand clothing store.

Hauck checked the neighborhood carefully before parking two blocks away. He saw nothing suspicious but the city itself. That a city once so great and powerful could be so wrapped in such decadent decline disgusted him. A glance overhead at the morning sky caused him to lower his eyes. Orange-brown smoke puffed up toward the clouds. Hauck grimaced at the idea that a city he once admired had become little more than an acid rain production factory.

When he arrived at his destination, Hauck saw that the Red Calibri lettering on the front door's greasy glass was still visible through the iron bars. It read *Traxler's Bibliotheca*. Rare books and manuscripts buried under the rubble of a twenty-first century Oz whose city used to drive the world.

The cracked ceramic buzzer screwed tightly to the doorframe looked as though it hadn't been touched in decades. When he pressed it, he saw dusty grime on the fingertip of his leather glove. The P-64 9 mm. tucked in his navy pea coat pocket was heavy as his past. It wouldn't be any use against the Instructor anyway. He'd be dead before he tried to use it. He consoled himself with the idea that it was for emergencies, for the unexpected. For Anna Kazokova's squalid little criminals since he now assumed that it would be totally useless against Drogol.

A hidden speaker crackled to life.

"Come on in. We got coffee."

The Instructor's voice was edged with nervous energy, and Hauck immediately began to worry that he'd made a mistake.

A metallic click as the door unlocked. Neither the Instructor nor Traxler would wonder whether he was alone. Traxler was as bad if not worse than he was himself. The entire street would be wired with enough high tech micro-cameras to start an electronics store. The old man would have enough computing power locked away for facial recognition programs to sweep the streets, looking for threats. Traxler had spent enough time in prison that he didn't plan on going back.

Hauck entered a vestibule and cleaned his shoes on a thick mat.

A thin, smoky light lit streams of dust motes that swarmed through the two story interior like tiny bees hunting honey. Stacks of books ringed the room in concentric circles like castle walls buttressed by towering mahogany bookshelves. Scattered throughout the room were browsing tables, straight-backed chairs and green glass banker lamps.

It was uncomfortably silent.

He stood out in the open, waiting to meet the most dangerous man he had ever known, wondering if even he would be up to the task of killing Drogol.

From behind a book stack, Rudolph Traxler suddenly appeared, dressed in a dark suit and an open-necked blue shirt. His moustache a thin line above his lips, his gray hair perfectly cut and eyes bright as though he were accepting an Oscar.

"Ah," he said, "so nice to see you again, my friend."

Traxler was tall and fit looking for his seventy-six years, and he walked with a confident stride.

"The feeling is mutual," said Hauck.

"Good, then I'll take your pistol, if you don't mind."

It was impossible to know where the sensors were, but walking into Traxler's Bibliotheca was like walking through an airport scanner.

"Certainly," said Hauck, and he handed over his pistol.

When the old man pocketed it, he reached out again and shook Hauck's hand. He leaned forward slightly and said, "He's in a good mood."

"I was afraid of that," said Hauck.

"Whatever it is you've brought him here for has him excited like the old days."

"I'm afraid it's gotten even more complicated."

Traxler raised a quizzical eyebrow.

"Well, then, let's not keep him waiting. Come with me."

They wound through the stacks until they came to a windowless office with a simple desk and stacks of books piled high on it, as though it were a researcher's table. Traxler waited for Hauck to join him inside, and then closed the door behind them. The old man smiled, then reached in his pocket. Moments later, the entire office descended.

It was a simple yet effective trick. As the office went down, another office exactly like the one they had entered lowered into position to displace the first. The entire building was a maze of hidden doors, rooms, hydraulics, sensors and electromagnetic locks. Hauck thought of it more as a machine than a building. It was a reflection of Traxler's mind, the way he concealed the complicated within the simple.

When they reached bottom, the door opened into an underground workshop and storage area replete with rows of automatic rifles, pistols, explosive, flame throwers and gas canisters. It was like an underground gun and knife show for elite clients.

At a table in the middle of the room stood a short man with a thick neck and powerful shoulders examining a sniper rifle. He tested the weight and then hefted it into the air as though about to fire a round into the ceiling. With a snort, he laid it back on the table, and then looked up at Traxler.

"This new stuff," he said, "it's like carrying nothing. This thing's got no weight. I love it. I love all of this space-age plastics bullshit. How you doing Hauck? You look like you ain't been sleeping. You got to get some sleep. Look at me, I'm in my eighties and I move like a teenager."

"You do at that," said Hauck.

"Come here, give me a hug," said the Instructor.

"Pardon?"

"I'm shitting you. You try to hug me and I'll kick your ass. Rudolph, you got any more coffee?"

"I can make another pot."

"Yeah, do it. Hauck here looks like he's going to fall asleep if we don't pump some caffeine in him."

Traxler walked away, leaving the Instructor and his pupil alone.

"So this is no bullshit, right? This thing in the video, I mean."

"No."

"Fuck me," said the Instructor.

"And there's more. Worse. I have some new video footage to show you when Rudolph returns."

"Video? You mean you're shooting motion pictures of this thing but you're not shooting it like for real?"

"We've tried," said Hauck.

"Is that so? What does that mean? Evgeny's gone blind?"

"No."

"Spotter's drunk?"

"I wish," said Hauck irritably.

"This just gets better and better," said the Instructor, and then he lifted his thick arms in front of him, rubbed the palms of his hands together and smiled. Hauck shuddered involuntarily.

*****

"Here," said Hauck, pointing at the computer screen on one of Traxler's tables.

"That's not possible," said Traxler. "Some kind of video anomaly, perhaps."

The Instructor stood to Hauck's right. He was only slightly taller than Hauck, who was sitting down.

"Show me that again," he said.

Hauck did so.

"It's not an anomaly," said Hauck. "It's real. It takes the impact and isn't so much as knocked off balance."

The Instructor ran a hand over the top of his shaved head.

"This ain't good," he said. "It's like he's made of Kevlar."

"Impossible," said Traxler. "Movie stuff."

"The beast himself is only barely possible," said Hauck.

"Still," said the Instructor, "anything can be killed. You try gas yet?"

Hauck stared at him.

"Gas?"

"Yeah, so there's nothing to stop, you know? It's got to breathe, for fuck's sake. It's got a nose, doesn't it? How about we hit it pretty heavy with something like knockout gas, then cut off its head while it's out. You think about that?"

"No," admitted Hauck.

"That's why you pay me the big bucks," grinned the Instructor.

"It might work," said Traxler. "But I have a question. What exactly is this thing? I admit it looks like a gigantic wolf on two legs, but there's something vaguely … alien about it."

Hauck took in the thought slowly, and then nodded.

 It did indeed.

For the first time since last night, he wondered if Zoe and Sveta were still alive.

Chapter Sixteen

Sveta woke to a pounding headache.

She was lying on a cot, staring face up at a plank wood ceiling. The room was lit with the same golden glow she remembered from the underground complex. It was somehow reassuring. Zoe lay on a cot nearby, her head bandaged and her left arm in a makeshift sling. Drafting tables covered with papers and stacked with books were scattered about the large room. There was only one window, as though she had woken up in a prison. Drogol stood looking down at her.

"No," he said gently, "do not get up. Rest. You are badly bruised, and you have broken three fingers."

Sveta sat up quickly, but the blood seemed to drain from her head and she dropped back down to the mattress.

Drogol leaned down and placed a bandaged hand against her chest.

"Rest, I tell you. You have been through much and more lies ahead of us all."

"Which ones?" asked Sveta.

"Which ones what?"

"Which fingers?"

Drogol appeared confused.

"Which fingers are broken?"

"Ah, those of your right hand."

She closed her eyes and breathed a sigh of relief.

"I shoot best left handed."

When she opened her eyes again, her vision cleared and she saw to her surprise that his face was battered and an ugly cut stitched across his jaw. He seemed to lean to one side, as though it were painful to put weight on his right leg.

Drogol's face twisted in pain for a moment, and then he regained control.

"Forgive me," he said hesitantly. "More and more I have less and less control. And there is so little time before I have no control left at all. The beast will then come when it wills, and I fear I will never see this world again."

"What is that thing?"

He looked away in shame, put his hands behind his back and began to pace back and forth. When he reached his hand up toward the ceiling once, she thought he was about to answer her, but he only shook his head and continued to pace. After a moment, he whirled awkwardly on one leg and stopped before her.

"Look at me," he demanded. "Who do you see? What do you see?"

She thought before answering.

"I don't know what you mean."

"Look at me. Really look at me. Use your heart. What do you feel?"

The painful urgency in his voice confused her. His words were alive with angry embarrassment. He seemed to pulse with a nervous, desperate energy.

"I see, I think, a tortured man."

His head bobbed up and down enthusiastically, a teacher urging his star pupil onward.

"Go on," he said.

"I see a man," she said hesitantly, "a man who does not fit well with this time."

"Good, good. This underground laboratory is dedicated to the sorcery of the very man who has cursed me these so many years. I am a man alone looking for salvation while hidden from the rest of the world within the genius of my tormentor."

Sveta felt dizzy. The agony and anger of Drogol's words seemed to press her hard against the mattress. She had no idea what delusion deranged his mind, but she had to get away from him before he turned violent.

"Ah," he said, pulling away from her. "Forgive me again. Twice I ask forgiveness from the same woman. What is happening to me? I cannot bear this."

With an effort, Sveta raised her hand, and was shocked to see her bandaged fingers. Her whole right hand felt numbed so that she still did not feel the pain; that would come later.

"It's too much for me," she said. "I don't understand anything you're saying."

"You who do not believe in the unseen, how can you comprehend the curse pronounced on my soul?"

Slowly, and with her muscles screaming for her to lie back down, she rose and propped herself on elbow. She was suddenly angrier than she had been in a long time.

"What I can't understand is all this vague bullshit," she said. "Just tell me what the fuck is going on here. Who are you, what is that thing and how can we get out of here without it eating us?"

From the other cot came agonized murmurings as Zoe attempted to roll over, but instead fell quiet again lying on her back. Drogol walked over and stared down at her as though willing her to heal.

"Rest, child," he said gently.

Suddenly, Sveta blanched. She reached for the pistol tucked in her belt.

"Where is my gun? Where is that monster?"

Drogol's mouth tightened and his eyes blazed.

"It is gone. Gone now and I pray that we do what we must do before this night is over so that it will never come back again."

Sveta's eyes locked on a stack of weapons to the side of her bed.

"Give me a gun."

"But it is gone. You are safe."

"Can you guarantee me that?"

Drogol hesitated, and she saw that the anguish in his expression was real.

"I think yes."

"Not good enough."

She sat up again, slowly this time, and then tried to get out of bed and retrieve a weapon. Drogol laid a hand on her chest.

"Wait," he said. "Rest. You are safe for now."

She struggled against him, but was no match as he pressed her back down onto the bed.

"Please," he said. "I will watch over you."

He looked away, unable to control his emotions.

"What is that thing?" she asked again.

"It is a demon from Hell."

"Just give a straight answer, please."

"You would not understand," he said and he turned away to pace the room, wringing his hands.

"Whatever it is," she said, "you've lost control over it, haven't you? We're all in danger, aren't we?"

Drogol picked up a wooden table and threw it straight through a window which exploded outward as though it had been hit by a cannonball. Sveta cringed at the sight and sound.

"Leave me alone, woman," he cried with his back still to her. "This is more than I can bear."

He covered his face with his hands and began to sob.

Sveta was stunned by his rage and violence, but the sight of his anguish frightened her even more.

As he turned back to face her, she asked him, "Did you really bring Zoe back at the warehouse, or did she recover by herself?"

"I did nothing to help her. Can't you understand that? You saw it yourself. God lifted her up. Tell me, why is it that you doubt the power of the Spirit? Even I, I who suffer under the affliction of this unnatural curse, even I see the Divine at work. I am only a man. By myself I have no power."

"I'm too old to believe in faith healers," said Sveta.

"Perhaps you are a little too young."

Even propped one elbow, his last statement made Sveta laugh bitterly. The sight of him wiping away tears made her angry. This man's beast had nearly killed both her and Zoe.

"In my line of work, you grow up quickly," she said. "Nothing like a little death to educate you."

"Only life educates us," he said with a dark look. "There is nothing to learn from death except to look toward life."

"Whatever. If you want to say that I can't understand so you won't tell me what's going on, then screw you. Just give me my gear and I can hit the road. The two of you can face your monster and Hauck all on your own."

"Then go," he said, and turned away from her. "Your bag and your weapons are near the door. Take them when you are ready and leave. The beast has gone for now."

Although she didn't believe he knew exactly where the beast was, she didn't think Drogol would knowingly send her out into danger.

Then again, two days ago she didn't believe Hauck would be hunting her, either.

As she lifted herself up, pain electrified her back, but she kept going until she was sitting. Her biggest fear was internal bleeding, but she had suffered that before and knew something of what it felt like. At least she hoped she did. There was no chance that she could enter and be treated at a hospital without Hauck learning about it, tracking her down and killing her. She had betrayed him; he couldn't afford to show mercy.

Drogol turned from her as though she weren't there and sat in a chair near the head of Zoe's bed. He reached over and stroked her dark hair as though she were a child, acting as though Sveta were already gone, as though she had never been there to begin with.

It was an irritating, arrogant side of his personality that made her want to scream in frustration. So typical. Like all Russian men. Brutal, needy, generous and vain.

With a painful grimace, she held her body upright as she swung her legs over the side of the cot one at a time. Sveta had been through the process before; she knew the routine. Stop before each major movement. Let your body get used to the change. Clench your jaw. Move again.

When an IED exploded and flipped her jeep, she'd been pinned for seven hours while the driver bled to death beside her. There was nothing she could do to stop it. But when she'd finally been rescued, she'd felt a lot like she did now. Pain. Dizziness. Wanting to throw up or cry.

Sveta knew the routine.

The edge of the cot wobbled as she got her first foot onto the floor. Then the second. She took her time, tried to feel her balance, then leaned forward and began to stand.

A hot sparkler jabbed into her hip as her legs began to shake, but she pressed a palm against the edge of the cot's railing to steady herself. Her duffel bag of weaponry, clothes and cash seemed to be a mile away as her vision waivered. She closed her eyes and slowed her breathing.

Five steps maybe to the first drafting table. She could make that. She could do that.

Her stomach growled so loudly it sounded like she was concealing a wild animal beneath her shirt. Her injuries weren't the only thing weakening her, she realized. She needed food and water. Too much action, too little nourishment.

She took her first step with her chin up just enough to show that she was in control and could make it to wherever she needed to go.

Drogol expelled a bitter laugh.

"What are you waiting for? Go, go out into the night. Spit on my offer of help. Talk to me profanely like a profligate. Treat me like a peasant. Go, I do not need you."

Now she had to make it. No way would she quit.

She saw a short piece of wood that could be used as a cane underneath the drafting table. Holding firm to the edge, she bent down and grabbed it. As she got hold of it, she became dizzy. She stayed squatted down long enough for her head to clear.

"Are you not able to stand?" asked Drogol. "Would perhaps like me to carry you to the street?"

"I've been hurt worse," she said, and slowly, very slowly, stood up again.

"You are a stubborn woman."

"Better than staying down here with you, kept in the dark."

"It is daylight above," said Drogol. "They will find you and kill you or worse."

"That's between me and them," said Sveta.

She started walking again.

Twenty maybe twenty-two steps to the door. Her makeshift cane helped. She had maybe ten steps left to go when she collapsed and hit the floor. As she lay there helpless, she heard something crash to the floor just outside of the door. Panic raced through her nervous system like lightning through an ungrounded network. When she tried to pull herself up on one elbow she fell back down.

"Where is your strength now, woman?"

Sveta closed her eyes and drifted away.

*****

His voice was as soft and seductive as Hauck's. Her head was held in the soft vise of his hands, one open palm pressed on either side of her head.

"Do not open your eyes," he said. "Rest and God may heal you."

Drogol began to speak in a strange language; his rhythm and powerful deep voice caused her to think it was a liturgical benediction.

"What are you saying? What is that language?"

"Always, always your mind devises questions. I am asking God to heal you. I am saying I face perhaps the greatest dangers of my life. I implore God for divine mercy, saying my enemies swarm about me, and pleading that I need his help to survive and become victorious."

She nodded slowly, afraid to move her head. A field of warmth covered the sides of her head and started to spread down her face and neck to warm the rest of her body. A faint electrical tingling surged through her spine and moved throughout her body; her broken fingers felt on fire. But it was an oddly pleasant feeling and she relaxed into it.

"The language is the language of my people," explained Drogol. "I was born in a remote part of Siberia. It was a place of holy languages brought to us by pilgrims looking to see the face of the divine in nature. Those who survived the journey were strong in spirit and favored by God. There is much to learn from such souls."

"We are such long distances from our homes," murmured Sveta.

She felt as though she were lying in a warm blanket, bundled in her mother's arms. Safe. Warm. She felt a sensation of well-being flood through her body. Like drinking hot tea on a freezing cold night, feeling its heat radiate throughout her body.

"And we are strangers in this world. Betrayed and hunted. Yet we are fearsome creatures, weak only in our loneliness."

His words seemed to flow through her like a river of hope; his voice was strong and deep, filled with lonely passion.

"Are we safe?" she asked.

There was no reason to ask him, she knew. His beast was out of control. And he could not know how close Anna Kazakova was to finding them, or how close Hauck was either, for that matter. For all his strangeness Drogol was, after all, only a man.

"We are never safe," he said. "Never."

The warm tingling sensation that began with Drogol's hands held to either side of her forehead continued until she felt it even in the soles of her feet. She smiled without thinking; health and goodwill lit her heart. But when she thought of what Drogol said, she opened her eyes and stared up at him, searching his face for a hint of hope.

"What is happening to me?"

"The Divine has chosen to heal your body," he said. "Give thanks and rise."

Sveta had scarcely seen the inside of a church since childhood.

"Where's the duffel with my guns?"

"Are you so afraid of Heaven's gifts?" he asked, his face incredulous.

His hands came away as she sat up. The dizziness and sense of immi-
nent nausea were gone. She felt ready for action. Like a soldier called to
duty, she swung her legs over the edge of the bed and got to her feet. A
stretch and twist of her upper torso. A rise to her tiptoes that bunched
her calf muscles together like squeezing fists. She was good to go again.

"Thanks. I don't know how you did it, but I feel better than I did
before all of this started."

Drogol said nothing.

"What?" she asked.

"I did nothing, nothing at all. God is real. His gifts are real. Do
you really believe that I have power to heal you? Look at me; I am only
flesh and blood like you."

"I don't know how it works and I don't care how it works," she said
irritably. "All I'm saying is thanks and I have to get going before Hauck
or the others show up here."

He stood like a defiant king.

"This is my home, my only hope," he shouted. "Whoever violates
this space, whoever would destroy my hope is already dead. I will kill
them with my own hands."

His face was flushed bright red, and his eyes lit with a terrible light.

"Calm down cowboy," she said quickly. "All I'm saying is that I can't
hide here forever. You don't know Hauck."

Drogol raised his hand, and then flipped it as though knocking
away an annoying fly.

"I knew him long before you did," he said dismissively.

"Oh, that's right. You murdered a prison full of men where he was
stationed, didn't you?"

"It was a military prison. I was a prisoner against my will. They
were going to experiment on me. Can you really mourn such men?"

"I understand all that. You did what you had to do to get out."

Her bag was sitting on a drafting table nearby. Drogol had swept
away books that now lay scattered on the floor to make room for it.
She walked over, pulled out her 9 millimeter, checked the clip and the
magazine, flipped the safety to the "off" position, and grinned. The way
she held the pistol, her intent was obvious before she spoke.

"And that's what I'm doing, Drogol. What I have to in order to get
out of here. Don't try to stop me."

"Go," he said.

"I don't need your permission," she said. "I'm armed."

"I see."

"Glad we finally understand each other."

"I think not," he said. "May I show you something before you leave?"

"No time."

"It is on your way to the stairs. You can look and then continue. I have no power to keep you here."

"You have no power over me period."

"So true."

"Okay. Show me."

A sudden pang of conscience hit Sveta. She looked toward Zoe out of the corner of her eye.

"How's she?" she asked.

"She is well," replied Drogol. "I am only giving her time to recover fully."

"You gave her something to help her sleep?"

"I sang to her, so she sleeps."

"Let's get going," said Sveta. "Remember, you stay in front. I'll have a gun at your back all the way."

"How powerful you are," said Drogol.

"Shut up and start walking."

*****

When he opened the door, Sveta waived him through first with her pistol. She took stock of her situation. She had cash and new clothes in the bag, which meant she would have enough to survive. Zoe was on her own with Drogol. She would have to make her own decisions when she woke up. Sveta had to concentrate on survival.

The golden light seemed brighter than she remembered it, and the strange electrical equipment shone as though polished especially for her awakening. Yet she cringed, too, because the beast could be hiding anywhere, ready to leap out at her without warning.

Forty feet ahead, she saw the train lying on its side. One last car and the caboose miraculously stood standing upright on the track as though the initial impact from the beast had been so quick and brutal that it had cut the trains in half like a cleaver cutting a snake into two parts with a single vicious slash.

One of the great bells was knocked loose from its giant frame, and landed a good fifteen feet away from where it had been. Wisps of steam drifted up from various parts of the complex, as though the beast had cracked or broken steam pipes that must have provided some of the location's heat.

"What is that?" asked Sveta.

She was pointing toward a smoky glass cylinder taller than a man and three to four feet in diameter. It was mounted on a blue-black platform eight feet square and just as high. In an odd way it reminded Sveta of the Plexiglas cylinders that drive-through banks send about through pneumatic tubes.

"My salvation, if I am favored by God. My destruction if I am not."

Drogol was moving in long strides toward the back end of the train. His high-collared vestment seemed more natural on him than it had on the surface, where time seemed to have passed his fashion sense by. Down here, surrounded by electrical equipment from a bygone era, he was not hanging in chains. He was the master of this place, and he walked quickly, confidently through it.

His back was a good target, but if he tried to bolt she would shoot him in the legs. Drogol had not harmed her. He was crazy, yes, but he had not hurt her when he had the chance. He might even, she thought, be able to heal himself if she didn't kill him.

Spooked. She must be spooked. What happened to all the questions she wanted answered before she left? She knew the answer to that. Even so far below the surface in this hidden world of Drogol's, she worried that Hauck could track her. She couldn't get it out of her mind. Something. She was missing out on something and she just couldn't get a handle on what and that spooked her.

They had come to the second car from the caboose, approaching it from the side opposite to where the other cars lay across the track like felled game.

"This is what you want me to see?"

"No. Follow me inside and I will show you."

"Go," she said, pointing her pistol at him.

He saves me, he heals me, so I point a gun at him, she thought.

At the top of the metal stairs, he opened the train car door inward and waited for her to follow him in. She hung back just a little, instinctively aware that there was something in this car that she did not want to see.

He walked a short way in and turned to her.

"Come. Come in. There is nothing to fear. Only a gift I give to you for your journey."

"Move in a little further," she said.

Drogol obliged her, and then waited with his arms folded.

"Okay," she said as she crossed the threshold, "I'm in. What do you have for me?"

She hadn't noticed much about the other train car that she and Zoe had cowered in as the beast was trying to kill them, but now she saw that the cars were elegantly, even beautifully equipped with marble, brass, and velvet. However these cars had been transported underground they had been meant for rich, powerful people.

"I have a knife beneath these robes," he said. "I need to remove it to cut free my gift to you."

"Uh-uh," said Sveta. "Point me to it and I'll cut it down. You sit in that seat over there, and lay your knife on the seat in front of you. I'll do the cutting."

Drogol laughed.

"As you say."

He sat down slowly, exaggerating his harmlessness. Next he pulled aside his robe to reveal the knife, slid it out and laid it on the seat in front of him.

"Now, do you see how safe I am?"

Sveta began to feel more and more nervous. This was a bad mistake. Just like coming here in the first place. She scooped the knife up with one hand while keeping the pistol pointed at him with the other.

"What am I supposed to cut down?" she asked.

He nodded his head to the far end of the car.

She risked a quick glance and could see nothing of interest other than a square of gold-edged red velvet hanging on the wall as though it were covering a picture.

"What's back there?" she asked. "A safe with something in it?"

"Something more precious to me than gold," he said. "But hurry, I know that you must want to leave so very badly. See what I am giving to you so you can rush away."

It could be anything behind that piece of velvet, she knew, but she was tired of his games. She stood to one side, tugged a little gold cord, and watched the velvet fall away.

Behind it was an old, sepia photograph about the size of a coffee table book. A regal woman, a man kneeling before her.

"How did you do this?" she said, swinging round quickly and focusing the pistol at the center-point of his forehead. "And why did you do this? What is your game?"

"I have no game," said Drogol. "Go ahead. Take the photo. It is old and I am tired of it. And no, it was not created with a computer. I have no use for such things."

"Bullshit."

"But I should know. I was there when it was taken."

"But that's a picture of me in a dress standing next to you. I don't wear dresses and I've never stood next to you in my entire life. One last chance. Tell me how and why you did this or I'll blow your damned brains out."

Slowly, with great dignity, Drogol stood and stepped out into the aisle.

"Shoot me if you have to, woman. I offer you a gift for your journey and you threaten me. You slap me in the face with your accusations. I tell you that is me in that photo. As for the woman, you should know her."

"I know my own face," said Sveta in a quiet, menacing voice.

"Perhaps so, but the woman in that picture is Alexandra, the last Tsarista of the Romanov's."

Sveta struggled to understand.

"It is your father in the photo, then?"

"No child, it is me in the photo. Why do you think my enemies pursue me?"

"You're crazy."

"I was born on the twenty-second day of October, 1869 in a wilderness village named Pokrovskoye."

Sveta's face went blank.

"What are you saying?"

He stepped closer and she raised her pistol.

"Look at the photograph. See what you see. See that I am me. Understand why they hunt me. Anna Kazakova is old and dying. I am a hundred years older but strong and vital. I have power in my body, power in my blood. She thinks I have the secret of immortality flowing through my veins. The other would kill me for revenge and he does not care what is lost by my death. He thinks I killed his brother in that prison forsaken by God."

He took another step closer and instead of pulling the trigger, she turned her head to stare at the photo again. It *was* him. No denying it. And it looked to be a genuine old photograph, cracked and peeled and browned at the edges. Desperately she looked for a date or a name plaque, but there was nothing to show the names of the two people in the picture. The man on bended knee, his head inclined before the Tsarista of all Romanov Russian. The man who was clearly Drogol.

Sveta felt him close behind her. Very close.

"Who are you?" she whispered.

"I am," he said in a low growl only inches from behind her ear, "Grigori Yefimovitch Rasputin, and I did not die in the Neva River in 1916 as that traitor Prince Yusupov told the world."

CHAPTER SEVENTEEN

"Hey, Sasha, wake up. You have a visitor," yelled the guard.

"Fuck you," said Sasha without opening his eyes.

"Suit yourself. I'll take the cigarettes."

"Wait."

Sasha opened his eyes and sat up in the cage.

"What time is it?" he asked.

"What's the difference?" said his guard.

As he ran his hand over his rough cheeks, Sasha realized that he had been drugged for so long that he now had a hangover of sorts. He felt like he'd been out drinking all night, got in a fight but didn't get laid. He hadn't shaved or showered, and although someone had thought to put a cushioned floor in the cage and a raggedy blanket, his joints and back were stiff.

"So who is here?" he asked.

There was a light shining directly down on him. The purpose was two-fold, he knew. First, to keep him disoriented by preventing him from getting a good night's sleep. Second, it kept his guards in the shadows so that he never knew if they were watching him.

"So it's okay, yes?" asked a familiar voice.

"The Iron Lady says it is okay, then it's okay," replied the guard. "She says I shoot you, I shoot you."

"She said I should check in on him, make sure he's healthy and see how his spirits are."

"She said that?"

"Not really all that."

Sasha finally recognized the voice. It was Dr. Pazyryk.

He closed his eyes and listened to the conversation.

*****

"Didn't sound like her," said the guard. "She throws somebody in a cage she don't ask how they feel about it."

"Well here's how it is," said the doctor, "she wants to know if he's healthy, and although I can tell a great deal about him from a physical examination, I'm not going into the cage with him. He bears a certain animosity toward me, you see."

"We got him chained. One chain each to the manacles on his wrists and ankles angled from the four corners, and another one from the top coming down to a metal band around his neck. He ain't going to hurt you. You want to see?"

"No, he'd strangle me with the chains while you were eating lunch or something. So I'm going to look at him over through the bars and talk to him."

"Talking helps you diagnose him?"

"Certainly. Besides, he might slip and say something important Mrs. Kazakova needs to know."

"You're a smart guy, doc."

"So that's him over there?"

"Only one I see chained in a cage."

"Yes, of course. He was hunched over and I couldn't see his face."

"Sure."

"I didn't know how many people we had in cages here."

"Yell if you need help," said the guard.

"Of course. Thank you. I will be sure and tell Mrs. Kazakova what a magnificent job you are doing."

"Don't say nothing about me to her, if you get what I mean."

"I will, of course, respect your wishes."

*****

The guard sat down, opened a desk drawer and took out a can of potato chips. He laid his pistol on the table within easy reach.

Dr. Pazyryk set off for the cage in the center of the floor, roughly thirty feet away. One guard visible, empty warehouse space with a titanium cage in the middle. Probably a sniper or two in the rafters or somebody watching over the cage with nano-cameras. That would be his luck. He wondered briefly if there were microphones. That could be a problem, but the idea seemed ridiculous. Bugging a cage? Not likely. But Hauck had already thought of the possibility.

His apprehension grew with every step. It was the first time that Hauck ever requested anything like this of him. Normally he just reported in on what he learned. He never had to *do* anything before this. Not really. This was serious. This could get him killed. But anything Hauck asked you to do could get you killed.

His body temperature increased even in the cold and forbidding emptiness of the empty room. A trickle of sweat ran down his neck. This was not about a patient, it was about *him*, and the thought of being discovered terrified him.

Sasha sat cross-legged in the cage, looking straight at him like a sinister yogi in the lotus position. A dangerous animal not to be trusted. A dangerous creature that did not trust its captors. The pure agony and hatred emanating from the young man was tangible.

"So," said Sasha. "You betrayed me."

"And so nice to see you, too, Sasha."

"You drugged me. It was you who did this to me."

"Indeed it was."

"You confess?"

"I do."

"I will peel back your skin when I get out of here and watch you die of infection."

"Now is that any way to speak to the man who saved your life?"

Sasha spit at him, but the doctor moved aside.

"You? You saved my life? This is what you call saving my life? Chained like a dog in a cage?"

Dr. Pazyryk remembered what Hauck had told him. Let the boy vent his rage. Act hurt. Act wounded. Then tell him their version of the story.

"How can you talk to me like this? First I risk everything to save you, now I risk my life to come and give you hope, and you treat me this way. I should have never come in the first place. Like a good friend, I even brought you cigarettes."

Sasha was about to say something, but the doctor caught his eye. He slid the cigarette pack out of his pocket, opened the box, and slid up a tiny screen hidden between the box and its foil liner. He shook his head at the young man to warn him into silence. It continued to display a faint green light, which meant there were no electronic transponders in the cage. He slid the card back into cigarette pack again.

"Okay," said the doctor nervously. "We can talk. Not much time, so don't say anything unless I tell you to, okay?"

Sasha, his eyes lit with new hope, nodded his vigorous agreement.

"Good. Now I think you've been wronged by all of this. I am loyal to your mother, but you are her son. I know that you don't think much of me, but I have always admired your courage and determination. You are the logical heir to her empire. But she is ill, and her mind has gone, I believe. It is possible Ivan has been slowly poisoning her with a metallic compound that has permanently damaged her brain and she is now insane. Do you understand?"

This was Hauck's idea. Even though chained and caged, no boy easily turns on his mother, not even Sasha. So the blame had to be shifted to another party. It was important, too, that the insanity be unable to be reversed because otherwise Sasha might try to save his mother.

"You are saying that pig drives her crazy with his herbal poisons?"

Dr. Pazyryk appeared to seriously consider the thought, as though weighing a terrible matter.

"Reluctantly," he finally said, "I believe it is true. Such damage cannot be undone. Your mother is not the same woman as before."

A fine point of instruction from Hauck. Such language implied that Anna Kazakova did really not disown her son. Anna Kazakova was gone. In her place was a crazy woman. It was important to reinforce that his mother had not betrayed him, but that Ivan had substituted a paranoid creature for her.

"I will kill that man," said Sasha. "I will stick a pistol up his ass and blow his balls off."

The doctor did not take time to explain the medical impossibility of such a plan.

"First we must get you out of here so that you can plot your revenge."

Sasha's body fell forward a few inches and his chin dropped.

"Look at these chains, at these bars. It is hopeless. Why? Why has this happened?"

"Keep your voice down," said the doctor. "Words might echo in here."

Sasha nodded morosely.

"Listen to me. In addition to the brain poison, Ivan convinced your mother Drogol's blood could cure her disease. At first she thought that your blood could do this. She had me test samples of your blood on her to see if they could cure her. Her instructions to me were to take blood from you as though for a routine physical exam, and then use it to experiment on diseased mice using those samples. I'm sorry, Sasha, but she would have killed me if I disobeyed."

"You used my blood on diseased mice?"

"She thought you shared enough genetics in common with your father to possibly cure her."

"That man is not my father. She is ill. My father died in the war and she knows it. This is all a mistake."

Dr. Pazyryk stayed the course. Convincing Sasha was completely necessary. Then, when he helped free the boy, the grateful young man would help him escape as well. The doctor knew sooner or later Ivan would figure him out, and he wanted to be long gone by then.

"No. It's not a mistake. It is the work of that albino magician. He knows that once he gets rid of your mother, you are the next in line to take over as head of the organization. With you both gone, he will grab the reins of power and claim ownership of all that your family has built."

The silence that followed was so loud that Dr. Pazyryk began to get nervous. The guard at the far away table looked to be sleeping, but that could be an act. Perhaps sound carried so well that even with hushed voices he could hear them and was pretending to be asleep.

"What are we to do?" asked Sasha. "Tell me, what are we to do?"

"First, I tell you that your mother, under the influence of Ivan, wanted you killed. Why, because she hates Drogol and believes that you are his child. You and I know that this is bullshit, but Ivan kept pushing the idea on her. I had to convince her that it was necessary to keep you alive for bait to catch the beast. Ivan wanted you dead."

"Thank you so very much, Doctor. You have saved me to be an animal staked out and soon eaten."

"Have a little trust, Sasha. I have to go now, but I will be back. I will be back to give you a sedative that will actually only be sugar and water. Do you understand?"

"Why would you do such a stupid thing?"

"I have convinced your mother that with further study of your physiology we may yet find a cure for her illness within you. I begged her to bring electronic scanning equipment to use in my research and she agreed."

"You are going to cut me open?"

"Don't be an idiot, Sasha. I must leave now. But when I come back, I will give you something that is supposed to put you to sleep. You will pretend to be unconscious. Do you understand?"

Sasha agreed with a nervous *yes*.

"Then, when I have declared that you are, to my satisfaction, completely unconscious, the guards will unchain you and strap you to a gurney. You will be wheeled to a separate room for a CAT scan. There will be only one guard outside of the room, and I will drug him. When he is down, I will free you and we will escape together. Now, I must go."

The look in Sasha's eyes told Dr. Pazyryk that he had won his confidence.

"Doctor?"

"What is it?"

"I will not forget your friendship."

"I am risking my life for you, Sasha."

"I will not forget. But one more thing, Doctor?"

"Yes?"

"Make sure that you find a way to get me an automatic weapon and lots of ammunition before we try to escape."

After a slight, awkward nod, Dr. Pazyryk began the lonely trek back across the cold concrete floor. He very much hoped Hauck knew what he was doing or he and Sasha would be dead before the end of the day.

He had not walked twenty feet before he heard the guard shout out, "Mrs. Kazakova wants to see you. Now. They've located the car they got away in. It had a GPS link in it."

Dr. Pazyryk almost fainted mid-stride.

CHAPTER EIGHTEEN

I don't like this sitting around and talking," said the Instructor. "It's boring. It's fucking-A boring. I like to do things; I don't like to drink coffee and yak. That's why I hate coming in to the middle of something—especially if it's a goat rodeo like this. But I ain't going in blind. So I want to know everything you know that's worth knowing and no hiding shit from me. That way we're through and I'm only bored for just a little bit. We all together on this?"

"Yes," said Hauck through gritted teeth.

"So let me see if I got this straight," said the Instructor. "Anna catches this werewolf guy when she was with the KGB. Am I right?"

Hauck looked at the options list of anesthetic gases Traxler had handed to him.

"Exactly," he said, without looking up from the paper. "We had no idea what we were getting into. He was a madman with a small, underground army of followers to protect him. They were like a cult."

"And you had to go into the sewers, which wasn't exactly what you guys trained for. Had to be careful pulling the trigger underground or you'd set off an explosion. Shit like that."

Hauck looked up and far away, remembering some of the people he'd lost to Drogol.

"A lot of good men and women died that night."

"You can tell me the details someday if we get drunk and play pool. Right now, I'm more interested if you saw anything that night should have tipped you off how bad it was going to get."

"Nothing," said Hauck, "until it was too late. It went through men like a propeller cutting through water in those sewers. One man made it back and started babbling about a monster. I thought perhaps a diseased gorilla had escaped from the zoo and was wandering the underground. So I ordered up all the high tensile strength nets and cables I could get my hands on. And I brought in animal control teams. Everything happened so fast I can't tell you how we actually trapped him."

"Bullshit," said the Instructor. "Don't lie to me. Don't ever fucking lie to me. Do I look like one of your stooges? Now it's a simple question: how'd you bring him down?"

Hauck looked the old man straight in the eye.

"I'm telling you that I don't know. It was Anna's show. Only she knows the full details. Communications were terrible. Everything was out of control. One minute we were dealing with a monster and the next we were dealing with Drogol. But we only got him because he was where the beast was. The beast itself was … gone."

The Instructor grimaced.

"So is this about a guy and his pet freak monster, or is it about a guy who turns into a monster?"

"I don't know," said Hauck.

"So you see anything good on that list from Rudolph?"

"Everything is good on the list from Rudolph," came a voice from across the room.

"Bullshit," said the Instructor. "I mean really good, humpa-humpa stuff; you know what I'm saying?"

Hauck held up a hand.

"I think I see what we need. There is no way, of course, to calculate the effect of gas on the beast."

"Everything's got to breathe," said the Instructor.

"The only thing we do not know is how much it will take to put it to sleep," said Hauck as though the Instructor hadn't spoken.

"Maybe we should just flat out kill it. Poison it, I mean. Why take a chance?"

"Too risky," said Hauck. "My operatives may be there. If they aren't with him, I doubt Drogol will show up."

"Or if we get him cornered we take him out with a rocket launcher. Or if we can get a line on where he's at, we blow the whole place up. He might be able to dodge a few bullets, but he ain't getting away from a rocket."

"That's not the way."

"I know, I know, you're worried about calling down those pricks at Homeland Security on us."

"We can't expect them to ignore an explosion in Detroit. Detroit's on their watch list so they've got the personnel and resources to take us down."

"Then we gas it. You want this thing dead? Then don't fuck around with knockout gas. I should have known better. It ain't good to be nice. We use poison gas and get it over with."

"No," said Hauck. "I won't kill my own people."

"Who we talking here? This Zoe? She your girlfriend or something? You banging her?"

Hauck could feel Traxler staring at him, but refused to acknowledge the awkwardness of the moment. The Instructor looked at him with just the shade of an innocent smile tugging at the corner of his mouth.

"No. I'm not *banging* her. She's an agent, nothing more."

"How about the other chick? What's her name? She going to be there?"

Damn the old man, thought Hauck.

"I don't know if she will be or not. We don't even know if we can set in play another controlled meeting with Drogol yet."

"What's her name again?"

Hauck let out a long, painful sigh.

"Sveta."

The old man crossed his hands behind his back and began to move idly about the room, paying attention to a pistol here, a grenade launcher there, and occasionally picking up a knife and holding its blade up to a light as though looking for imperfections.

"So, you banging *her*?"

"No."

"You want to?"

"Sveta's an agent," snapped Hauck. "Nothing more."

"Got it bad for her, huh? Well here's the deal, slick. That thing in the video? It ain't rolling over and passing out because we ask it to. And we don't kill it, it sure as hell is going to kill us. You getting this?"

"I will not murder my own agents," repeated Hauck.

He had about enough of where the conversation was leading.

Traxler moved over to a computer and began typing, trying to stay out of the line of fire. The Instructor walked past him and stopped to stand before a piece of quarter inch thick diamondback steel plate. He turned to look back at Hauck, as though waiting for him to say something. Without warning, he spun back to face the steel plate and his fist shot out so quickly that Hauck only saw a blur. The crack of his calloused knuckles against steel rang out like a dull bell.

"What in God's—" said Traxler.

He spun his chair around and was staring in disbelief at the fist-sized dent in his piece of metal.

"Hauck'll pay you for it," said the Instructor with a dark grin. "I'm just letting off a little steam. I didn't come all this way to babysit. You agree with me, Rudolph?"

"I respect both of your opinions," said Traxler. His eyes were locked on the impossible dent.

"You're so full of shit. And Hauck, you get this straight—my old lady hates your guts and I'm beginning to get pissed off at you myself. You used to have a brain so I liked you, but now I think you're going soft in the head. If your women are stupid enough to be in close with that thing when we go after it, then they're just going to have to die unless you can think of something better. Besides, didn't that one bitch turn on you?"

"She was out of the loop. She didn't know how she fit into the plan. I can see how she might have misinterpreted events. I might have done the same myself."

"Uh-huh."

"She's a good soldier in a bad situation."

"We're going to have to gas them all anyway."

Hauck rubbed his hand across his forehead and wished that Zoe would make contact and tell him what the hell was going on.

*****

"You want to know what I think?" asked Yuri.

"No," said Evgeny. "I only want to hit my target. Thinking is no good for accuracy."

"It must be boring inside your head."

"It is very peaceful," said Evgeny.

Yuri watched the sniper cleaning his rifle. For a squat, solid man, Evgeny's fingers moved across his weapon like a violinist's across a Stradivarius. Deft, graceful and purposeful. An act of love to bring forth the essence of the instrument for the musician, an act of will to bring forth the end of another's life for the sniper.

They were in a converted firehouse built in the early nineteen hundreds. The dull metal pole that ran between the floors was so discolored from neglect that it looked like a giant pencil lead instead of a fireman's pole. The windows onto the street were tall and arched at the top as though taken from an old church. A six foot neon-ribbed picture of Elvis Presley flashed above a wet bar put in long after the firehouse tenants were dead and gone.

Eight of Hauck's men rotated in and out of the building. Two were downstairs with the vehicles, Yuri, Evgeny and two shooters called Filipp and Feodot rested in their cots. A heavyset woman named Alyona and a Georgian man named Bagrat were out following down leads and making arrangements for Hauck.

Yuri sat in a leather and chrome chair, his feet propped up on a thick wooden conference table while he stared idly at a row of screens and rubbed his cast with his free hand.

"This is starting to itch."

"You took so many pills you can't feel your arm," said Evgeny. "So how can it itch?"

"No, I mean it. It's like poison ivy."

"Quit whining."

"I'm not whining," said Yuri. "I mean it, I can feel it itch."

"Take another pill."

"I don't need another pill. I need answers. I wouldn't itch if I had answers."

"What answers? You talk much but you say nothing. You are like American television."

Yuri swung his legs down to the floor, sat up straighter and glared at Evgeny.

"You're so smart, you tell me. What kind of thing is this that we track? You don't miss. I know that. You know that. So how come it didn't go down?"

"I hit it," said Evgeny.

"Hit what? A werewolf? A ten foot tall werewolf? And silver and

mercury do nothing to it? What kind of werewolf is that? What if …
what if it isn't a werewolf at all? That's all I'm saying."

"You keep saying the same thing all of the time."

"That's because I have no fucking answers. I have no information
to even start looking for an answer."

Evgeny held up two gray-black sections and snapped them together
as smoothly as if he'd been born doing it.

"So what," he asked without looking up, "is your question?"

"Okay, here is what has been nagging at me ever since we started
this project. Say you were a Russian."

"I am Ukrainian."

"Thank you, Evgeny, for sharing that with me. But if you were
Russian like this Drogol."

"He is Siberian."

"Russian, Siberian—"

"Not the same."

Yuri looked at him in surprise.

"Maybe something there, okay, I give you that. But let's stick with
Russian for now. Why would Drogol leave Russia after so many years
to come to the United States?"

"Easy," said Evgeny. "He comes here to hide from Anna Kazakova
and Hauck."

"Ah, but why to Detroit?"

"A good place to hide."

"Think about that, my sniper friend. A six foot six Russian with hair
like a wild man comes to Detroit. Does he fit in so well?"

"No," admitted Evgeny. "He is like a polar bear in Africa."

"Exactly. So you see my question—why is he here? If we could
figure that out, maybe we could use it to catch him and stick a spike
up his ass."

CHAPTER NINETEEN

I will guard the door," was all he said to finally convince her.

A quick shower.

A quick meal.

A mug of coffee, real coffee.

Three minutes for the shower. Two to get dressed. Five minutes for food and coffee. Ten minutes total and she was off and running. Showered, fresh clothes, fed and caffeinated. Jacked with cash and weapons and a vehicle, she could go anywhere in the United States without crossing a border.

But first she had to know.

Hot water ran over her naked body. She ran one trembling hand over her face and neck to wipe away the grime. The other hand held her pistol wrapped in a clear plastic bag that stopped just before her elbow. Her weapons and cash duffel were tied off inside a black garbage bag. She moved quickly, worried that she was making a mistake, taking chances she didn't need to take. She was a fool to do this, but she had been too dirty and ragged to go back onto the streets. People would notice and remember her. Maybe a cop.

Sveta closed her eyes and quit thinking.

She scrubbed herself with mechanical efficiency, and then slowed to simply enjoy the heat and pulse of the water. Somewhere within the underground complex was a boiler or a means to heat the water. How this had all come into being, how it was maintained, all of this she put aside for the simple languor and comfort of a hot shower.

From somewhere outside the door, she heard a deep, throaty growl and she stiffened.

She heard Drogol's voice.

"Grigor," he said sharply. "Leave Ilya alone. Go hunt the rats and leave your brother be."

Wolves, Hauck had said. *He kept wolves in Moscow.*

With a turn of her wrist, she turned off the water.

"Is it safe to come out?" she called.

"If you are dressed, certainly," came the reply. "Sometimes my pets can be temperamental, but they are always obedient to me."

From inside the garbage bag that protected the duffel, she withdrew a towel and began to dry herself. When she finished, she dressed in black jeans, black boots, black shirt and sweater and then threw on her black leather coat. Her hair was short and she brushed it quickly. On a good looking woman, much was excused. And Sveta knew she was a good looking woman.

Duffel over her shoulder, pistol held before her with the barrel up; she pushed open the door to the shower. Drogol stood twenty feet away, his back to her with his hands at his sides as though standing at attention. He stood before an odd assortment of crystals that glowed with soft, shifting colors.

"Beautiful, are they not?" he asked without turning around.

"What do they do?"

"Truly," he said as turned around and spread his arms out, "I do not know. There are mysteries within this place that elude me. Still, it is here that exists whatever hope I have of finding a cure for this curse that the new god of your world has sent down upon my head."

Sveta holstered her pistol.

"I don't have much have time," she said. "Are you going to start talking so I can understand you or am I going to have to leave?"

"Come, walk with me. Listen to me, and I think you will either stay, or run for your life."

"So long as we walk towards the stairs leading up to the surface."

Drogol nodded.

They walked side by side through stands of bizarre equipment that Sveta couldn't understand or recognize. There were what looked to be giant vacuum tubes. Blinding white lightning bursts spontaneously erupted within them from to time to time with whip-like cracks that startled her. Drogol looked around the room, lost in thought, oblivious to the mysteries surrounding him.

"I am Siberian originally, and at first, as you must no doubt know. From there, I went to Moscow and gained notoriety. A simple mistake for a simple man. I was an embarrassment to the royal family in unfortunate ways, but they kept me close when, through me, God took mercy and healed their child. Again, you are Russian and know all of this."

Struck by an impossible thought, Sveta said, "This place is like a picture I saw of Edison's laboratory."

"Very good, child," laughed Drogol.

Sveta glared at him, but he gave no notice.

"I was, I admit," he continued, "in a desperate state. A decadent city like Moscow was no place for a holy man. I had fallen under its spell. Its debauchery dirtied my soul. So I decided to return to the Siberian forests in shame, to confess my fallen state to God, and seek him out among the innocent trees of Tunguska, where many a holy man has found again their faith."

Sveta touched his sleeve.

"I don't believe," she said, "that you are Rasputin. I don't believe that I am the reincarnation of Alexandra. But I do believe you must hurry. I cannot stay here long. We both have a price on our head and they will eventually find us if we stay in one place too long."

Drogol looked tired for the first time. His shoulders slumped just a little, and the wrinkles at the corner of his eyes seemed to deepen with sadness.

"How do I tell you a lifetime of pain and suffering and exile and, yes, longing, in only a few moments. You asked who I am and what this place of hope and horror is and how it came to be. It is the secret of why we are both hunted, woman. Leave if you must. Run away if you are afraid. But if you wish to understand your enemies, to know what they do not know so that you can use it against them to save your life, then listen. Simply listen."

It was, she felt, an insoluble problem—dangerous for her to stay, but perhaps more dangerous for her to leave without hearing what he had to say.

"Go on," she said reluctantly.

He started walking again, leading them past the suspended bells, and then stopped. When he turned to her, his gaze was focused far away on a distant past.

"I went to find the God that I had once known, but instead, in that Siberian forest, I found the god of this place. I found the god that the whole world would come to worship. You look at me as though I speak in riddles, but I tell you what I found in that Siberian forest was not God, the Father or God, the Son of my faith. Neither the Son of Man nor the Son of Heaven. That day, on June 30, 1908, I came face to face instead with the father of science, the religion with no soul that possesses your world. There, starving and exhausted, as I rose to my feet to beseech God, I saw the largest, most ferocious and rabid wolf I had ever seen charging toward me like a demon from the Pit. I know now that it was a bodark—a werewolf. But before its foaming jaws seized me, the very air came alive with a surge of energy unlike any the world has ever known."

"What are you saying, Drogol? You're not making sense. Just spit it out."

"It was a burst of energy one thousand times more powerful than the atomic bomb dropped on Hiroshima. Over eighty million trees were flattened in an area over eight hundred miles square."

"The Tunguska meteor. Every Russian knows of that. You tell me nothing new."

Another grim laugh as painful memories floated through his eyes like dark clouds.

"It was no meteor."

"Then what was it?"

"It was a beam of energy sent around the world by a madman. A madman the world now reveres. All the way on the other side of the world Tesla, the great Nikola Tesla, tested his death ray at that very moment, aiming for the Arctic Circle but instead scorching the countryside where I stood. I became his sacrifice to the god of science. You look at me as though I am mad, but I am not mad. This is history, woman, and unlike you I have not only read about it, I have lived it."

With an abrupt turn he grasped her arms and squeezed them hard. He stared into her eyes with an intensity that shot through her like a jolt of electricity.

"It ripped my very soul from me. I felt the fabric within my spirit tear wide as if my soul was split by a hatchet. And something, something dark and ravenous, something malevolent and insane from the other side stared through me from its world of nightmares into our own.

Through my eyes. Through my eyes, I tell you. It saw the rabid wolf-beast leaping at me and in an instant it pulled that wild animal within me and consumed its disease. The energy field increased so quickly that the world around me lit with painful, blinding black radiance, and then, I was no longer there."

"Let go of me," said Sveta. "Or I'll shoot you."

But his eyes burned with conviction and he clung to her as though she were a lifeline. He was mad. She could see that plainly now. Yet he exerted a magnetic pull on her that she could not explain. He believed what he said with an intensity that was beyond question.

"Suddenly," he said, "I was in a dark world of horrors. A world of dark caverns and ever burning liquid rocks. A sulfurous, smoky mist hung in the skies and pale skinned monsters with glowing red eyes and leprous skin hunted in the eternal night of that wretched landscape. Always they hunted. And I knew that I was no longer on this earth."

Sveta tried to pull away, but his strength was too much for her. She could have fought him, but his eyes held her in place.

"I saw herds of animals running, always running from gibbering creatures. Screams bloodied the night like the red phosphorescent fungus that grew everywhere.

"Can you imagine the overwhelming terror that gripped my soul? I searched the forests of my youth seeking divine epiphany and thought I had been cast into Hell itself by God. I did not know that I had survived the greatest disaster in mankind's history by being thrown into another dimension because of Tesla's energy machine. I thought that God himself was judging my sins and sentencing me to eternal damnation."

His face twisted in epic torment, he raised his fists toward the heavens and shook them as though exhorting God.

"Have I not suffered enough?" he cried. "Must I be cursed by this god of science? Will you not yet forgive me?"

"Let go of me," Sveta said.

Drogol snarled and stepped back away from her.

"You think that I'm crazy, don't you? But you have seen with your own eyes the beast. And it is from that world that he comes. I don't know why or how, but sometimes I am sent into its world and it is sent into ours. It is not I that it is the beast, don't you see? I am innocent, truly innocent, but still they hunt me."

Sveta did see.

Drogol was really and truly out of his fucking mind.

Worse, she now knew that he had not released a beast the night before, he *was* the beast.

CHAPTER TWENTY

C ome closer to me, Ivan, and tell me again of the beast."
"Yes, Mother."

Anna Kazakova let out a long, painful sigh. He knew how weak her body was; if they did not capture Drogol soon, she would certainly die from the stress.

"It is a comfort to hear you call me mother, now that I have no son."
"Indeed."

The door was closed and locked. No one would disturb them. He was a pale white specter, leaning against a side wall, listening to her breathing, remembering other old women he had attended. Remembering other old women whose last breaths he had captured in his smooth hands to feel their death slip through his thin fingers. It was a sublime feeling for him, a fleeting moment of exultation.

"Mishka is organizing the men and their weapons?" asked the old woman.

"He is."

"Water in a vodka bottle."

"Pardon?"

"Clear like vodka, but with no strength. He is not man enough to run this cell of our organization. When we have what we want, you must dispose of him. It must be ... instructive to the others."

Ivan nodded in the darkness. His eyes suffered so from bright light that he was never without his sunglasses during daylight hours. But at night or in darkness, his eyes could see without pain. The old woman did not mind that he turned the lights out. She did not fear the dark. In the thin quiet of the office room that had been cleaned out to accommodate her, the only light was that faint shadow of fluorescence that came from beneath the door. Somewhere in the building, hard men were loading up automatic weapons and ammunition into dark SUV's, but Ivan could scarcely hear them. None dared disturb the rest of Anna Kazakova, the Iron Lady of Ryazan prison.

"As you wish."

"But enough of that, Ivan. Come to me and tell me of the beast."

Ivan moved through the darkness to stand behind her. She lay on the medical cot, hooked to wires and electronic devices that could do nothing to save her from the disease that ruined her body. He reached out and ran his hand across the few wispy hairs that clung to her cold, sweaty scalp.

He began to speak, and his voice was warm and relaxing, deep and resonant with secret knowledge.

"Siberia is the land closest and dearest to the gods of the seven levels, Mother, and from there come the only true priests, the Weavers of Worlds. Seven bloodlines run throughout its peoples, but only one of these is chosen by the gods. These are the Buriat people. And in ancient times only one family among the Buriats was chosen to see the mysteries and to travel between the seven worlds, to attest to the divine knowledge and presence of the gods.

"Over the generations, these people grew arrogant, and defied the gods of the seven levels by intermarrying with those not blessed by the gods, and so not all of that family's descendants were able to be Weavers of the Seven Worlds. Each, therefore, had to be tested. Most were found to be hollow of spirit, and the shamans began to fear all was lost. But after many years, one qualified person was found, and his name was Rasputin, whom we later named Drogol. This boy passed all tests given him."

The old woman coughed. Her body palsied, but when Ivan placed his hands on her, she grew still. He wiped her mouth and chin clear of spittle with a clean cloth, and then let her sip water.

"Shall I stop, Mother?"

"No. Tell me the rest."

Ivan folded the cloth with which he'd wiped her face, and then threw it in a wastebasket before continuing. The smell of her drool was death's own.

"They began to teach him in the old ways. When he was ready, he was given herbs to unbind his mind. One teacher blindfolded him and made him sit, and then poked and prodded him to make sure he was no longer in a waking state. When he did not respond, that teacher began to beat him across the back with a switch while others sang. Another teacher slapped him on the forehead to help further loosen his thoughts. Sacred plants were burned and the night air filled with the perfumes of magic. Teachers gathered around him and began to chant. This continued through the night until the moon rose to its highest point in the sky."

He told her this story many times. But over the last several months, she asked for it more frequently, as though to reaffirm her sanity.

"When the moon rose to its fullest height, the cloth was taken from his eyes and if he saw a red moon, pale like thin blood, then he was a true Weaver of Worlds. That boy, called Rasputin, saw the blood moon that marked him as a true Buriat. The knowledge of the blood moon is the knowledge of the sacred. Because of this, we named him Drogol.

"It is our way that after that night, he be sent into the forests alone. There, he must make his way for the passing of one cycle, or what you call a month. At the end of that time, his teaching and obligation to the people would begin. He would be a true Weaver of Worlds. This as it always has been and always will be."

"But he betrayed his heritage," spoke the old woman.

"Yes, Mother, he betrayed his heritage. While in the forests he met a hermit who, when he learned why the boy was alone in the forests, began to lie to him, to tell him that he was deceived by demons. And before the cycle was through, Drogol denied his heritage and his obligation and became a holy man of a foreign faith. Because of this, the gods of the Buriat cursed him.

"For this has always been so, that whosoever is chosen by the gods of the Seven Worlds must accept that honor and obligation. Whosoever turns away from them is cursed and cast out. And I was chosen by the elders of the Buriat to kill this man who violated our faith. It is a great honor for me, to be chosen to kill this traitor."

"And so you will," whispered the old woman.

"Yes, Mother."

"Ivan?"

"Yes, Mother?"

"I want a computer screen in here with audio/visual feed. I want to see everything that those men see. Do you understand?"

"I do."

"Then you, you personally see to it that no one kills the beast until the doctor has samples of its blood. I will not die an old, sickly woman when Drogol lives on filled with vital energy. I want his blood. I want to live, damn him. I want to live for over a hundred years and more and stay young like he does. If one of those men kills him, I want you to chop of his head and feed it to the others. Do you hear me?"

Her voice had risen to a raspy scream so quickly and unexpectedly that Ivan involuntarily stepped back.

"Yes, Mother," he said. "I hear you."

"Then go bring me the blood of my enemy."

*****

Dr. Pazyryk stood smoking a cigarette, watching men loading a generator and metal nets onto the back of a truck placarded "Detroit Utility Repair." Three men loaded flame throwers into a van while others dragged the propellant and flammable liquid containers toward the same van.

"Hey," he yelled out, "are you crazy?"

The men kept walking.

"I said, are you fucking crazy?" he screamed.

Suddenly, the three men carrying tanks turned, set them down and stared at him. Not good. He had seen men like this before. Tattooed necks, short, cropped hair and dead eyes. The doctor let his cigarette fall to the concrete and then nervously ground it out.

One of the three smiled at him, made a hand motion and said, "Come here, little girl."

This man was the shortest of the three, but he had shoulders wide as a forklift with a neck so thickly muscled that his head looked too small to be his own.

"Actually, I was just trying to keep you from getting hurt," stammered the doctor.

'You called me crazy," said the man, and he pulled out a long, thin knife from somewhere beneath his jacket. "So you come here and blow me like a little bitch or I come to you and cut your throat."

The doctor ran his eyes around the room looking for Mishka or anyone else he knew.

"I'm with Mrs. Kazakova," he said in a voice tight as a garrote. "I'm her doctor."

"Is that right?" said the man, and he took two steps forward.

"That's right. She wouldn't like it if you annoyed me. She's not in a very good mood anyway and you know what she did to her own son, don't you? And besides, I was trying to keep you from getting hurt. If you drove around with flammable gases in your car then just the slightest leak and maybe a spark and you'd be blown to bits. Mishka would be upset losing a perfectly good van. He's not a very nice man, you know."

The man's face went pale, and he stopped where he was and started to back away.

"I didn't mean nothing," he said. "Nothing at all. Sorry. Thought you was someone. Someone else."

"What's your name?" asked an emboldened Dr. Pazyryk. "I believe I shall have to report you."

The man held up his hands in horror. The two men behind him picked up their tanks and moved quickly toward an empty pickup truck.

"Please. Sorry. So sorry," said the man as he turned and followed his comrades.

Dr. Pazyryk looked around to see that other men were turning away from him as though they had seen nothing. He straightened himself and nodded in satisfaction. There were certain advantages in being Mrs. Kazakova's person physician.

"May I speak with you, Doctor?" came a voice from behind him.

He swallowed painfully and turned to see Mishka standing only two feet behind him.

"So I take it I didn't scare those men off?"

The handsome young man narrowed his eyes and shook his head.

"That short one is very bad. You don't want to know how bad. You should stay away from him. He enjoys hurting people very much. Do you understand?"

"I was only trying to save his life. Did you see him? He was going to put flammable materials in an enclosed van. Even if the cylinders leaked but the gas didn't ignite, they could still be suffocated by the gas."

Mishka put his hand on the doctor's shoulder. A bright sparkle of diamond flared by the overhead halogen lights caught his eye. It was the biggest diamond ring that Dr. Pazyryk had ever seen.

"Will you take a walk with me, Doctor? We need to talk and time is short. Can you do that?"

"I'm waiting for Ivan," said Dr. Pazyryk, looking around nervously.

"Who exactly is he?" asked Mishka. "Tell me how has he gained so much power that Sasha is locked away in a cage?"

"You'll have to ask Mrs. Kazakova."

"My guard tells me you went to see Sasha."

"What is it you want?"

"Are you his friend?"

"I am a loyal member of the organization."

"That's not an answer to my question."

"As I said, you'll have to talk to his mother. I am loyal to her."

Mishka moved to stand beside the doctor, grabbing his elbow as he did so.

"Walk with me, Doctor. I believe we have things to discuss. We have mutual concerns, I think."

"I should wait here," said Dr. Pazyryk nervously.

"Voices echo a long way in big, empty storage rooms, did you know that? Would you like me to repeat what you said to Sasha while you were there?"

Suddenly the loading and staging area seemed much too small. The doctor looked about frantically for Ivan, but all he saw were Mafiya soldiers loading weapons like they were going to war with the entire city of Detroit instead of just one old man named Drogol.

"Ivan said to wait here."

"Tell him you had to go to the bathroom."

"You don't know Ivan. He's as scary as her."

"We have to chance it. I don't know which of my own men to trust anymore and time is very short. And you, you are not safe either. This is my building. I have surveillance equipment installed everywhere. Would you like to know whether you'll be leaving this city alive? I can let you listen to what your patient had to say about that. You wouldn't like it. She has plans for you. You won't like them either."

Overhead fans kicked on to exhaust the emissions from the vehicles as drivers turned over their engines. Things were moving much too quickly.

"Then we'd better walk while we still have the chance," said Dr. Pazyryk. "Because I know what her plans are for you and they're probably worse."

"I don't think so," said Mishka.

The doctor blanched.

"We have to get away before they move on us."

"They'll wait until after the raid."

"We can't take a chance."

"We have to free Sasha. I have a few men I can trust."

Dr. Pazyryk had an idea, a sudden flash of inspiration.

"No," he said. "I can bring help, but I have to know where that car is."

"Help? From who?"

"No time. That's Ivan. Coming our way. No don't look around. Where is that car?"

Mishka told him.

By the time that Dr. Pazyryk put his cell phone back in his pocket, Ivan was on them.

"Doctor, hurry," said the albino. "We are ready to leave. Where is your medical equipment?"

"In the transport van," said Dr. Pazyryk. "I was told to wait for you here. But I would like to check on Mrs. Kazakova before we leave."

"She does not wish to see you."

The doctor nodded nervously and clasped his hands together. It was clear from his face that this news frightened him.

A small man in a navy pea coat and wearing a roll-down cap approached them.

"Excuse me, Mishka," he said. "Everything is ready for your inspection."

"Go, make sure everything is ready," said Ivan. "The doctor and I will ride together. We have much to discuss."

But before Mishka could leave, the room was filled with screams of "I am innocent. Unchain me. I will kill you all if you do not set me free."

Sasha was being moved to the medical van on a forklift that carried him cage and all. He looked like a feral animal. His face was distorted by rage and terror. The workers pretended as though he were not there.

"Where are you taking me?" he shouted and rattled his chains like a madman.

Ivan shook his head and then spoke to Mishka.

"It is not good to choose traitors for friends," he said sadly. "Now go, redeem yourself with Mrs. Kazakova. Make sure that we have what we need then report back to me."

Mishka stared as the forklift driver slid the cage into the ambulance, then withdrew the forks and drove away. After a few moments, he gritted his teeth, turned and left.

As the young man walked away, Ivan stared after him, a pale white figure whose eyes burned with barely disguised arrogance beyond his pinkish-red sunglasses. He ran a thin, neatly cut fingernail across his lower lips as if to test its sharpness.

"What were the two of you discussing?" he asked as he turned his face toward Dr. Pazyryk.

The doctor stared back at him, willing his face to be blank, willing his knees not to shake and his brow not to sweat. Before the drinking and the deaths, he had been a good surgeon, with solid, unshakable nerves. But this was a different situation, and he was now a different man. As a surgeon, one small slip could mean the death of a patient. Here, one small slip could mean his own death.

"You," he said finally. "We were discussing you. He asked who you were. I told him you were a holy man in some backwater Siberian cult that Mrs. Kazakova had come across. He asked what she needed a holy man for."

A tight smile appeared on Ivan's face. A tremor in his jaw muscles told the doctor that he was fighting for control.

"And what did you tell him?"

"I told him he could bloody well ask the old woman himself. I said I was a medical doctor not a witch doctor so it wasn't my department."

Seconds passed.

Ivan did not move. He did not speak.

"What?" asked the doctor.

"A sufficient answer."

Ivan drew out the word *sufficient*, elongating the sibilance of the letter *c*.

"I still think I should see her before we leave."

"Get in the van, Doctor, and wait for me there."

Dr. Pazyryk counted off the seconds, not breaking away from the red-eyed man's stare. But as the seconds passed, he felt sweat forming on the back of his neck.

"Very well, but I will see her immediately when I return. Her health is my responsibility."

"That is why you will oversee the collection, purification, and injection of the wolf-beast's blood."

Having made his point in a small measure that he was personal physician to the Iron Lady and could not be pushed around, the doctor nodded and started in the direction of the medical van.

"And doctor?"

"Yes?" replied Dr. Pazyryk with stopping.

"I would very much like to see your cell phone before you take another step, if you please."

Dr. Pazyryk's stomach clutched like a tight fist.

CHAPTER TWENTY-ONE

Twenty two launch fired gas tubes," said Traxler. "Ten of one, twelve of the other."

He ran an age-spotted hand over his forehead.

"You understand," he continued, "how lethal these canisters are? You need to choose your poison."

"What are the two gases?" asked Hauck.

"Arsenic pentafluoride and hydrogen cyanide. They are quite deadly, Hauck. Whatever or whoever is exposed to either of them will not last long."

"So which one would you pick?" asked the Instructor.

"Hydrogen cyanide gas is both lethal and an extreme fire hazard."

"So, like, if it ain't killing it, we could blow it up?"

"Something like that," nodded Traxler.

"That could work," said the Instructor.

"But it is sub ambient, isn't it?" asked Hauck.

"Sub what?" asked the Instructor. "I hate it when you use those big shit-eaten words. Why can't you just talk normal English?"

The Instructor had his black sweater off, and because he wore only a short sleeved black t-shirt beneath it, Hauck could see the man's massively rippled forearms. They were so out of proportion to the rest of his body that it was as though his arms belonged to someone else.

"What I'm saying is that hydrogen cyanide is a liquefied gas stored under its own vapor pressure, and its vapor pressure is less than the normal pressure in a room. So when you open the valve, air is sucked in instead of the other way around."

"Is he shitting me?"

"No," said Traxler, "but these tube canisters are slightly different from cylinders of hydrogen cyanide that you might find in a laboratory. First, they are combined with a moderate pressure component that releases upon impact like an air bag and spreads the poison. It will fill a room quickly. You need to stay around one hundred and fifty feet away to be safe. Even then, a spark can ignite the dissipating gas and shoot a flashback fireball straight back at you."

The Instructor strode toward a case holding a display of swords. He was so short that some of them looked to be almost as tall as he did. One in particular seemed to catch his eye.

"What's this?" he asked Traxler.

"That is a Persian sword," said the weapons supplier. "Made from the finest Damascus steel. I have it on good authority that it was the personal weapon of a member of the Assassini."

"Is that right?"

"They were the original assassins," said Hauck. "Feared more than any other by the Crusading armies of Europe."

"I know that, you fuck. What I want to know is if it's any good."

"Against who?" asked Traxler.

"You ever answer a question with an answer instead of another question? All I'm asking is if you'd use it to cut somebody's head off. Does it cut better than a machete, if you know what I mean? And just give me a yes or no, will you?"

"Yes, I would use it myself if I were in a *jam*, as you would say."

"Good," said the Instructor. "And throw in this thing so I can strap it to my back. Hauck here will buy it for me."

But Hauck held his hand to one ear, blocking it off while he cupped his other hand behind a Bluetooth earpiece. He nodded once, then said, "Say again?"

"Trouble," whispered Traxler.

"Get Evgeny and the team mobile. They're already on their way? Good work, Yuri. I'll contact you after we're mobile as well."

Hauck clicked off the Bluetooth connection and then looked down at the tube-canisters.

"We'll take them all, Rudolph. And the protective suits and breathing apparatus to keep us alive when we use them so we can work in closer if we have to. Anna's men have located the car that Drogol got away in. Seems it had GPS installed and nobody thought to look for that signal until half an hour ago. So we have to move quickly or we'll just be cleaning up the mess her people leave behind. Have your men load everything including the automatic weaponry in my SUV and I'll wire you the money now. What is your price?"

Traxler told him.

"Shit," said the Instructor. "This is why I always make you buy the weapons."

"Keys?" asked Traxler.

Hauck held up a key ring and then handed it to Traxler. When he tried to pull them out of Hauck's hand, Hauck smiled a thin smile and held up his other hand.

"You get the car yourself."

He told him where it was parked and how to use the electronics attached to the key ring to unlock the doors.

"I want you to personally drive it into your loading area and to personally oversee every aspect of loading the equipment into it. And these keys never, ever leave your hands."

"You were so much more fun in your thirties," said Traxler.

"Wasn't he though?" added the Instructor. "Now he's as exciting as watching shit burn."

"What a lovely example," said Traxler.

"Thanks. Hey, can you throw in that rocket launcher over there?"

*****

"I have lived many years," said Drogol, "and I am no longer an ignorant peasant. I have studied much science with many great minds. I have learned to read and write many languages over the years. It is true that for some time I lived a life of debauchery, but I was frustrated and alone. Who could I tell? Who could I trust? I walked out of the Tunguska devastation, transported back from one hell to another. All around me was death and destruction. Eighty million trees destroyed. Eighty million, it is beyond the ability of a mind to comprehend such numbers."

They were seated on the platform before the eight foot tall brass-rimmed quartz tube. Their legs dangled over the edge as if they were father and daughter enjoying time alone. The constant hum of electrons singing back and forth to each other lit the golden globes scattered through the labyrinth construction.

"This place," said Sveta. "It's like being in an amusement park by ourselves when all of the people have gone home for the night."

Drogol stared at her.

"I am an ugly man, am I not?"

"Why would you care?"

"I know the standards of beauty in this world."

"We don't have time for this," she said. "And I don't want to hear anything more about you being Rasputin. Why did you come here? Do you seriously believe there is something here that can *cure* you?"

"Behind you," he said, and slid off the platform to stand upright on the floor and raise his arms into the air dramatically. "Behold, the Resonance Tube of Nikola Tesla."

Sveta cocked her head over her shoulder.

"You didn't answer my question." she said.

"But I did," said Drogol. "Tesla's Resonance Tube can change the resonance of anything or anyone inside it. From my research I believe that it can return me to the man I once was. Look at it. Look at it. I dare you."

She stood up on the platform and looked down at Drogol.

"You're serious about this?"

With an easy leap, with a cat's grace, he was on his feet beside her. Sveta looked down to ground level and tried to imagine if she could do make the same jump.

"I am indeed. Magnetic and mechanical resonances were the capstone of Tesla's work. He believed that understanding these twin attributes of matter were the key to all transformation. It is a body of knowledge ignored today in its fullness by scientists because it is in truth magic."

It was cool to the touch, and she marveled it actually looked like a test tube except for the wires emerging from its cap and the brass discs bolted into place above it.

"What are those things?" she asked.

"Wireless electromagnets. In his journals, Tesla writes that mechanical resonations were actually more important than magnetic resonance, but my experiments reveal that the magnetic resonation is still critical."

"What exactly do they do? How do they work?"

Drogol smiled at her interest.

"A portion of the tube slides open so I can put things in it. A person can fit inside quite comfortably, don't you think? Or, an animal. Or an object. You next close the door."

"And then?"

"And then, my dear, the tube is pulsed and vibrated and those waves are transmitted to the subject. I have personally tested over one hundred rabbits in this tube."

"Did this help them in some way?"

"Actually," he confessed, "it killed each of them except one."

"But it killed a hundred others?"

"I prayed for them both before and after they died."

"Never mind that. What killed them?"

"The sound. This tube can generate resonating frequencies. Resonating frequencies are much more deadly even than high-intensity focused acoustics."

Sveta rapped her knuckles on the tube. It clunked as though defective. She held her palm against it, like she was feeling for a pulse.

"Sound dampened," explained Drogol. "Each time before I use it, I have to release the dampeners."

"And you think because one healthy rabbit came through healthy that proves it can help you?"

"I have no more time to experiment. I must act. In Tesla's journals, which I have here underground, he writes that it must work. And work it must, because I am losing more and more control over the beast with each passing day."

"I hope Tesla knew what he was talking about," she said.

Drogol grasped her hand and gently pulled it away from the tube's surface. He turned it over and looked at her palm.

"Let go of my hand," she said.

His hands were rough as planked board. Her hand felt small inside of his.

"I said let go."

"I am only looking for your future in your palm."

"I don't want to know my future. I just want my hand back. Now."

He ran a fingertip along a line that ran from the base of her palm up to another line that ran horizontally, cutting her palm sideways like a knife scar. Finally, he let go.

"So," he said. "Now you know much more than you did and so do I. Will you stay or will you go?"

He moved to a complex panel of switches and dials and began adjusting them. Lights appeared and electrical gauges sprang to life. A deep humming like that from a transformer filled the air.

"Before this night is through," Drogol said, "I will enter this chamber and attempt to cure myself. Will you stay for me?"

"Any other ways in and out of this place?" she asked.

"There are more hidden entrances and tunnels in and out of here than ever were in Ryazan prison. Why do you ask?"

"Do you have weapons down here?"

"I need no weapons, Tsarista."

"I'm not your Tsarista," snapped Sveta. "We already went through this, remember? I'm who I am and it's not her. Got that?"

Drogol's mouth set in a thin straight line, but he nodded.

"One more time," she said. "Have you got that?"

"Do not test me, woman. Why do you wish to know about exits and weapons?"

"Because they'll find us here eventually. You have to know that. Hauck always finds everybody eventually."

Drogol waved his hand dismissively.

"He is so not so good that one. I have myself eluded him for thirty three years. So if you will stay, stay without fear. Stay to learn. Stay to help me cure myself so that this curse is gone from my life."

For the first time since everything went wrong, Sveta smiled. He had a point. Thirty three years was a long time on the run. So maybe Drogol was right, maybe they had time. They hadn't caught him in all that while. With luck, maybe even Hauck and Anna Kazakova would give up. After all, anyone that knew of this underground laboratory complex was dead except for Drogol, she and Zoe.

"You see? You smile. Come, we will go check on young Zoe and eat. And then, you will assist me as I step into Tesla's machine."

"I have to know one more thing," said Sveta. "Make that two."

"Always one more thing, then another and still another. But ask, ask me if you must."

"First, what exactly is this place?"

"Look around. What do you see? All men would be Prometheus and steal the fire from heaven. Up above was a city of great wealth, the engine of the world, and its great men lost their way. They plundered what they could not create, stealing from minds they could not understand. This place is their storehouse. In great secret, the pirate industrialists of that time began robbing what they could from Tesla and other men of genius. Down here, beneath their quickly corrupting city, they began building a model of the technologies they would unveil to the world for their great price. And down here, they hid the one device I needed to try and restore myself."

"So how did you find this all?"

"Much research over more years than you have been alive."

"But what happened to these men?"

"It is of no concern to you."

Seeing the look in his eyes, she did not push the matter.

"Okay, then the last question—what were you doing at that house at the edge of Detroit? This is where you live, so why were you there?"

Drogol smiled as though she had finally asked an intelligent question.

"The girl. Zoe. She saw in a dream that if I went to my old house, where I used to study the old texts in my search for a cure that you would come with others to kill me. You would try, but not succeed. Then, she would come to you and offer her help and I would then come to you."

"So you put yourself in that situation waiting for me to come and kill you?"

"I believe in the ability to see the future. I spent many hours with this woman making her acquaintance, learning to appreciate her abilities."

"How did you meet her?"

"What does this matter? I am a man of the Mysteries, and I know another true seer when I meet one. Come, enough of this, we must go to her so she may help me. I will enter this chamber, she will turn the dial to where I show her, and then we shall see if God has forgiven me. But you, Tsarista, you who do not believe in reincarnation, spirit healing, or prophecy, tonight you shall see that all are true."

But Sveta knew that it did matter very much how Drogol met Zoe, because she suspected now that Zoe worked for Hauck and that the whole thing had really been a trap.

CHAPTER TWENTY-TWO

Listen to me, everyone on the net," Hauck said as he steered down back alley shortcuts, swerving to avoid rusted out mufflers and broken whiskey bottles. He jerked the wheel hard to avoid a man who stepped out suddenly from behind a dumpster pointing a pistol at the car and yelling like a lunatic. The man fired off a wild round then jumped back behind the dumpster.

"I like this town," grinned the Instructor.

The old man had a Benelli pump lying across his lap, jacked and ready to go.

"It's like a half empty asylum at war," said Hauck.

He turned a corner and up ahead they saw a bright, burning fire in a fifty-five gallon drum. Four men huddled around it holding out their hands to keep warm. Hauck honked the horn once, twice and three times, but the men only turned to stare at him.

"Ram 'em," said the Instructor.

At the last possible moment, Hauck spun the wheel hard again, and turned into a small field. They did a full circle and then he had them back in the alley.

"The fuck you learn to drive like that?" yelled the Instructor. "That was beautiful."

"Should have run them over."

Remembering what he had to tell the men in transit, he clicked his earpiece /mic again.

"Listen up, everyone," he said. "We can't all show up en masse. The Kazakovas have their soldiers in route, too. They're further out than we are, but I want you to remember this. This is a Port Town. Homeland

Security is big here. Detroit may be half empty but the other half is filled with criminals, police and Homeland Security. We can handle the first two, but the third is a nightmare. We don't want to attract attention by a massive firefight that shows up on television. Are you all clear on that?"

Everyone acknowledged his instruction.

"Boss?" asked Evgeny.

The Instructor sat beside Hauck in the front seat, running his hands idly over the shotgun's barrel as though he weren't listening to Hauck's side of the conversation.

"Yes?"

"Why are we all on our way to the location if we have to stay low? It's almost totally empty so we'll stick out like tourists with guns."

"He's right," Yuri checked in. "We're going to look like a convoy."

"One moment," said Hauck, and he clicked off.

He turned to the Instructor, who was looking out the window.

"This neighborhood blows, you know," said the Instructor. "There's no hookers anywhere."

"We have a problem. Anna's men will be showing up in force. They're too stupid to think about Homeland Security, television crews and kids with cameras. We have to get out of this town cleanly after this is done. Mistakes will get us killed."

"Yeah?"

"I am out of plans."

"That means you don't know what to do and you want me to figure it out for you, is that it?"

"Yes."

The Instructor rubbed his chin.

"You know what I like about this Benelli?"

"Please."

"I point it, pull the trigger, and anything in front of it is dead. So here's what you do. You send the sniper and the others to go blow up something. They got to make it look natural and it's got to be noisy. Nothing pussy. But nothing that's going to pull in the Feds. You and me, we park near a sewer entrance close as we can to the neighborhood, and we go underground."

Hauck almost slammed on the brakes.

"Why in the world would we do that?"

"That's where you found him last time, wasn't it?"

Hauck swore for the second time in two days.

"Yuri," he said as he clicked his mic back on. "I need some cover. And I want it to be very, very noisy. And bring up a map of the sewer and drainage system in the area of the house. We're going in from the bottom up."

"You know the only thing I hate about all this?" said the Instructor.

"Tell me."

"I hate putting on these gas suits and breathing tanks. They ain't natural."

"They will protect us from the gas."

"But I'm okay with the rocket launcher."

*****

Zoe woke but didn't open her eyes.

She felt warm and safe and wanted to stay that way.

There was silence all around, and she felt none of the stress that afflicted her body with tension and insecurity. She'd worked undercover for so long that she welcomed moments such as these, knowing even as she did that they wouldn't last. People that worked for Hauck either learned to handle the tension or left his employ. Zoe considered that option as she laid there, her eyes closed, her mind resting on the silence like she was floating on warm milk.

How could she have known when Hauck first assigned her to impersonate a psychic that her target was not in fact a horrific madman, but instead a holy man from another century enduring a curse that she could not imagine? Drogol had been kind to her. In fact, she believed that he'd truly brought her back from the dead or close to it. Either way, without him she would be dead. How could she betray his kindness by contacting Hauck and revealing the existence of the man's underground sanctuary?

But that was what she did.

Spies betrayed people.

Gradually, carefully, she opened her eyes to find that she was alone. *What if,* she thought, *my phone doesn't work underground?*

She hoped that it didn't. If it didn't, she wouldn't have to make a decision. There would be no chance of betraying Drogol. No chance of causing his capture or death.

What a weakling I am, she thought. *I have a job to do; now I just have to do it and this will all be over.*

As she sat up on the cot, her hand subconsciously rubbed over the spot where she she'd been stabbed. She paused, and leaning over, she lifted her shirt. Her stomach was flat, lightly muscled, and her skin was unblemished where there should have been a scar. The watcher who tried to rape her got worse.

I can't do this, she thought. *I can't call Hauck and betray Drogol.*

But that's what spies did.

Spies betrayed people.

Zoe saw her coat on a paper-strewn drafting table. Her satellite cell phone would be in her right pocket. Like any other person getting up to go to work, Zoe stood, stretched, and thought that if she knew how to do anything else, she would find another job.

*****

Dr. Pazyryk sat in the backseat of a black Lexus while Ivan, who sat on the opposite side behind the driver, examined the doctor's cell phone. A layer of uncomfortable sweat began to form along his shirt collar as he watched Ivan pry the device apart with a thin screwdriver. Although he'd never fired a gun before in his life, Dr. Pazyryk was quite sure that if he had one now he would kill the pale-skinned priest without a second thought.

"Well, Doctor, your cell phone seems to be just an ordinary cell phone, but you understand that I must be protective of Mrs. Kazakova."

"By breaking apart my cell phone? What did it ever do to you?"

The priest stared at him thoughtfully before he spoke, as though weighing what to say.

"I am convinced that we have a traitor in our midst still. Everyone, including you, is suspect until this is over. She is unforgiving on the issue of loyalty and depends on me to protect her."

Especially, thought Dr. Pazyryk, *since you have her son locked away in a cage.*

The tension in his shoulders eased just a little. The electronic square hidden in a second pocket of his coat contained all the electronics necessary for his coded communications with Hauck. Unless the two were connected together, there was no way to understand how or if the cell phone was used to transmit or receive.

"It will give you something to do while waiting for Kirill to bring you to us when we have captured our prey," said Ivan.

Dr. Pazyryk looked toward the heavyset driver whose shoulders filled half the front seat.

"Don't worry," said Ivan. "He will protect you."

"I've seen that thing in the video. I don't think whatever he's carrying will even slow it down."

"You worry too much, Doctor. Kirill would be a last resort. The beast will be unconscious long before then. We have equipped our men with the tranquilizing rifles we brought along with us on the plane. One such dart would take down an elephant. We have automatic weapons for backup, but Mrs. Kazakova wants it alive so that you can draw its blood."

"And you?"

"Don't become inquisitive, Doctor. It could become fatal."

Dr. Pazyryk looked out the window at the construction barrels, signs lit by hidden spotlights and the endless mounds of brown grass that passed for scenery. He wondered how his life could have come to this moment, how one night of drunken surgery had resulted in the destruction of his career, his life and his future. Sitting in a limo with an albino maniac obsessed with religious vengeance. He might as well be strapped to a bomb with the timer running.

"But I will tell you this," continued Ivan. "When you are through with your science, when you have drained enough blood from this monster to satisfy our mistress, then it will be I that cuts its throat and drinks whatever will be left."

Hauck, get me out of here, thought Dr. Pazyryk. *I'm a wretch with a burned out soul, but surely even I deserve better than this.*

It was at that exact moment and just over one mile ahead that a fifty foot high fireball burst over the freeway. So bright did it burn that Ivan screamed and slapped his hands over his sensitive eyes in agony.

Kirill instinctively threw up his arms to cover his face and forgot to brake. The car ahead screeched sideways and they crashed into it. Airbags exploded into the car and squares of the windshield broke away.

Everyone inside the vehicle slapped into the airbags and fell backward.

The sound of blaring horns, emergency sirens, and the smell of burning rubber filled the night air.

*****

Anna Kazakova lay in her medical bed, the room lit only by the soft green and white screens that flashed her vital statistics. Her eyes were dry, lips parched, and still she did not reach for the water pitcher and glass sitting on the metal stand near the side of her bed. She breathed in, felt the air fill her lungs like dust pouring into thin paper bags, and cursed every unfiltered cigarette that she had ever smoked.

Outside the door, two bulky men stood guard in the near empty building. They were hard men, who would defend her with their lives, but she knew death came quietly, unannounced, and there was nothing their guns could do to stop him if he came calling. Death, she believed, was always a man. Women gave life. Men took it away.

Men like Drogol.

All men, no matter how charismatic their words or charming their ways, were beasts inside. They lied to women to ravage and control them. They took what they wanted and went their way.

Drogol was the worst. His dark, brooding eyes tinged with the madness of conviction. His wild hair and repressed vitality. His obsession with the long dead Alexandra. How could she, Anna Kazakova, have been so utterly and completely under his power?

He was not handsome, no not at all. He was strong, immensely strong, but his arms were too long, his hands too big and his shoulders too narrow. His nose was too large and yet his eyes, his eyes would sometimes glow as though lit by an inner light.

When he took her he was overpowering, as though he were wrestling her into submission. And he took and he took and he took.

She hated him.

So when Ivan had come to her, she listened to his entreaties, heard what he desired, and licked her lips with anticipation when he offered himself as her long arm of vengeance. Ivan would punish Drogol in ways that her frail body could not. Ivan would bring her first his blood, and then his soul.

Blood trickled from the corner of her mouth and she wiped it away with her sleeve. Water, she must have water. Her lips were cracking like desert parchment.

Wires and tubes dangled from her arm as she reached for the pitcher. Her fingers were only inches away from its handle when she felt something clamp down on her heart. She gasped with a pain like nothing she had ever felt before and her arm went numb. Harder it squeezed and harder and her eyes locked as wide open as her mouth. Her extended hand began to shake and spasm and she knocked over the pitcher. It crashed in broken splinters that shot across the floor.

Hear that, she screamed to her guards.

But the scream was in her mind.

No thought. Too much pain. Just a scream.

I won't die like this, she thought. I will not die without seeing Drogol's face again.

She tried to rise but it was as though someone had thrust a knitting needle through her heart and pinned her to the bed. The Ryazan prison massacre video was the last thing that flashed through her mind before she died.

CHAPTER TWENTY-THREE

Yuri sat at a keyboard typing furiously. His mouse hand circled, clicked and moved on. Diagrams popped up on one screen, slid to another to be replaced by still another. He was a conductor exhorting his electronic musicians to fill the room with information. Top of his game, best in the world and, more importantly, the highest paid person in Hauck's organization. This was why Hauck paid him twice what he himself took in. He could penetrate any network and make it his own. He typed twelve hundred words per minute and was pushing for more.

I'm no tourist, he thought. *I own Detroit.*

And own it he did. His brain was an eidetic sponge absorbing information.

He pulled up schematics for the city's underground water system and any associated information that he deemed helpful. Newspaper clippings scanned into storage appeared on the screens like an electronic exhibit of tired paper.

"Yuri," came Hauck's voice. "What was that?"

"What?"

"Answer me. Where are you?"

"I'm here. Where else would I be?"

"Check the police scanners. What was that ignition?"

"That what? You mean Evgeny's fireworks? He's closing down I-75 north of the city like you asked him to."

"What the hell did he blow up?"

"Later, okay? Right now I've got some interesting stuff for you. You ready for this?"

"Don't try my patience, Yuri."

"Right. Well, Detroit's like an underground parking lot in places. No, not like a parking lot, it's like an underground city. They built all sorts of stuff over all sorts of other stuff, if you get what I mean."

Silence from the other end.

"Okay, let me try it another way. Area you're headed to has a lot more underground than just sewers and maintenance tunnels for gas and electric. What I'm looking at here is an assortment of projects going back maybe fifty to seventy years. Excavations for this or that. They're in the paper; they're not in the paper. Blueprints filed with the city that don't match what's supposed to be going on. Very weird stuff. Hard to say exactly what you're going to run into down there. There's been some heavy tampering over the years is my best guess and I think we've got a network of tunnels and abandoned construction projects that could hide an army of Drogols."

"Yuri?"

"Yes?"

"Shut up and find me the best way in."

*****

Dr. Pazyryk came to with his face pressed against the unbroken passenger side window. He heard sirens and what sounded like distant foghorns but could only have been the sound of approaching fire trucks. He pulled his head back and rubbed his hands over his face. They came back bloodied.

"My head, son of a bitch, my head."

Gingerly he moved his head back and forth to reassure himself that his neck wasn't broken. He blinked the blood out of his eyes and saw Kirill pressed between an inflated air back and his seat. But neither Ivan's nor his own airbag had remained inflated. Whether defective or by design, they had both hissed away their shape sometime after the doctor had passed out.

Ivan lay slumped forward, held up only by his seatbelt. In the beams of headlights that shone on him from cars spun round in collisions and pointing at their car, Dr. Pazyryk saw him as though he were on stage, held up only by a seatbelt marionette wire before the spotlights.

Car doors slammed and he heard shouting.

Kirill was down.

Ivan was unconscious.

A glance over his shoulder, shielding his eyes against the headlights shining through the shattered back window. Where were the other Red Mafiya cars?

Somewhere in the distance, he heard the irritating, continuous blare of a jammed car horn. Everywhere was confusion. His head started to pound as though it would never stop and he looked down at his palms and stared at the blood.

What was the worst case? He had a concussion? Internal injuries? Whiplash? He seemed to have no broken bones. He ached all over and knew it would get much worse but could he run?

Maybe he could.

With a thumb and forefinger he un-clicked his seatbelt, watching closely for any sign of consciousness on Ivan's part. Nothing. Not a fluttering of eyelids; no sudden movement of his fingers like the Frankenstein monster coming to life. Nothing.

He reached for the door handle, and then stopped.

What about Hauck?

They had an agreement. If he would spy for Hauck, then Hauck would get him out; give him an untraceable new identity, money, and protection. It was a good deal. No one could escape the Iron Woman and her albino priest without help and protection. And it was not good to betray Hauck. If he broke and run, would both Hauck and Anna Kazakova be after him? What would his life be worth then?

Running.

Since that night in the surgical theater he had never known a moment when someone was not after him, nipping at his heals. The Moscow police. He shuddered at the thought. It was an accident. He was drunk. The scalpel slipped. It could have happened to anyone. Anyone that was drunk. They had called for him. He protested, saying he was drunk, but they told him to come anyway. The State apparatus would not be denied, of course; the State apparatus could never be denied. It was always benevolent in its errors. There was always a citizen to be blamed. The State itself was never wrong. Only the citizens.

So when Anna Kazakova saved his neck, she owned him.

When Hauck promised to get him out from under the old woman's thumb if he spied for him, then he owned him, too.

But now he saw a chance to get away from them all. Outside on the freeway, the night was chaos. He was used to chaos and the streets of Detroit were enough like the streets of Moscow that maybe, just maybe, he could get his life back and disappear somewhere in the big country that was America.

To hell with the Moscow police, to hell with the state police, to hell with Anna Kazakova and Hauck the invisible spy. This was his chance and he was going to take it.

Without even a look over his shoulder, he grabbed the door handle and pulled it. Locked. No, it moved, just a fraction. Jammed, maybe in the collision. He removed his seatbelt entirely and threw his shoulder into the door. It opened an inch further. Again, this time with more force. Another inch. Once more he slammed his shoulder against the door, this time with the full weight of his desperation behind it. Ivan had checked his cell phone before they left. The strange priest suspected him. That wasn't good.

The door came open all the way and Dr. Pazyryk spilled halfway out onto the asphalt freeway. He thrust his hands forward to protect his head but ended up slapping down on his forearms. The shock of the impact jarred his jaw and cracked his teeth together.

People were milling about in the middle of the freeway like zombies, staring at the bright burning catastrophe somewhere up ahead. In the confusing glare of headlights and taillights and the smell of radiator fluid pooling on asphalt, he saw an opening between two cars, a glittering corridor of windshield fragments that shone like jewels in the reflected light of the overhead halogen lamps. Beyond that were cold, empty streets, abandoned buildings, and many, many places to hide.

Keep moving, he thought.

He placed his hands flat on the ground and pushed up enough to pull himself out of the car. There was a small grassy hill after the concrete embankment followed by a long cyclone fence. No barbed wire. No gun turrets. Just a simple fence. He would do this and never look back.

But he did look back, and saw Ivan leaning forward to grab his ankles.

Panicked, he pulled himself out of the car and took a step toward the concrete embankment just as three black cars and a van drove up between him and his destination. A door sprang open on one of the

SUV's as Dr. Pazyryk turned his head looking for another way out. A grim-faced man swung out onto the street with a black pistol hanging loosely from his left hand.

"Get in," he said, motioning to the doctor.

The doctor looked back as Ivan pulled himself out of the wrecked car and into the street. He was brushing himself off and straightening his robes.

Behind him.

The doctor looked back toward what used to be oncoming traffic but now just a narrow parking lot. Could he lose them in the confusion?

Two more car doors opened; two more men stepped out onto the side of the freeway with pistols.

"Move," said Ivan, thrusting him forward with the palm of one hand.

"Kirill," protested the doctor. "He might be hurt."

"He is dead, Doctor. He came to but could feel nothing in his legs. "

Dr. Pazyryk regained his balance, and as he was hustled into a car he called out, "But I thought you said he was dead."

Ivan, his red sunglasses in place now to protect him from the car headlights, said, "He is. I cut his throat myself. Men who cannot walk are not needed. Now get in the car."

The last thing that Dr. Pazyryk saw before the car door slammed shut on him was Ivan wiping off his jewel handled knife on a dark rag. His eyes were fixed on the doctor the entire time. Although it only lasted a moment, in Dr. Pazyryk's mind, it stretched to the edge of sanity.

Men who cannot walk are not needed.

He felt like throwing up.

*****

Evgeny pulled into a dark side street with his headlights turned off. The mixture of houses and empty lots were silent.

Like Moscow, he thought. *When the fox comes calling, the chickens cower in their coops.*

But maybe not this time.

Maybe this time, the chicken coops were filled with wolves.

He U-turned and parked his truck facing back the way he came.

With his left forefinger, he turned off the GPS. He could see his destination two streets over. He knew where he was going.

"I don't think this is a good idea, Evgeny," came the voice in his ear. "Hauck's going to string us up. You're supposed to be running interference against the Kazakovas. I'm supposed to tell him where you're at."

"Then tell him. I did my job. I slowed down the traffic. Now I'm scoping the area for him. Put him on with us. You worry too much."

"Hang on," said Yuri. "Hauck? It's me, Evgeny, and you. That's it."

"Did you find me the quickest way in yet?"

"We need to take care of something first. Evgeny's a couple of blocks over from the house where our info said Drogol's escape car is."

"Good. Evgeny, what do you see?"

"Nothing. But it's too quiet here. Just as dark as the house last night. Same feeling in the air. Not even gangs or dope dealers."

"Nobody's home in that part of town" said Yuri. "But Hauck, did you okay Evgeny moving in on the house."

"What's your point, Yuri? It was his original destination before I sidetracked him."

Evgeny grinned. He could feel it coming. Yuri was always, always the untouchable. He got paid to know everything. He got paid to keep Hauck and the teams informed and out of harm's way. Everything was supposed to go to him.

But Evgeny knew that Yuri was always suspicious of a back door channel. Nothing he could ever identify. Nothing blatant enough to question Hauck directly. But he didn't like it that he couldn't be sure.

"Nothing, I just got the impression that you wanted him to continue to run interference between us and the Kazakovas."

"No," said Hauck. "I wanted one major distraction and now I want him on point to watch above ground while we enter from below. Are we clear on this?"

"What about a spotter? Shouldn't he have a spotter, too? He always has a spotter."

"What information did you uncover about his last spotter?"

"Point. I get your point. Just had to make sure. It's what you pay me for."

"Right now I'm paying you to find me the best entrance. Get me an answer."

Evgeny bit his lip.

"Okay, you heard the man," said Yuri. "Got to go to work."

"Hey."

"What?"

"You remember what you were saying earlier, about not knowing why he's in Detroit?"

"Sure. You got an answer?"

"No," said Evgeny. "But I have a hunch we're about to find out."

Yuri clicked off.

Hauck always had his secrets.

What Yuri didn't know was that he and Hauck went way back. Everyone on the team owed Hauck something, something more than their work for hire arrangement except maybe Sveta. It was how he bound them together. Hauck never completely trusted anyone who worked just for money.

*****

"Ten blocks away?" Hauck asked. "That's the best you can do?"

"You asked for the best way in," said Yuri. "It's like a maze down there. The tunnels are different ages and different sizes. Some dead end or are closed off. This is the cleanest shot you've got. I could bring you in closer but the tunnels are in ruins."

"What's he saying?" demanded the Instructor. "Put him on speakerphone. You have a speaker phone on that fucking thing?"

Hauck linked his cell phone to the car's computer system and switched over to speakerphone. He had Yuri repeat what he just told him.

"No wonder this city smells like shit," said the Instructor. "The sewers are no good."

"I'm giving you the best way in," said Yuri.

"Don't give me that, you little asshole," said the Instructor. "You've never been down there so you don't know crap from shinola. All you know is some city blueprints and whatever you can pick up from some jack-assed search."

"It's all we have and we don't have any time to get more information," said Hauck.

"Say anything about rats in that crap you're pulling up on line?" asked the Instructor. "They got those big, filthy rats with rabies?"

Silence for a moment.

"I don't know," Yuri said finally. "There's nothing I see so far that—"

"How about sewer gas like methane and all that? Is the air clean enough to breathe?"

"How the hell would I know?" said Yuri.

"Exactly. Why don't we just use a crystal ball?"

"I'll keep looking."

"For what?" said the Instructor. "We go with what we got."

"Tell me where we're going in," said Hauck. "Then keep researching the area. There's a reason Drogol went to ground here."

"That's what Evgeny said."

"Who said that?" asked the Instructor. "That little prick with a rifle? The one that couldn't hit the ten foot monster with a high powered rifle and a six thousand dollar telescopic sight? Yeah, now I'm feeling better."

"Enough already," said Hauck. "Yuri, you heard me. Keep digging and see if you can find out why he's here. We're running short on time and this location is the first new variable we've had to work with. Get to it."

CHAPTER TWENTY-FOUR

Zoe was no longer asleep. She was sitting on the edge of the cot where they last left her, looking down at her feet.

"You see, God has healed her because of her true heart," beamed Drogol.

When Zoe looked up at her, Sveta stared her down. The girl knew that she knew, she saw it in her eyes.

Drogol went forward and took her hands.

"Can you stand, my child? We have much to do together, and I need your help."

Zoe looked about like a trapped animal, and then, with a look of resignation, she stood.

Sveta appraised her. Young, pretty, and with a certain look of helplessness about her. A perfect choice to gain Drogol's confidence. She would never be perceived as a threat. Now if she could just get her away from Drogol long enough to ask her whether or not Hauck was already on his way.

"How much does she know about you?" Sveta asked Drogol.

"Enough. She knows that I am a man in search of regaining his soul, and although she did not know of this place or the cursed technology I will now make use of, she knows my pain and I believe she will gladly help me. Is that not so, dear child?"

Zoe's eyes darted between Sveta and Drogol, bewildered.

"Why do you hesitate? Are you afraid, little one?"

Finally she answered.

"No, Father."

I hope that cost you, thought Sveta.

"Then come—the time is upon us. Come with me."

He put his arm around her waist, concerned for her, and like a father leading a child, they began walking. Sveta, having no good choice, followed silently behind them. He would never believe the girl was a traitor and he was not stable. Having seen what he was capable of and not knowing the real truth about the beast, she would have to wait for the right moment and then make a break for it.

Her hatred for Hauck and his entire world of betrayal grew with each step she took. Drogol was mad. Hauck had no such excuse.

*****

The Instructor picked the lock on the concrete bunker door in less than ten seconds. They were in and down the iron rungs wearing their fire and chemical resistant suits and their weaponry. They wore headlamps, and moved through the knee deep water and the cement tunnel like coal miners from a different era. Hauck led the way, following Yuri's directions, stopping occasionally to check in and make certain of their location.

They heard nothing but themselves as they sloshed through the water. It was as though they were in the catacombs beneath a European city, exploring hidden secrets while those above slept or moved about unawares on dark, rain-slicked streets.

"Yuri, can you hear me?"

"You're breaking up a little, but yeah I can still hear you."

"There is a fork in the tunnel here, which way do we go, left or right?"

"Give me a minute. There's no fork in the schematics I'm looking at."

"Take your time and give me your best shot."

"I'm working on it."

Hauck felt the Instructor's hand on his shoulder and turned to face him. In the beam of his headlamp, he could see the transformation. He was on the hunt now, moving in for a kill. No mercy in his face. No more banter, no jokes. Just an overwhelming sense of dark focus.

"Here's the deal. We find this thing, and anybody between me and it is going down, you understand?"

"I understand."

"Good. And here's the deal with the old lady and me."

Hauck tensed so hard his back muscles hurt.

"She wants the thing alive. I told her to fuck off. Then she talked to me about taking you out. She doesn't know I'm working for you now."

"That's acceptable."

"But after her guys have captured it or I've killed this whatever it is, she wants you put to bed. I told her I'd wait three days. If she's still alive, then I'm coming for you. If you take her out first, the deal's off. You got that?"

Hauck searched the old man's face. Somehow he'd believed that it would not come to this, that the Instructor felt some small degree of affection for him, and would not have accepted Anna's offer. But he was at least giving him a way out. That had to count for something.

"You got three days to whack the old bitch. You take care of business and you and me are good. I figured you could handle that. She paid me half up and I get to keep that. So that's the deal. It was good money. I figured three days was enough time for you to take her out. Can you bury her that quick?"

Hauck nodded again.

"Then let's get moving."

"Yuri is trying to find which way will take us there. We have to wait."

"Yuri's a dumbass. We go left. Let's get moving."

Hauck started walking. He gripped the gas gun tighter and began to consider what to do about Anna Kazakova, because he very much wanted to stay alive.

"Evgeny," he said, "can you hear me?"

"I'm here."

"I have a new assignment for you."

"Not a good idea, the competition is arriving."

"Already?"

"Like I said."

He was beginning to have a bad, very bad feeling about this.

"Listen to me carefully. No matter what happens tonight, your new priority is to track down Anna Kazakova's location and eliminate her, is that understood?"

Silence.

"Evgeny, are you there?"

But Hauck had lost radio contact.

*****

"Here is close enough," Ivan told the driver. "Tell the others."

They were only a block away, but he did not want to be too far in case things got out of hand.

He felt the presence of his old enemy and could barely contain his excitement after so many years of hunting him. At last he would fulfill his destiny. The beastman's blood would be his, Anna Kazakova be damned.

"Roll down my window," he instructed the driver.

As the glass lowered into the door, he felt the cool rush of moist night air and listened to the pitiless night wind pushing down empty streets. There were no streetlights in this section of town still working. Most had been shot out and left that way.

Detroit was a city that he could understand. It was as brutal in its way as Siberia, but with a colder heart. A machine's heart, without feeling, without remorse.

Ivan looked at his driver, a man whose bulk was that of a small bear. His bearded face was expressionless, a man who did what he was told with no regrets. He stared straight ahead, waiting for instructions.

Anna Kazakova had armies of men like this scattered all over the world. She ruled them like a monarch. Those who obeyed and executed her orders without question did well. Those who failed her expected no mercy.

Before the disease had overtaken her, her brilliant mind and ruthless ambition had propelled her to the top of a criminal empire that generated more wealth than many countries. Blackmail, greed and brute force had been her weapons. Those whom she could not co-opt with blackmail, she lured in with money. Those whom she could not control with such means, she terrorized by executing their close friends and family members until they finally submitted.

As her health failed, she had brought her son into her business. He lacked her analytical mind, but his zeal in dealing with her enemies won her confidence until Ivan began to undermine it. It was the method of his sect to rise to power by gaining the position of advisor to the powerful, then weakening them by planting the seeds of suspicion until they destroyed each other, leaving behind the spoils.

Ivan had a true hatred for all Russians. For centuries they exploited and repressed his people. But Siberians were the ones destined to rule, not Russians. There was a saying among his people that no Russian was fit to wear a Siberian's shoe, and Ivan believed it with every fiber of his being. When he had the beastman's blood running through his veins and Drogol was dead, he would demonstrate just how true that saying was by taking over the empire that Anna Kazakova had built.

"Vasily, you will be by my side at all times," he said to the driver. "We are hunting tonight, you and I. We will be the *zayats*—the hunters of this night. We must let the others be the dogs who charge into the bushes while we are patient and wait to shoot what comes running out. Some dogs will be lost. Perhaps many dogs will be lost. But the hunters must live to claim the game, yes?"

The thick-bodied Russian nodded his agreement. Once up and once down. His face as severe as a stocky Lenin, his nod of agreement slow, thoughtful and final. He had the chin of his famous ancestor, who received the order of *Hero of the Soviet Union* for his brilliant marksmanship and ferocious combat accomplishments. He had the shoulders of his famous ancestor. They were broad and densely packed with muscle.

"In the heat of the hunt," continued Ivan, "some dogs may turn on the hunters. The smell of blood may drive them mad. They must be put down quickly."

Ivan waited a few moments for a response, but when the driver said nothing, he continued.

"So if anyone turns and runs, shoot them down."

This time, Vasily nodded with enthusiasm.

*****

Dr. Pazyryk sat on a plastic crate at the back of the van behind Sasha's cage. Sasha lay sideways on a metal bench, still chained into place like an animal. His eyes were closed and he wore the same clothes that he wore when the doctor last saw him.

Near the double doors sat a guard on a plastic folding chair. His head was bald and gleamed softly in the muted moonlight filtering through the windows. He casually held a dark pistol that rested across his knees. When he felt the doctor staring at him, he turned and smiled a metallic smile.

A pair of pointed scissors on an open shelf only two feet away was the only weapon that Dr. Pazyryk had been able to find. Compared to the dark pistol, they hardly seemed like a weapon. Besides, what would he do with them? He had never struck another man in his life and certainly never stabbed one with a pair of scissors. But being a doctor, he knew where to do so.

It had to be from behind, he knew that. The idea of stabbing someone from the front seemed like a good way to get shot. No, he would have to bide his time until a situation presented itself where he could grab the scissors and drive them straight into the spot at the base of the man's skull, severing the nerves and preventing him from getting off a shot.

"May I have a drink?" he asked. "Perhaps you have a flask?

The man turned his deep-set eyes on him again.

"Maybe you could shut your fucking mouth."

He raised the pistol and pointed it toward the doctor.

"I could do that."

With his free hand, the man pulled a flask from beneath his coat, placed it between his knees and unscrewed the cap. Lifting the liquor to his lips, he stared at the doctor while he took a long pull, then returned the flask beneath his coat quickly and efficiently, like a magician finishing a trick.

Dr. Pazyryk decided that if he ever got the opportunity, he would gladly stab the man just to get at his flask.

CHAPTER TWENTY-FIVE

The van doors opened suddenly, and Dr. Pazyryk saw the crowd of dark men standing outside. Mishka must be among them, but the doctor could not make him out.

"Doctor," he said, "how is our bait?"

"Out cold."

"Then inject him with something to wake him up. Soon we may need him to play his part."

"I can inject him with the stimulant, but he will wake up groggy. It will take time for him to be fully awake."

"Just do it."

"Too much too quickly could damage his heart."

"Just do it," hissed Ivan, then turned away. "I have received word that his mother is dead. His utility to us is much less."

His men followed him, leaving only the open night behind them. They were in a neighborhood that defied polite description. Somewhere in the distance were the blurred lights of the city, but here there was only darkness and cool, moist air. A light rain drizzled down, and the doctor tried to see something, anything that would indicate which way to run when the time came, but then his guard closed the doors.

The Iron Woman was dead. He was her doctor. His utility was less, too.

"I need my medical bag," Dr. Pazyryk said.

His guard kicked it across the floor toward him.

"Be careful with that. You might have broken the syringe and then—"

"Shut up."

He obediently quit talking, picked up his bag and opened it, rummaging around as though looking for the syringe although he already knew where it was. It was the gleam of his scalpel that had immediately captured his attention. With it he could cut the man's throat in an instant. He looked up to see if the guard was staring at him, but the man had turned away. With a deft motion of his hand, he palmed the scalpel and slid it into his coat pocket, then picked up the syringe.

"I need you to open the cage."

The man grunted and tossed him a set of keys. Sasha lay still, although the doctor had earlier only injected him with a harmless solution.

Now the critical part, to see if the keys to Sasha's manacles were on the key ring.

"Will one of these open the manacles so that I can get at his arm?"

"What for?"

"I have to do this right. Just one wrist is all I need to undo."

The guard looked at him for a long moment.

"The long thin one," he said finally, then looked toward the back windows.

The doctor's hands trembled as he bent to pick up the keys. The guard was still looking the other way. If he got to his feet and took a few quick steps, he could use the scalpel and slit the man's throat while the others were looking for Drogol.

Just a few quick steps.

But all the guard had to do was turn a little in his chair and shoot him.

He wondered what it would feel like to be shot. Not good he suspected, not good at all.

"Could you hold your gun on him while I'm doing this so he doesn't hurt me?"

The guard looked back at him over his shoulder.

"You want me to hold your hand while you do it? He's not going to bite you."

The doctor shook his head no and tried to appear chastened.

"Then just do it. You talk more than my kids."

In the darkness, Dr. Pazyryk blanched. *Kids*? Did the man say kids? How could someone like him have children? And if he killed him, they would be orphans. Suddenly the thought of murdering him in cold blood seemed horrific.

He stood with the syringe in one hand and the keys in his other and moved toward the cage.

There were three keys on the key ring. He thought about that. One key for the cage, one for the manacles, and the other for … what?

The first key he tried opened the cage door. It swung back noiselessly on well-oiled hinges. *How thoughtful*, he thought. Someone actually oiled the hinges to the cage. Perhaps they had a mechanic whose sole job was to keep cages and chains and torture devices well-oiled. But to his dismay, the door swung open the wrong way. It now stood directly between him and his guard. To cut the man's throat, he would have to close the door again. The inside of an ambulance had never seemed so small.

As he looked over at the guard for a moment, he reconsidered. Perhaps the man's children would be better off without a father, especially a father like him.

The second key did not fit the manacle on Sasha's left wrist and Dr. Pazyryk wondered again what it was for until he saw that the lock on the neck ring was different. The third key undid the wrist manacle with a soft click.

He lifted the syringe and was about to pretend to inject it when the guard turned and shouted "Watch out." The doctor jolted backward so quickly he almost dropped it.

"Sorry," said the man. "I thought he was going to bite you."

"Very funny," said Dr. Pazyryk. "I almost dropped the syringe."

The man turned back to look out the windows.

Bastard, thought the doctor.

Throughout the entire incident, Sasha had not moved. He played his part so well that he looked dead.

Better to look dead than to be dead, he thought.

He moved forward again, lifted Sasha's arm, and jabbed the needle into a pinch of sleeve, injecting the fluid harmlessly along the man's bicep. Sasha would pretend to wake slowly in a few moments. He must have heard the discussion with Ivan a few minutes before. Whatever else his failings, the young man had iron nerves.

After quietly laying the syringe on the floor of the cage, the doctor slid the scalpel out of his pocket and concealed it behind one hand as best he could. Then, he took the keys in his other hand and backed out of the cage. The cage door closed without a sound.

As he approached the guard, he jangled them to make enough noise that the guard wouldn't be alarmed. To his relief, the guard merely extended his hand and curled his fingers, indicated that he should drop them in his palm. Dr. Pazyryk stepped dutifully forward, then taking a short intake of air to fortify his nerves, he dropped the keys in the man's hand, leaned forward, extended the scalpel and slid his hand around the man's neck. With a quick slice, he cut completely through the man's throat and pulled it around to sever his ceratoid artery.

*****

Mishka led the men to the building.

The formed a net around it of thirty men wearing night vision goggles and riot gear. One man popped the garage door, while the others trained their weapons, ready to shoot. At the back of the garage, they saw a door, and, weapons still raised, they approached and opened it wide. Mishka gave the signal and they went in one at a time then reformed inside the empty building. When the all clear was given, Mishka went inside. His nerves felt thick with fear. Even in the video, the beast was terrifying. Now, he was about to enter its den.

"No sign of them," whispered one man into his ear. "Place looks like nobody's been in here for years. There's dust everywhere."

Mishka breathed a sigh of relief, grateful that tonight he would not be facing the monster. Then, from across the room, one of his men motioned near a closed door. Mishka walked over and saw the man point down.

A line of disturbed dust in the green light of their goggles showed that the door had been opened recently. Mishka gave another hand signal, and men fanned out. He stepped back behind them then said quietly, "Go."

It was unlocked. His earlier relief dissipated.

Down the hallway they went in silence, two abreast, weapons at the ready. The tension was as oppressive as the stale, tasteless, dead air. He began to sweat underneath the weight of his gear.

Mishka thought about his cousin, who had brought him all this misery. If only she were here tonight with the man they were hunting. He would shoot her himself. Back at the warehouse he had slapped her for show in front of his men. Now, however, he would gladly beat her to death before he shot her.

He put the thought on hold while they moved through the hazy green of night vision.

Down they went, asking no questions, a small army of killers ready to shoot on sight. They walked silently on thick-soled boots. The hallway began to feel confining and Mishka smelled the stink of his own fear. He held tightly to his AK47 as though it were a talisman that could ward off the evil at the end of the dark hallway that seemed to go forever down. Finally, they came to the massive iron door.

His men moved aside so he could inspect it. Somewhere deep inside, he knew that it was the gate to Hell itself. He would be shot if he went back. Beyond the door might be the beast. He faced death at either end. Suddenly Sasha's cage seemed a much safer place to be.

"Blow it," he said.

A man stepped forward and began putting plastic explosive in place.

Mishka, who did not believe in God, began to pray anyway.

CHAPTER TWENTY-SIX

Dr. Pazyryk threw up on the man he'd just killed.

The ambulance filled with the stink of his vomit, and his knees buckled. Before he could hit the floor, he caught the side of the cage. The taste in his mouth was awful.

"Don't pass out before you unlock me."

"I'll try."

Sasha was nodding his head at him like an understanding friend.

"First time's the worst."

"I don't want to have a second time," he said.

"Then unchain me. I'll take it from here."

The tone in the young man's voice caused the doctor to look over at him.

"Hurry, we don't have much time."

The doctor wiped his sleeve across his mouth, searched for and retrieved his keys and crawled into the cage again. He tried to open the locks, but his hands shook so badly that he couldn't even insert the key. Sasha took them from him with his still free hand and undid the others while the doctor collapsed back against the bars and watched.

"The other key, that's for the band around your neck."

"Speak quietly unless you want company. Leave the locks to me. You get me his gun. His gun," Sasha repeated. "You know, so we can shoot back. Hurry. We need a weapon."

"I feel sick.'

"Better than dead."

Although Dr. Pazyryk was well familiar with dead bodies, he had never touched the body of a man that he himself had murdered. The urge to vomit rose in him like an eruption, but the thought of being gunned down in the ambulance by Ivan's men caused him to suppress the desire. Things were totally out of control now. In the past being caught and killed had been only theoretical. If he was careful in his communications to Hauck his betrayal of the old woman would not be discovered. Those days were long past. There was no longer any possibility of him staying alive unless he escaped.

So he moved.

He crawled over to the guard's body and searched for the pistol. The stench of vomit grew so strong that it hurt his eyes. In the confined space of the ambulance, it was overpowering. But he continued because he could imagine no other choice.

He felt around the body, as though creating a chalk outline. Then, reluctantly, he worked at the edges, and grimaced as he pushed his fingers through his own vomit. If there was anything he most wanted at that moment, he realized with disgust, it would be a gas mask and a set of rubber gloves.

No gun.

He realized that it must be under the man's body. He closed his eyes just for a moment. He heard Sasha swear.

"What's wrong?" he asked.

"Fucking lock. Don't worry; I'll take care of it. Just get me his pistol."

Dead bodies were harder to move than living bodies. There was a reason for that, but it escaped Dr. Pazyryk. Perhaps it would come to him later, if he lived to see later. There was not much light, so he could not easily see the matted black weapon. He had to find it by feel. With one hand he kept the corpse pushed on its side. With the other he felt through the blood. He kept his lips compressed and tried to breathe in through a corner of his mouth in the vain hope that he could tolerate the smell. His fingers closed on the barrel of the pistol just as he threw up again.

"Would you stop that?" said Sasha. "It smells like shit in here. Have you found the gun?"

"It's covered with blood."

"Tell me you didn't throw up on it."

"Just blood."

A satisfying click and Dr. Pazyryk knew that Sasha was free.

"Wipe it off and give it to me," said Sasha as he climbed out of the cage.

"On what?" asked Dr. Pazyryk.

"His pants, his hair, his ass—I don't care. Just do it and give me it to me."

Obediently, the doctor cleaned the pistol on his guard's pant legs, then handed over the weapon.

Sasha leaned toward him, and then dropped to one knee to appraise him.

"Are you ready for this, Doctor? Freedom is on the other side of those doors and if you aren't ready to break out of here, I'll just leave you. You saved my life, but I can't carry you. Can you get yourself together enough to move?"

Freedom.

Freedom through those doors.

The look on Sasha's face was fierce. He wanted revenge. No one would stop him tonight.

Dr. Pazyryk just wanted to get as far away from these psychotics as his legs would take him.

"I can do it."

"Then get up and let's go. We're going after that *holy man* who poisoned my mother. I'll open the door and you hit the ground running. I'll cover you."

"Shouldn't you go first? You have the gun."

"And leave you behind without a gun?"

The doctor considered.

"Okay, I'll do it."

Freedom lay on the other side of those doors.

"Good. You're tougher than I thought."

Sasha looked through the van windows again before opening the door just an inch.

"Ready?"

The doctor nodded.

The young man flung open the door and the doctor, after a moment's hesitation, jumped out and began running down the street. His arms pumped up and down like a true sprinter. The rush of cold, clean night air into his lungs was painful, but it was a good, bracing pain. He ran a total of twelve steps before Ivan's driver raised his rifle and fired a bullet into his right eye. The impact of his head hitting the pavement cracked his skull, but he was already dead.

*****

Sasha forgot his stiff joints and launched out after he guessed the doctor had distracted whatever shooters were left behind when the others moved on the house. He felt his extended right foot slide when he hit the pavement and he went down. His pistol skittered away across the cement. As he dropped a hand to the sidewalk just outside the ambulance bumper, he looked up and saw Dr. Pazyryk take a bullet.

The shooter was a bulky man carrying a rifle and Sasha knew right away he was in trouble. He looked over at the pistol again, but did not move, willing Vasily not to see him. Ivan stood just behind the man's left shoulder, his face difficult to read in the darkness. Sasha stayed as he was, his legs splayed like a gymnast, breathing quietly, hoping against ridiculous odds that they would not see him. That they would walk over to inspect the doctor's body so that he could get up and dive for his gun.

"Get up, Sasha. You look like a fool," called Ivan.

Sasha slowly, very slowly, got to his feet, treasuring every moment that Vasily did not shoot him. Nonchalantly, from the corner of his eyes, he looked toward his pistol. One, maybe two long steps and a dive, grab it as he spun and then come back to one knee firing like a professional stunt shooter. But he was not a professional stunt shooter. In fact, Sasha, for all the men he had killed, was quite a bad shot. He'd had to stand very close to his victims to shoot them.

"Go ahead," said Ivan. "Go for your gun. Vasily is, as you must know, a bastard descendant of the great Vasili Grigorevich Zaytsev, the famous sniper who killed 242 men in one year using only a standard issue Mosin-Nagant rifle. Is that not so, Vasily?"

His driver said nothing.

"He speaks very little, Sasha."

Somewhere several miles behind Ivan, auto horns blared like angry fans whose team was losing. The lighted outline of Detroit broke the night, and Sasha knew that they must be at the edge of the blighted city, separated by blocks and blocks of darkness, where people moved in the shadows and slept on cardboard.

He said nothing.

"Do you know why?"

"No, I do not know or care why."

"Never offend a sniper," said Ivan.

"Why? He will shoot me now or you will throw me back in chains. What is the difference? I will be dead either way."

"He does not speak because your mother had his tongue cut out for mispronouncing her name."

"I see."

"And before you die, I must tell you that your mother, too, died tonight. Congestive heart failure, perhaps."

"You poisoned her," shouted Sasha.

"Keep your voice down or I'm afraid Vasily will shoot you this moment."

"The doctor told me everything."

He pointed to Dr. Pazyryk's body.

"I know that it was you who convinced her to put me in chains."

"The doctor? Don't you mean Hauck's spy?"

Sasha felt the blood drain from his face.

"What are you saying?"

"I'm saying that you really are too stupid to live," said Ivan. "Kill him now, Vasily."

The bastard descendent of Vasili Grigorevich Zaytsev raised his rifle into position, aiming directly at Sasha's heart. Sasha felt warmth on his cheeks as his tears flowed—not out of fear, but for the loss of his mother. He was about to close his eyes when he saw Vasily take a bullet in the throat.

After a moment's confusion, Sasha looked away from the dead sniper and back toward Ivan, who stared at him in bewilderment.

*****

On a nearby rooftop, Evgeny looked through his scope and smiled at his handiwork. Although he did not know the man he had just shot, Dr. Pazyryk had been one of Hauck's own, and there were rules to the game.

CHAPTER TWENTY-SEVEN

Brass piping and steam wisps, gauges and dials, levers and knobs as large as a fist. All around the base of the platform were scattered machines and devices that looked to Sveta as though they had been taken from the engine room of the *Nautilus*. A shaggy white wolf appeared in an aisle between electrical equipment and was shooed away by Drogol.

"Beasts like Ilya and Grigor have been my only companions here beneath the city," he told Sveta and Zoe. "They guard me day and night. Even a monster such as me must sleep."

"You aren't a monster," said Zoe.

"But I am," he said. "Ask this woman. Tell her, Sveta."

Sveta was impatient for him to climb into the tube. The moment he did and Zoe flipped the switch to start the machine was the best moment for her to make a break for it.

"Tell her what?" she asked.

"Tell her what you believe. Tell her you don't think it is a beast from some other world that comes through me. Tell her you think that is only an aspect of my poor irradiated mind manifesting. You think Rasputin is an insane monster who transforms into a vicious beast but cannot admit it. You think it is Rasputin who becomes the monster. Tell her."

"How long have you lived?" she asked irritably.

This appeared to confuse Drogol.

"How long? Perhaps over one hundred and fifty years. Why? What for do you ask?"

"Don't you ever get tired of listening to yourself?"

As though moved by a suddenly revealed moon, one of Drogol's wolves howled somewhere off behind the upended train cars. Drogol held up his palm toward Sveta and tilted his head to one side. He sniffed the air. Something. Maybe nothing.

"Sometimes," he said, "the rats irritate them."

Zoe edged closer to Drogol.

"Do not fear the wolves," he told her. "They are good and steady companions whose only desire is to protect me."

"The rats. I don't like rats."

"No one likes rats," said Sveta, "not even other rats."

She glared at Zoe as she said it.

If Drogol noticed the animosity in her voice, he ignored it. Women had always fought over him. Men had always died around him.

"Even in so many years here, I have not truly explored this fabulous city. In fact, so bitter am I against Tesla, that, although I admire this underground city's so cold beauty, I cannot truly love this place. Yet it is all that I have. So many years I wandered alone, looking for something to keep me from becoming a monster. In the beginning, have I told you, during the cycle of the full moon."

For a moment, they inhaled the silence that more than anything else defined Drogol's world.

"There was no peace for me," he said. "The moon comes and goes in the night sky, waning and waxing as God commands. I was at its mercy. When it grew in fullness, I would … transform. I came to fear the moon. Yet it was not always so for me.

"When I was a boy, I would walk the forest paths of Siberia, wandering the night. I had always two friends with me. The moon would accompany me to show me the safe way. My wolf would stay close by to protect me. I carried a stick, a stick maybe as long as you, Zoe. Can you imagine this?"

Zoe looked as though she would cry.

"You must have been afraid," she said.

"Hah. Afraid? I was joyous. The moon to show me a safe path, a wolf to protect me and a stick to walk with. What more could a boy ask for when traveling alone?"

"A rifle," said Sveta.

Drogol laughed so hard that he bent over and slapped his knees in delight.

"Yes, a good rifle," he said finally. "Tsarista, that is true."

"I'm not—"

"Tell me, Zoe. Who is this woman to me?"

The two women looked at each other.

I dare you, thought Sveta.

"She is your heart's desire," said Zoe. She looked down at her hands and wiped them on her coat.

"Yes, she is. Though she has no memory of who she once was, so she is in truth only an image of my heart's desire. Because of this, she is perhaps reincarnated in face only. No matter. I have been alone for a long time in my despair, and you brought her to me that I might have hope and strength again to do what is right."

Grabbing a brass lever as long as his forearm inset into a control board, Drogol pulled it upward, and then pushed it forward. Suddenly the room was filled with a sound like piano wire unwinding from a spool.

He looked at Sveta.

"The house where you found me is one of many where I worked at the hermetic arts. Mine was a disease of the moon. The science of that earlier day had nothing that would cure me, so I became both a student and a practitioner of the Hermetic Arts. The world may laugh now at Astrology, Alchemy, Tarot and Magic, but I tell you truly that it was within these arts that I discovered something to suppress the curse."

"You found a cure?" asked Sveta

"No, not a cure. What I found was that certain preparations of colloidal gold held the curse at bay. Common lore had it that mercury or silver would be effective, but they were just superstitions. A disease of the moon can only be cured by a preparation of the sun—gold, of course, being the metal of the sun. So it was in that house I first created something that would keep me from turning into a monster every full moon."

He walked underneath the platform and began making magnetometer measurements. Zoe followed quickly, not wanting to be left alone with Sveta. For a time he said nothing, his attention focused on the work he was doing. All the while Sveta counted the minutes, growing increasingly agitated. She knew that Hauck was not far away. When he finished, he turned to them again.

"And now," he said, "all is ready. I will show you where to set the dial, I will give you my confession, and then we shall do this."

"Your confession?" said a bewildered Sveta. "We're not priests."

"I have confessed to God, now I must have witnesses. Such is my way."

Sveta hoped his confession was short.

He led them out from under the platform, walking until he reached the bottom of the steps. After climbing halfway up, he turned and sat down, expecting them to stand looking up at him. His face was calmer than Sveta had seen it since she first laid eyes on him.

"We become what we fear most. This I have learned in my long lifetime. But there is no place for fear in God's love, and to harbor such fear therefore keeps us away from God. Listen to me. My father was a terrible man who beat my mother and myself unmercifully. We lived in terror of his anger."

Oh my God, thought Sveta. *He's going all the way back to his child-hood. There's no time for this. I should just shoot him and get it over with.*

"He and my mother died when I was young. I was left to take care of myself as best I could. It was a hard life, children. I was sickly and weak. I came to covet power and influence over others so that I would never be victimized again. I feared my father's power over me, so I coveted that same power over others.

"I was alone and starved too often. So one day when the holy men of our pagan faith came to me and asked me to come with them, I went. I accepted their faith; I had nothing and they would take care of me. Eventually, I turned away from these people and their faith when I met a true holy man in the forests. He told me about the real God who would reveal himself to me if only I would seek him out. And his words were inspired. I did find God—not in scriptures or religion, but in seeking him. God spoke to me, and gave me the gift of influence and bestowed upon me the honor of administering his healing abilities to those in need. But I misused these gifts because I could not put aside my need for power.

"God lifts up those who are weak, but I wanted strength and power because I so feared it in my father. One day God punished me for my arrogance by allowing the god of science to deliver upon me this curse.

"Now, I have great power. But I cannot use it for good because when I transform I become a raging, terrible beast whose needs are only to destroy and devour. It was to be many years before I learned to control this with the alchemical formula I spoke of moments ago.

Before that success, I killed many innocents. More than I can now consider without sinking into abject terror and remorse.

"You may ask why I have not killed my miserable self. Why, you may ask, did not Rasputin take his own life? I tell you that it is a sin to do so. I would be permanently separated from God.

"So tonight, I instead attempt to restore myself to who I once was so that I may live and die a normal death, taking each day hostage as though it were the last. I would do good in the world. I can no longer live as a monster. You, Zoe, will help me in this. You, Sveta, will kill me if I fail. Through the monster I am a murderer, and the penalty for murder must be death if I cannot be cured."

Sveta and Zoe exchanged glances. Sveta spoke first.

"How can I kill you?"

Drogol opened his coat, and withdrew a long bladed knife, which he then handed to Sveta.

"Should the time come, you will use this to cut off my head. It is the true way to kill me. Can you do this for me?"

She took the knife.

"You're sure this will work?"

Drogol tugged at the edges of his beard and appeared to consider the question thoroughly. It began to irritate Sveta, as she began to think that Hauck and his team would find them before she could escape.

"I know much, very much about this curse and those who have been afflicted with the wolf-bite," he said finally. "On this earth I am the only man who knows anything at all about the effects of being exposed to Tesla's Tunguska disaster. And even *I* do not know that you will be permitted to sever my head."

Anything to get you into that tube so I can get out of here before Hauck shows up, she thought.

"Okay," she said. "If this thing doesn't work and you still want to die, I'll be your executioner."

What Sveta planned on doing was being long gone before Drogol came out of the tube.

"No," said Zoe. "You can't ask her to do that."

"She has already agreed. As the Tsarista Alexandra knew so many years ago, I am too dangerous a man to let live."

Damned straight, though Sveta.

Without another word, Drogol stood, turned and walked up and into the tube. The quartz door hissed closed. Vapors began to swirl around his feet and soon the tube was filled with a soft mist. He smiled at them once, and then bent his head as though praying.

"Hauck put you up to this," Sveta said to Zoe.

"I was following orders, but now I don't know. What if this works? What if he's normal again?"

"You explain it to Hauck. I'm getting the hell out of here the minute you throw the switch."

Zoe looked desperate.

"It was the only way," she said.

"It's what spies do," said Sveta, and she shook her head in disgust. "Go ahead, turn the knob. I'm out of here."

The brass dial turned easily beneath Zoe's fingers. The sound in the room came alive with a high-pitched frequency. The tube began to charge with silver light that grew in intensity as Zoe moved the dial slowly towards its mark.

When Sveta looked up at Drogol she saw him standing straight as a cadet, his eyes wide open, his lips pressed tightly together. His eyes began to glow like liquid metal and she saw swirls of blue light pulsate around him, wrapping him in bands of energy like an electric snake.

Time to go, thought Sveta, but she was transfixed by the sight.

Drogol's mouth opened in a silent scream and Sveta saw tears streaming from Zoe's eyes. The golden light that lit the complex began to swirl and spark as though alive.

Now or never.

Sveta grabbed her gear and was about to step off the platform when she felt the ground shake from an explosion somewhere in the direction of the entrance.

Too late.

Hauck had arrived.

CHAPTER TWENTY-EIGHT

But it wasn't Hauck's team that exploded their way into the underground complex—it was Ivan's.

The first few men through the door stopped suddenly at the unexpected sight of the immense complex. Behind them, men started shoving and pushing and asking what was wrong, but no one could hear each other because their ears still rang from the percussive force of the explosion.

What the men that came through first saw astounded them. It was not the size of what they had stumbled into that caused them to stop and gape in wonder, it was the simple fact that moments before they were armed and dangerous men who filled a dirty, descending, half-constructed passageway with impending violence. Now they were face to face with a golden world of arcing technology in a cavern the size of two football stadiums. Hardened killers pushed their way out onto the first platform to stare at bursts of blue steam that shot up from hidden pipes, copper-ringed towers that crackled with power and shot brilliant rays of light across the spaces to bounce off each other to another and yet another such tower.

"Where are we?" said one.

"What?" said another.

Earplugs could only do so much and most of these men simply didn't put them in because they didn't really believe the sound of an explosion could hurt their ears. Half of them had been street criminals that Sasha bought from overcrowded Russian prisons and shipped to Mishka and the others were Russian Mafiya thugs.

"Mishka's coming through," said someone else.

Some men pressed against the side rails to make space for him, but none turned to face him. Instead they stared out at the underground city in awe.

When Mishka arrived, he, too, stared in disbelief.

What is this place? he wondered. *What have we found?*

Try as he might, he could not devise an answer. Whatever it was, it was a secret that in some way might be worth a fortune. Or, it occurred to him in a flash, it could be a death sentence. What if this was a secret military installation of the United States government? But if it was, where were the soldiers? Maybe a research facility, but if it was, where were the scientists? Even without descending to ground level, he was intuitively certain that the place was empty.

Except, perhaps, for the beast who had slaughtered his men at the warehouse.

"What do we do?" asked one of his men.

The mood in his group was changing. They could smell the money. He might be able to use that to advantage. No. He could use nothing to advantage down here. Ivan would have made sure to pay at least two or three of these men to kill him when the shooting started. Executions were easy enough to buy. He ought to know; he had paid for enough of them himself.

He could expect no help from Sasha's men, for his friend was somewhere above ground chained and caged. They were both dead men before the night was out.

"What do we do?" the man asked again. "This place is so big. How will we find the one we're looking for?"

Mishka had an idea.

"We go down," he said.

"Yes, but where do we begin looking? He could be hiding anywhere."

That was what gave him hope. It was a place big enough to get lost in. A place so large that, when the shooting started, he could double back and get out the way he came in. He didn't know who Ivan paid to kill him, but he could improve his own odds by ordering the men to split up in groups of three. Whoever came with him, he would have them take the lead and, when the time was right, he would dispose of them.

It might work. If he could get away, he would find a way to leave the country, maybe find a way to return home someday. Even Moscow was safer than Detroit.

"He's right," said another. "Where do we start?"

Mishka looked out across the complex, and somewhere near its center he saw a pulsating pillar of white light calling him like a lighthouse beacon. He had no idea what it was, but it was clearly something important. Something was going on there.

"There," he said, pointing at it.

His men only knew that they were chasing a dangerous man who sometimes kept vicious wolves. Mishka knew that tonight they would face much worse.

"Go," he said.

They began moving carefully, quietly down the stairs as though whatever waited for them in this strange world had not heard the explosion.

*****

Sveta grabbed the telescope barrel and swung it up and around to face the entrance. She bent over to the eyepiece and looked in. Nothing but a blur. She swore, and then began adjusting the focus knob, then re-aiming, then re-adjusting.

"What is it?" said Zoe. "What's going on?"

"Your friends are here. Weren't you expecting them?"

It was impossible to quickly find the right spot for viewing the way the telescope was configured. It was an ancient astronomer's instrument, meant for slowly turning the gears toward a particular section of the sky with identified coordinates. Whoever had crafted it hadn't planned on it being used to track a fast-moving incoming SWAT team.

Automatic weapons fire from somewhere near the stairway.

"Shit."

"What?" asked Zoe.

"What are they shooting at? There's no one down here but us, is there?"

"Wolves. Maybe they're shooting at the wolves."

A second later Sveta though she heard a wolf yelp. Snarling and more rifle fire.

"Bastards."

Sveta bent back over the telescope and tried to block out the thought of what was happening.

Behind them the Tesla tube began to ring with resonant notes, as though the tube itself were a variable tuning fork. Drogol could be seen, had they been looking back at him, only as an image that faded in and out like a bad cell phone signal.

At last an image came into view of a man's head.

You son of a bitch, she thought.

After some quick trial and error, she was able to control the telescopic direction and magnification so that she began to get an idea what was going on. Hauck probably thought that he came with enough men, she thought, but he hadn't counted on a place this big. There were too many places to hide.

They were far enough away that she had a little time, so she started counting. Maybe fifteen, maybe twenty men by the time she was through. It was hard to tell through the telescope. She was getting nauseous just looking through it.

"What do we do?" Zoe asked.

"We?" Sveta said without looking up. "I'm getting out before they get here. Right now I'm just sizing them up. Oh shit."

Zoe grabbed her arm and tugged.

"What is it?"

With a quick motion, Sveta pulled her arm away and stood up.

"You called Hauck, didn't you?"

"I had to," said Zoe defiantly.

"I don't give a damn about that now. You know who's over there coming in the same way we did? No? It's my cousin Mishka, the same asshole who threw you into a closet and left you to die at the warehouse. Red Mafiya. And he's got about twenty men with him now. Probably more up at the surface. So how the hell did he find us down here? Are you in with him, too?"

"I don't even know who he is," protested Zoe.

Long, drawn out tones began to vibrate through the platform. The Tesla tube light show began to pulse more slowly, each note longer and deeper than the other. Drogol was visible within the tube, but the energy flux made him look more like a created hologram. There was something soothing about the sound and light imagery.

Sveta slapped her.

"You wearing a transmitter?"

"No."

Sveta hit her again.

"Tell me."

"I'm not wearing a transmitter," screamed Zoe.

In a sudden spasm, she doubled over and grabbed the spot where she had been bleeding earlier. Her face seemed to turn pale white.

No time. Drogol in the tube. Zoe hurting. Mishka and his men coming at them.

A scream and more weapons fire. How many wolves did Drogol have?

Think. How did Mishka find them? And then it hit her. The car. Mishka's car had a GPS. She hadn't thought of it when they were on the run. So now she'd be facing Hauck's team and Mishka's gunmen.

I should have just sent out party invites, she thought.

"Shut the machine off," she said.

A bullet whined off a nearby panel board, and Sveta dropped straight to the metal platform.

"Down," she yelled. "Get down."

Sveta played it out in her head. Accidental shot. No one was firing at them. They were too far out. Mishka wasn't that stupid to let them open fire over such a distance. Wild shot by one of Mishka's men bitten by a wolf? Maybe worse. Maybe Hauck's team had showed up and they were fighting it out for who got to take Drogol's head home in a jar. Maybe that was better. Confusion was good when you were making a break for it, and Sveta had to make a break for it.

How long before they got to the platform. Five minutes?

A tight pattern of shots fired from a few feet away.

Sveta looked up to see Zoe with an automatic weapon firing toward the stairway.

"Stop," yelled Sveta. "What the fuck are you doing? You're telling them where we are you dumb bitch."

But Zoe, who had in the period of two nights been stabbed, died and resurrected, attacked by a giant wolf beast and having betrayed the man who brought her back to life, had gone over the edge. In the middle of the pulsing Tesla tube light show she stood like a mad-woman firing bullets at men she could barely see. Her shots clanged and careened off electrical junction boxes and shattered glowing quartz crystals.

Return fire came and all around the area Sveta heard bullets winging off of nearby equipment.

"Shit, shit, shit," she yelled.

Save your bullets, save your bullets, save your bullets, she thought.

A break in firing by Zoe.

Sveta brought her pistol up and was about to shoot her, when she saw the tears rolling down the girl's face and figured there was no point. Everyone knew where they were now. The tube behind them began to emit high pitched sounds and bright sharp colors and she saw Drogol shaking and shaking and she thought he would die in there for certain.

"Shut that fucking thing off," Sveta screamed.

Zoe looked down at her and seemed about to say something when she bucked backward as though an invisible hand had hit her. Her mouth opened wide in surprise and Sveta saw a bloodstain spreading out from her chest. The girl dropped her rifle, brought her hands up and began to stagger.

There was a sound that Sveta recognized instantly and she clapped her hands over her ears as she closed her eyes. Twenty feet away a projectile exploded. When she opened her eyes again she saw Zoe fall back against the pie-shaped dial that controlled the Tesla tube. As she continued falling, it moved with her until it stopped at the position marked "Maximum." A screeching cacophony of sound and searing light screamed from the tube and Drogol twisted and turned so fast inside its vortex that he looked like a life sized doll thrust into a blender.

Vibrations surged across the platform like angry waves. Sveta reached for a floor clamp to keep from being tossed over the edge without her duffel. She saw it sliding, let go and rolled toward it. It slid away but she kept after it and finally grabbed it with an outstretched hand. She began wiggling like a snake toward the edge of the platform, her body pressed down as much as she could to avoid catching a bullet. Behind her, a round hit the Tesla tube with a bright crack and pinged off like a cushion-shot without damaging it.

She risked a quick glance over the edge of the platform and saw that the men were closer than she thought, firing at the platform in steady bursts to keep her pinned down. She heard shouting and even though she couldn't make out what they said she just knew they were saying, "There she is. I see her, kill the bitch."

Keep moving.

If she slid over the edge without getting shot, she could make it underneath the machinery below and run out the other side and find one of the many exits Drogol had hinted could be used to escape. A blast of quartz crystal flashed past her before she could move. She closed her eyes and pressed her face down reflexively as a wave of heat passed over her. The smell of burnt hair filled her nostrils.

When the press of hot air passed, she started crawling toward the edge again. She was about to roll over when she realized that the entire complex had gone quiet. Then men who had been storming forward stopped moving. She saw one of them lower his gun and extend a finger toward her in fear. No one moved. Sveta held her breath as though by doing so she could prolong her safety.

Behind her, she heard a loud wail begin low and soft and rise in a powerful crescendo until it filled the cavern like a fire alarm.

Standing by himself where the tube used to be was Drogol. Iridescent energy seemed to ripple over him like a radiant blanket. She saw him look around, bewildered, hopeless. His eyes found hers and, for a moment, he seemed alarmed, as though he did not recognize her. He turned his head to one side, and then stopped searching when he saw Zoe lying flat on her back. Shaking like an alcoholic deprived of drink, he walked toward the girl. Crouching down next to her as the room remained quiet as though a truce had been declared for just a few moments, he touched his finger to her stained blouse. He stood again, and held that finger before his face like he was checking the wind direction as he stared at her blood.

Why isn't he dead? wondered Sveta. *That thing went to maximum. It should have killed him.*

He looked at Sveta, who forcefully shook her head and pointed toward the men who had been shooting at them. It was an instinctive action, decided on with neither strategy nor tactics, but the effect on Drogol was dramatic. He tilted back his head and screamed, lifting his arms upward as though calling down a rain of fire.

When his cry had echoed throughout the cavern for the second time, one of Mishka's men fired a burst at Drogol, who lowered his arms slowly to point a finger at him. The man stopped firing, but others started. It was too late. Drogol began to change. A dark rippling, a gasp as he covered his stomach where a bullet struck him and Sveta saw something dark moving within his form like before. It was a more powerful, demanding writhing energy, charged beyond sanity with the compounding effects of the Tesla tube.

God no, thought Sveta.

She rolled over the edge as a giant blackness of bristling hair and razored claws leapt over her toward Mishka and his men.

CHAPTER TWENTY-NINE

Mishka's men started firing as soon as they'd been attacked by wolves. In the confusing maze of machinery and electrical equipment, it was impossible to tell how many wolves there were. When the first wolf sunk his teeth into one of the men's thighs and ripped off a huge chunk of bloody flesh, the man's screams initiated a firestorm of bullets. Most simply hit equipment, bouncing off and hitting still other machinery. But the occasional stray bullet hit one of the men.

It was impossible to tell what was going on as wolves snarled and attacked the men firing at them.

There must a hundred of these damned things, thought Mishka. *It's like a fucking army.*

He didn't have to worry about his own men shooting him if he tried to get away because all of them were doing the same thing he was—trying to find something to climb up on to hide from the sharp teeth and snapping jaws and manic yellow eyes. As if he didn't have enough trouble, someone near the flashing cylinder up ahead on the platform was shooting at them with an automatic weapon.

Mishka ran with his pistol stretched before him.

As he turned a corner near something that looked like a mutated hybrid of a bulldozer and a radio headset, he saw a wolf crash into a man, knocking him completely backward onto the floor. Before Mishka could aim, the wolf was at the man's throat, grabbing hold and shaking him. With a quick, lucky shot to the back of its head, the wolf was dead.

They are huge beasts, he thought, *big as Siberian wolves.*

The wolf fell away and Mishka saw blood gurgling from the man's throat. Even with that horrific wound, his eyes blinked at Mishka, as though sending him a message in Morse code with his eyelids because he could not speak.

Mishka shot him between the eyes, then stepped over the man and the wolf and kept on going. He was looking for a way back to the stairs they had come down. But around the next corner, he saw something that looked like a flammable chemicals cabinet. It was made of thick metal and was about the size of a large bookcase but twice as deep. He could fit in there, he reasoned, close the door behind him, and be safe from both wolves and stray bullets.

It was at that moment he heard another explosion reverberate throughout the room.

Mishka peeked back around the corner and saw a tall dark man standing where once had been the glass tube that flashed a dazzling light show across this underground world. He knew instantly that this dramatic figure was Drogol by the power that emanated from him like the electricity in the air near a powerful generator.

In a gesture of despair, Drogol raised his arms and began to wail and such was its effect that Mishka felt an urgent need to raise his arms, too, and cry out with this man.

But a few seconds after the wail ended, the howling of the wolves echoed throughout the complex. It was as though they felt their master's grief. Mishka could not understand the source of such agony, but the howling quelled when the transformation began.

Drogol's body looked like it was in motion while standing still, as if something inside him were trying to burst out. Mishka could feel the rage struggling to consume this man, but a split second later when he saw the beast that destroyed his warehouse and slaughtered his men leap out from within that man, Mishka screamed.

He dropped his pistol, jumped inside the metal cabinet and slammed it shut behind him.

*****

Mishka closed his eyes and pretended he was not there.

Outside the thick walled metal cabinet he heard more automatic weapons fire and the sounds of flash-bangs. The faint smell of tear gas tendrilled into the cabinet, so he covered his mouth and nose with his coat sleeve as best he could. An explosion nearby actually sent a tremor through the heavy cabinet, but Mishka could handle that, too.

What were more difficult to endure were the screams.

So many men.

So much screaming.

And outside, splattered everywhere, would be so much blood. This thing could not be killed. He should have begged Ivan to shoot him instead of sending him down here. A bullet in the back of the head would be mercy compared to being ripped apart by this monster. It was the same creature, no doubt, but now it seemed bigger than it had been in the video he'd watched. Something had caused it to grow more massive and powerful. As it leapt from inside Drogol, Mishka had immediately felt the rage and lust to kill radiating from it.

"Oh fuck, oh fuck, somebody shoot me," he heard a man scream.

It was close, too close.

He could smell the odor of wet fur and blood. Heard heavy movement. He could hear whimpering. He couldn't tell how close, but it was enough that, moments later, he heard more plaintive screams followed by the snapping of bones. A pause, and then a very, very large crunching noise followed by a cracking noise and something else. Mishka did not want to know what it was; he did not want to think about what it could be.

Pacing.

The monster was pacing back and forth. The sounds of metal boxes tossed about. Snarling and glass breaking. An enraged howl so loud Mishka covered both ears to protect his eardrums from rupturing. He began telling himself over and over that nothing could get in, that the walls of his cabinet were too thick. His gun lay outside somewhere on the floor. If the beast moved away, if it left for long enough, he could chance getting his gun.

That way he would have something to shoot himself with when the moment came.

He pressed against the metal door gently, but it would not yield. There was no give at all. It was dark in the cabinet, so he probed for a handle with his fingertips. He began to panic when he realized that he had locked himself *inside* and the handle was on the *outside*.

Something hard hit the cabinet and it flew up and over and landed upside down on concrete with a bang. Sasha fell into deeper depths of darkness.

*****

Sveta ran hard toward the opposite end of the complex from where she, Zoe, and Drogol had entered because that's where Mishka's men were and, now, that was where the beast ran free as well. She needed a plan, should have already had a plan and cursed herself for listening to Drogol talk instead of taking action. Lots of ways out. He had implied as much, but was it true?

It had to be, she realized, because the air was breathable. There had to be active vents that connected this underground world to the surface. Otherwise the buildup of noxious gases would make the air un-breathable. So what was she looking for? She was looking for the ventilation system.

The screaming drove her to think more quickly than she ever had before. It was hard to see what was overhead or how high the ceiling was, but she saw no light coming in from overhead. But of course she wouldn't—it was dark outside because it was night. Then how to find the ventilation system—that was the question.

The beast was keeping Mishka's gunmen on the run, so she had a little while. This was slight comfort because she knew sooner or later it would run out of men to eat and would come looking for her.

She decided she had to get to higher ground to see exactly where she was and try to find the ventilation system. Scaffolding bracketed to the side of a network of steam and water pipes gave her a secure way to gain some height. Overhead she saw that there were service platforms roughly every twenty feet. The original engineers and construction people had been kind enough to weld in place a half circle protective cage onto the ladder rungs to prevent anyone from falling backward and killing themselves.

She took a quick look over her shoulder. Nothing. Up in the air she might be more of a target for Mishka's men, but wolves didn't climb utility ladders. And the half cage bolted to it was barely big enough for her and her weapons duffel. It wasn't big enough for the beast to fit in. She was definitely going up. Switching the duffel bag to her other shoulder, Sveta began to climb.

Behind her, the shots, the screams, and the explosions continued.

Halfway up to the first service platform she stopped. The beast couldn't fit inside of the protective cage around the ladder, but it could climb on the outside and reach in for her. The thought of it caused her to grip the ladder rungs so hard her hands hurt. She stayed there until she got it under control. No such thing as a perfect plan anyway, she thought, and started up again.

It was a better plan than she'd realized.

Each of the service platforms was four feet square and half a sheet metal wall three feet tall formed and welded inside the curved railing. She crawled out onto it and shoved her weapons duffel up against it, then shimmied the rest of the way and collapsed onto the diamond-backed floor. After a few deep breaths, she checked her AK and got to her knees to look over the edge of the sheet metal enclosure.

The beast crashed through structures and equipment like a giant wrecking ball with teeth and claws. Its rage filled the room like a presence as it snarled and barked, howled with released fury and bounded throughout the complex slashing and biting and tearing. It knocked over electrified towers like they were toys, and Sveta saw to her horror that fires had sprung up.

She realized that the smoke might be a way to find the exhaust ventilation system. If the beast didn't get to her first. It was beginning to rage in widening circles. She saw it hit one man with an open paw with such power that it completely separated his head from his body. Another man tried to hide beneath the upended train and it shot after him, lifting the entire car into the air and then dropped it on him.

But it suddenly reared up, sniffed the air, than began dashing toward something she couldn't see.

It's running straight into that bricked up portion of wall, she thought. *What the hell is it doing?*

*****

"Somebody blew up something," said the Instructor. "Let's get moving."

They had some distance left to go by Hauck's reckoning. The radio signal was still not getting through to either Yuri or Evgeny.

"What's your problem? Faster."

"I'm not risking falling down in this filthy water and ruining the gas gun. We're almost there, anyway. Can't be more than another five or ten minutes away."

Hauck could still communicate with the Instructor via their fire and chemical suit radios. The suits made them look like sewer rat spacemen splashing through the water.

"Five minutes? Ten minutes? Screw your gas gun. I've got a shoulder fired rocket launcher back here."

Hauck tried to move a little faster, but the water was too high.

"This water," he said. "It's almost up to my waist."

"Fuck you. Your waist is as high as my armpits so get the lead out. I want to get there before this thing gets away."

So they pushed forward harder. Little dark things hiding on the concrete ledges scurried away as they got close.

"Air's getting worse," Hauck said as he shoved a floating piece of darkness away from him. "Oxygen's going down and the methane's going up. I can't see the numbers for hydrogen sulfide on this wrist detector, though."

"What are you, the fucking weather man? We got filters and backup air tanks on so who the hell cares? Just get your ass moving."

They moved on in silence until they heard an impact explosion, like someone had just driven a truck into a brick wall. Hauck looked back at the Instructor.

"Still down ahead a ways. Hard to tell how far the way sound travels through these old tunnels."

"Get that gas gun of yours ready now. Get up on the ledge where there's that little dent in the wall there. There's another one back about twenty feet there on the other side where I'm going to set up."

"But we're not even there yet," protested Hauck.

The Instructor grinned behind his face mask. It was an eerie sight in the green light and Hauck thought he looked like an evil goblin.

"We don't have to get all the way there. Can't you feel the ground shaking? It's coming straight at us."

Hauck scrambled up onto the ledge and unhooked the compressed gas gun from his shoulder strap. He looked down at the surface of the water, and saw small tremors shudder the water as though someone were shaking the underground waterways.

CHAPTER THIRTY

Y uri, you there?" asked Evgeny.

Rain still misted down, and droplets ran off the edges of his pancho.

"I can't get hold of Hauck yet," Yuri's voice came back.

"Never mind that. I've this guy in my sights on the ground outside of the building. He looks weird, like some kind of an albino. You got anything on him?"

"Albino?"

"Yeah, looks like it."

"That would be … Ivan, the old woman's spooky bodyguard and counselor or whatever you want to call him. A stone cold dude. Into some weird religious shit."

"I'm going to take him out."

"Wait. Let me try to get Hauck one more time."

"Son of a bitch."

"What? What's going on?"

Evgeny swung his scope back to where the man Ivan's sniper was trying to kill was standing in time to witness a terrifying transformation. Tufted ears shot out from the side of his head. His jaws shot forward and sharp teeth sprang from his gums. An agonizing scream rent the night as the man arched backward. His shirt split open as his musculature expanded. Evgeny could hardly process the sight of the man's arms shooting out and sharp claws formed where he once had hands. In the gathered light of his star-scope, the metamorphosis was a black and white horror show.

It was the face of the monster that caused Evgeny to do what he had never done before that night. He pulled his eye from his scope in terror. But he had to look. He pressed the scope to his eye again even as he focused on controlling his fear.

Shreds of cloth clung to its torso as it writhed in agony. Dark fur covered its face. He watched as it bent over in pain. Then, it straightened and tore off its remaining clothing, like a snake shedding its skin. Evgeny saw it hold its clawed hands up before its face, clenching and unclenching them. As suddenly as it began, it was over. The monster stiffened and looked straight at Ivan.

*****

At the sight of Vasily's murder, Ivan felt the combined rush of rage and fear. His pale eyes narrowed as he scanned the area for the executioner. He did not duck or draw a weapon. He was a khylsty, a divine warrior whose anger was sufficient to confront the demons of hell. Under the protection of the old gods, no one could harm a khylsty doing their will. And their will was that he find Drogol and drink his blood. No man could stop him.

"Coward," he shouted. "Face me or flee."

The khylsty dagger appeared in his right hand, a slender sliver of silver. He had survived Anna Kazakova. No man could frighten him.

Nothing moved to up or down the darkened street. The houses stood lifeless and still in their desperate abandon. The distant lights of Detroit silhouetted the flat rooftops, but he could see no movement, no hint of the enemy.

"Run with the rats," shouted Ivan.

Truly, he had survived Anna Kazakova. He feared no man.

Movement and a curse.

Sasha. He had forgotten Sasha.

The young man squirmed and cried out as though he, too, had been shot. Ridiculous. If the Hauck's sniper had targeted him, Sasha would be dead, not wounded.

"Silence," hissed Ivan.

Sasha cursed again and arched his back so hard it ripped his shirt.

"Fuck, oh fuck, something's wrong. Help me. Somebody help me."

His torso twisted so fast Ivan thought his spine would surely snap.

"I said silence."

A step towards Sasha, the khylsty blade rising in front of him. All thoughts of Hauck's sniper forgotten, overwhelmed by disgust. What an affront this young piglet was to the magnificent and worthy enemy that his mother had been.

"You drop to the ground like a schoolboy screaming for his mother. You are not worthy of her memory."

Sasha covered his head with his arms and wailed.

Ivan looked at the clean, sharp edge of the khylsty knife that had bled so many of the unclean.

Will I never meet a worthy opponent? he thought.

*****

Aiming the rifle to the right, Evgeny brought Ivan into view. He stood transfixed, spellbound by the monstrous transformation he was witnessing.

Evgeny's finger squeezed the trigger, but stopped.

The albino's mouth was moving, chanting something as he lifted a long dagger into the air above where the man-creature lay writhing.

Evgeny re-sighted on the monster.

You first, he thought

But he was too late. The beast leapt up toward the albino with incredible speed. He re-sighted in time to see it leap on the other and sink its jaws into the man's face. Even though he was on the roof of a building halfway down the street, Evgeny recoiled at the ferocity of the attack.

"It's out here," he whispered into his mic. "It's eating the albino."

"Shoot it," said Yuri.

And Evgeny did.

Through his scope he saw the beast spin and snarl, looking for the source of its pain. It looked different than the animal they were chasing. Smaller, only a little bigger than its victim. But when it opened its jaws and howled, Evgeny shot it three more times square in the chest. It fell backward, hit the ground and sprung up. He almost pulled the trigger again, but the beast turned and roared at the building where a group of men rounded the corner and began firing at it.

Without any hesitation at all, it ran straight toward the shooters, snarling and snapping. The men continued to pump round after round in it but it still came at them. Panicked, the men began screaming and fell back, running for their lives. The beast was on one of them and bit off the man's arm with one bite. It caught another with its claws and ripped his throat out. More shots.

"What's going on?" said Yuri.

"Some of the Kazakova soldiers heard the noise, came running around the building and started shooting."

Evgeny wondered if Hauck and the old man were dead.

"And?"

"It's killing them."

"Did you hit it?"

Evgeny said nothing.

"I said to you hit it?"

"We all hit it," said Evgeny, "but it's still moving. It moves so damned fast I can't keep it in my scope."

"Shit."

"Yeah."

It was over in a few more seconds.

Torn bodies littered the ground.

Evgeny ran his scope around the area, looking to reacquire the beast. It was gone, blending into the night. He kept searching.

"I've lost it," he said finally.

"I just tried Hauck again. They're still out of reach."

Tilting his head slightly upward, Evgeny looked at the faint red moon. There was a name for it. Yuri had told him what it was, but he had forgotten it. Whatever it was called, it was a very bad omen.

"I'm going to stay in position in case Hauck and the old man show up."

"You're probably safer on the roof."

He was positioned against a crumbling brick chimney on an abandoned two story house. An old, tall tree grew on its east side, and he climbed it to get to the roof. The tiles were wet and slippery, but Evgeny had waited in worse spots.

Time passed. Heavy, dark clouds moved slowly through the sky, sometimes blocking the moonlight. But there was enough ambient light for his night vision equipment to give him a good view of the building and the area around it. Nothing moved, so Evgeny waited.

Patience was the sniper's way.

"Anything?" came Yuri's voice.

"Nothing."

"Still can't raise Hauck."

"Give him time."

"I—"

"Quiet."

He'd heard something. A scratching. He listened, but heard nothing. Yuri would hold radio silence until he spoke again. His scalp began to tingle. The urge to turn, and look behind him grew. After a full two minutes, he inched upward and back to gain purchase with one hand on a section of the rope harness he had put into place to keep himself from falling. It was secured around the chimney for stability, and he used it to turn and get to his knees.

The roof-peak was four feet away, but he would have to risk it.

With his rifle strap wrapped around one arm he slowly moved up, sliding his knees along the wet roof. The rope would hold him if he began to slip, but with his back to the street, he felt like a range target. He stopped halfway there, listened and heard nothing, then risked a look back at the vacant street below.

It took a long time for him to finally get one hand on the roof's peak. For a moment, he stopped again, listening. With a sigh of relief, he slid his rifle strap over again so that it was supported on one shoulder, placed the other hand on the roof's peak alongside the other, and pulled himself up so that his chin rested there.

Two clawed hands clamped onto his head and pulled him up so that he was face to face with the beast. Evgeny did not have time to scream before it was at his throat.

*****

There was a limit to how long Yuri could wait.

No contact with Hauck. No contact with Evgeny. Crue dead. Sveta on the run. This kept up, there wouldn't be anybody left.

"Evgeny? What's happening?"

No response.

"Hell with these assholes," said Yuri. "Nobody wants to pick up the phone. Nobody wants to call in. Everybody just leaves me sitting in this stinking cushy chair, spinning around with one broken arm and a bottle of pain pills in front of these big screens with no information. Find this, Yuri, what about that, Yuri. Well at least fucking talk to me."

"Quit yelling," came an irritated voice from across the room.

Two of his five bodyguards—he liked to think of them that way—were playing cards.

"You'd yell, too, if nobody called you."

"You got all those computers," said the man, "why don't you try an internet dating site. They got chat rooms. Pretty cheap. That's what I hear, anyway. Right, Igor?"

From across the wooden table, his concentration buried deep in five cards he held in his massive hands, Igor grunted.

"Oh, Jesus," shouted Yuri.

He slapped himself so hard on the forehead that he almost fell out of his chair.

"Thank you, thank you, amen."

"The fuck is wrong with you?" said the first card player. "You're nuts."

But Yuri was already working with his touch screen to bring up Evgeny's nano-cam. He was so stressed and so bugged out on painkillers that he'd forgotten Evgeny wore a camera like everybody else.

"Got you," he said triumphantly. "You don't' want to talk to me, I'll just spy on what you're looking at."

Yuri froze. He felt his pulse slowing down as the fear iced his heartbeat.

The nano-cam screen was filled with the beast.

His mouth felt dry. The creature was chewing on something. A big bone maybe. Chewing the meat off it. Yuri was going to be sick. Yet he couldn't turn away. Instead, without thinking, he took his bottle of vodka from his backpack and started pouring himself a shot in the glass he kept near his keyboard. The bottle clinked nervously against the glass as the clear liquor flowed up the glass and over the rim. A small pool of alcohol formed on the desk.

"Hey," called the first card player, "pour me one, too, will you?"

Yuri nodded, then tilted up his bottle and set it on the floor near his chair. He took the glass and began drinking as tears welled in his eyes.

At first, he had hoped that Evgeny was hidden, looking at the monster, watching it eat while waiting for a shot. But after a moment he realized that the camera angle was all wrong, that it was looking up and when the beast reached down to tug on something, Yuri saw the image shake. He knew then that Evgeny wasn't waiting for a shot while the creature ate. Evgeny was what was being eaten.

Yuri didn't know how long he sat in place, drinking and crying. He was about to shut off the remote camera, when in that peculiar blend of horror, pain killers, booze and trauma that ran through his brain, he realized something that he shouldn't even been able to think about in the circumstances. He took a snapshot of the beast's terrifying face and slid it on to a bigger screen.

I'm going to get you, he thought.

With a gamer's detachment, while Evgeny's remains were being devoured by the beast on the camera screen to his left, Yuri pulled up an image of the beast that had attacked his van. It was taken by one of the cameras on the van roof. He almost reached for the vodka bottle next, but instead arranged both beast images on the screen before him. In a moment, he had re-sized them, adjusted the image brightness and such, and had them up side by side to study them.

Another drink and he spun on his chair to shut off Evgeny's remote camera. The beast was gone, and Yuri saw only empty sky.

Never enough information, he thought, *and never on time*.

He drained the rest of his glass in an easy gulp, and turned back to the screen with the two images displayed.

"Well now, he said, we didn't know there were two of you," he said.

He had to make contact with Hauck.

*****

Sveta counted the minutes from her perch. She was safe for the time being where she was, but she could not stay on the maintenance platform forever. Looking over the edge of the sheet metal again, she saw that, although the beast had torn through Mishka's troops like a cyclone, destroying everything in its path, a few men survived. They were between her and the stairway exit, but better she shoot it out with them than run into the beast in the exit that he had blasted through the wall.

She was halfway down the ladder when she heard yet another explosion and swung around to see flames shooting out of the hole the beast made.

*****

It came hurtling down the tunnel toward Hauck.

In the light of his night vision, the monster's eyes glowed like hot green coals. Hauck felt again the same fear he'd known in the prison where the beast had killed his men. It was running on all fours like a wild animal. Water sprays shot up around it with each slap of its paws.

Hauck chocked the compressed air gun and fired when it was only twenty feet away, then pressed back hard into the wall's recess. He'd set the firing selector to full auto and fired all of the canisters in one assault. But the creature was coming so quickly it ran past him before it realized it'd been hit.

Poisonous corrosive gas filled the tunnel like deadly steam.

The tunnel was silent.

Inside his suit, Hauck prayed the seals held tight and his filtration system worked. He decided not to take a chance and switched to his breathing tank. After that, he risked looking out.

The creature stood fifteen feet down the tunnel surrounded by white mist, staring straight back at him. It roared and took a step forward. Hauck saw shiny, metallicized claws and a long, slavering set of jaws filled with massive fangs. Without thinking, he threw the compressed gas gun in the water, swung loose his automatic rifle and reached for the trigger.

Before he could finish the pull, he saw the Instructor come out of hiding. The rocket launcher was mounted on his shoulder.

"No," screamed Hauck. "The gas is flammable."

Too late. The Instructor had already fired. Hauck closed his eyes.

The missile hit it square in the back and the force of it set the beast flying toward Hauck just as its firing ignited the gas and the entire tunnel burst into flames. The blast was so powerful it flipped Hauck over in the air and sent him flying end over end until he landed face down in the water.

He blacked out so quickly he didn't have time to realize how lucky he was that he'd switched to his breathing tank.

*****

Hauck woke to the sound of someone knocking at his door.

"You alive in there?"

"Go away," he said.

"You wish," said a familiar voice. "Now come on, get up 'cause we don't have much time."

"What time is it?" asked Hauck in a distracted voice.

"Who the fuck cares? You want me to bang on your face mask some more? It's time to wake the fuck up before that thing comes back and rips us to shreds. How's that for what time is it?"

He felt himself being flipped over, heard water splash, and then was hauled up and dumped in a sitting position on a hard seat. There were water droplets in front of his eyes like rain on a camera lens. Everything came back to him.

"Did we wound it?"

"We didn't even slow it down. Blast took down part of the ceiling. I almost got hit in the head with that piece of concrete over there when it dropped, but last I saw our buddy it was hauling ass down this tunnel burning like a Christmas tree. Before it hit the first bend the flames were out and it just kept going. Whatever it is, I think it's fucking fireproof."

Hauck slid off the tiny ledge and stood up. He almost fell, but laid a palm on the concrete ledge for balance.

"My ears are still ringing," he said.

The Instructor slapped his helmet so hard Hauck's head bounced inside like a bell-clapper.

"I'm moving, I'm moving."

"Yeah, well not quick enough. You saw how fast that piece of work came at us."

"We keep going the way he came at us maybe we can find Sveta and Zoe."

"He probably already ate them. But it's better than going the way he went."

He probably already ate them.

Hauck tried to go faster.

It bothered Hauck that in spite of what just happened, the tunnel wasn't much different than before the beast ran them over. The water was still filthy. It was still dark. It was silent. And they still seemed like they'd never get there. Except for his headache, it was like it had never happened.

The only thing different was this time the Instructor was in the lead and the monster was behind them.

Age before beauty doesn't cover this, he thought.

Up ahead, the Instructor stopped at a bend in the tunnel and thrust one palm toward Hauck like a crossing guard.

"Did you hear something?" Hauck whispered into his microphone.

"No. We got light up ahead, rock star style. You stay here, I'll check it out."

The Instructor disappeared around the bend and Hauck realized that he was alone in the tunnel where they had just seen the beast.

"I'm coming up behind you," he said.

"Come on up, Dorothy" said the Instructor. "We ain't in Kansas anymore but I think we found Disneyworld."

CHAPTER THIRTY-ONE

Up again or back down?

Up high she could see what was happening. But the ladder didn't lead to an exit. It stopped where the piping dog-legged across the room.

Sveta opted to keep climbing down. So far she'd seen only a handful of men on the floor of the laboratory complex. More were likely upstairs, but unless she could find an air vent before she got to the far side, she would just have to take her chances. She had a duffel full of firepower with her, and, after all that shooting, they might be low on bullets.

By the time she made it to ground level, she heard voices coming from the other side. The difference between gangsters and military trained operatives, she thought, was that criminals always started arguing soonest and loudest. At least she would know where they were.

One thing she didn't have was a compass, and she doubted if she did have one that it would work because of all the electromagnetism. But she knew the rough layout of the place, even without knowing the actual north, south, east and west of it.

On a straight line between her and the stairs she had come down with Drogol and Zoe was the platform where the Tesla tube used to be. That was about half way. Roughly. The area between the long row of stairs and platform held what was left of Mishka's men gathering. She could still hear them arguing with each other like vicious children. Which was what they were. Vicious children with guns.

Best to avoid them if she possibly could.

To her left as she faced the platform was the side where the beast had run at and burst through a section of the wall. She could follow along the edges of that wall until it curved in toward where the long stairs came down. If Mishka's men didn't guard the stairs or left only a single man, she would have her chance. However, she might meet the beast coming back through the tunnel.

The opposite wall to that was unknown territory. If where she came down the stairs originally was north, just for sake of calling it something, then the remaining wall of the complex would be east. That wall seemed the safest. With any luck, she might stumble on the ventilation system and not have to shoot it out for the stairs.

It worked in her favor that the light throughout the technology maze was less. The beast had knocked over towers and globes that lit the place with golden light. There were fewer power beams shooting overhead in their wireless grid. Sveta now had shadows to use as camouflage. She would be less of a target. This was the way that she loved to work. No night vision. No nano-cams. No microphones or wrist screens. No partners. She was on her own.

What is all this stuff? she wondered.

The complex really was like a giant science museum, but without signs explaining what each piece of equipment did. If she knew what some it did, she might be able to use it get out, but that wasn't going to happen in the next few minutes. So no matter how wonderful or powerful these things were or whatever fantastic things they could do, to her they were only ground cover and bullet shields.

She heard only outbursts between the men near the long stairs, but she could no longer see them and moved carefully because she was not certain how many of them were left. Three to five seemed like the best guess. Leave two at the stairs, send the other three out hunting. A good way to do it, except for the monster that had killed their friends. No, Sveta was banking on them all staying near the stairs, however many of them there were. They'd be afraid to leave, but more afraid to stay. She could use that against them if she could just figure out how.

It took her a while to navigate her way over to the far wall. Once along the way she had almost fallen into a fifteen foot pit filled with a phosphorescent liquid that glowed and crackled with lightning-like charges throughout its depths. She grabbed onto a ceramic insulated copper rod to keep herself from falling in, and as she hung there for a moment, she thought that she was looking into a well of liquid lightning.

As she pulled herself back, she heard a faint scraping sound.

Shit.

With a deft, silent movement, she angled off, listening for another sound that would help her place her enemy. After moving ten feet or so, keeping behind a massive set of horizontal silver tubes resting on a skid, she heard what she was looking for. Now the question was go toward or away from whoever it was. The sooner she engaged, the faster her enemy could mount an organized response.

Move away.

As she was stepping over a rubberized black cable thick as a fallen tree trunk, she heard a pained whimper from the same direction. Probably injured. Maybe going to die. So what? Either way it didn't help her get to the stairs. There was nothing she could do for the animal. Besides, no wolf was ever truly tame. If she went to check on it, it would probably attack her. They were Drogol's pets, not hers.

Couldn't do it though.

No good reason.

Just couldn't do it.

Her sound suppressor was on her nine millimeter, so if it looked like the wolf was going to go berserk on her, she'd just shoot it. Best thing for them both.

She turned the corner of a gray motor control panel and there it was, lying on its side, panting like it was out of breath, looking up at her. One wolf looked like another, but she thought this animal looked very much like one of the two Drogol had shooed away. It was a magnificent animal, maybe three feet long and heavy-shouldered. Beautiful, expressive face. Maybe a hundred and fifty pounds. Sharp, long incisors.

The air was rich with the now familiar smell of wet fur and blood.

"You aren't going to make any noise, are you?" she whispered.

The wolf, of course, said nothing.

"What's wrong with you, big boy? Uh-oh. Can I see that paw?"

She moved closer and the wolf did nothing but continue to pant and stare at her with its hypnotic yellow eyes.

"Remember me? I'm the one was with Drogol, the big guy with the wild hair and the messed up beard. Thinks he's Rasputin and talks about everything but what you ask him about. I came down here with him so I'm your friend, okay? I'm not going to hurt you."

She knew what she was doing was stupid, but for some reason kept doing it anyway.

There was a piece of copper wire sticking straight up and through the animal's paw. It couldn't walk. If the wire wasn't removed, the animal would eventually die. If she pulled the wire out and wrapped the wolf's paw, then it would have a chance.

This is a really, really, stupid idea, she thought.

Wolves were intelligent, she knew. They had bigger brains than dogs. But they weren't domesticated. She dropped her duffel and then lowered herself to sit on the ground facing the wolf anyway. Her pistol dangled losing from her left hand while with her right she reached out very slowly to pet the animal. If it moved, she was going to have to shoot it. Maybe she should shoot it and get it over with.

But the wolf did nothing except lay there panting. After a tense moment, it allowed her to scratch behind its ears and talk softly to it. She moved back a bit to see what she could do. Maybe push it part way through, then pull it the rest of the way and try not to get her hand bitten off.

"Lay still, big dog. This will hurt a lot, but you can walk later and stay alive. And tell your other furry friends to leave me alone. Okay, you ready for this?"

As Sveta leaned forward, she slowly reached for the animal's paw. When her fingertips touched it, its eyes suddenly widened and its lips pulled back in a throaty snarl.

A fast, easy trigger pull, and she'd shot the wolf in the head below its right eye. She stared at the blood and pieces of protruding bone.

One second we're alive, she thought, *and the next we're dead.*

"You should have listened to the wolf, woman," said a raspy voice behind her. "Now drop the gun and turn around very slowly."

*****

One man, alone. That's all that's behind me, she thought, *and he's standing too close.*

Sveta put the pistol down on top of the wolf so the man behind her could see what was happening. Her other hand was blocked from his view, and she was in a squatting position, close enough to her ankle to pull free her knife. With a flick of her pistol hand she sent the handgun sliding off the wolf and onto the floor. Nothing threatening, just a millisecond distraction to allow her to spin and jam the knife into his abdomen.

And that's what Sveta did. Driving it furiously through his abdominal muscles and into his intestines, she sawed straight upward. The sheer shock and terror of this action paralyzed his nervous system. He did not pull the trigger on his weapon, he did not pass go. The blood came out in a rush but she kept the serrated edge cutting up still further. She smelled his urine and her arm was soaked with his blood. She hooked the back of his knee with her free hand and pulled to topple him.

Sveta took the knife out. She thought what a wonderful invention the blood groove was. Without that groove, the body's suction sometimes held on to the blade longer than field operatives liked. She wiped as much blood from the knife as she could on his pant legs, then slid it back into its sheath.

There was not much of use on his body.

She'd hoped for a communication link so she could hear what they were saying, but Mishka's thugs weren't all that high tech, it seemed. Big on guns, not so big on communications. Blast everything on sight and talk about it later. But she had all the weaponry she needed in her bag. After a moment's reflection, she scotched that thought and took his pistol and ammunition. It was a good thing, really, that he wasn't connected with a communication link. If he was and he didn't respond on time, the others would know that something was up.

A last look at the dead wolf and she started out again.

Twenty minutes later she was moving along the wall toward her objective.

*****

Still difficult to tell how many of Mishka's men were left.

Sticking her head around a steam boiler to take a look could reveal that she was still alive. Worse, it could get her shot right on the spot. She had to be more careful about this. The intermittent noise from light globes discharging and pressure relief valves releasing jolts of steam made it hard to hear sometimes. No way the man she'd ripped open would've been able to come at her without her hearing something normally.

Sometimes the underground equipment was completely quiet, and she could hear fragments of the men's conversations. Talk like: "I see that thing again I'm going to blow it the fuck apart."

Then the lucky break.

She came upon a giant brass and glass gauge the size of the Winchester Cathedral clock. It stood at a ninety degree angle between her and the bottom area of the stairs where Mishka's men congregated. She dropped down to her knees again to see if she could catch their reflection in the glass, which, although not polished after so many years of neglect underground, might still allow her to see exactly how many men there were.

There was a metal cabinet knocked over on the floor ahead, and if she pulled herself along on her belly, she could stay prone and keep behind it. Spotters looked for intruders at eye level. It was a natural human tendency. Sveta removed anything that could scrape against the brick floor, and then began pulling herself along.

It was a painful way to move, mostly because of her overwhelming fear of being shot in the back while she inched along the bricks. To occupy her mind, she remembered slithering through the mud in basic training while live rounds whistled over her. While she remembered, she keened her ears to anything that would tell her she'd been seen. By the time she made it to the metal cabinet, sweat beaded along her back and she felt as if she'd run five miles with a sixty pound pack strapped to her.

She risked a glance up at the huge gauge and saw three men smoking cigarettes, their automatic weapons slung carelessly from their shoulders. None of them had either hand near the trigger guard. Idiots. Amateurs. Good targets.

Three men out in the open.

Three clean shots.

Easy enough.

She rested for a moment, and slowed her breathing. They'd have to be dropped before they could get off a shot or anyone upstairs, if there was anyone upstairs, would hear the shots. But Sveta didn't think there was anyone upstairs, because no one had come running down for support when the beast attacked. They could be outside, though, on the streets. Still, more men should have come down. They'd been here a long time.

She waited and risked another glance up at the gauge. It would have to be done soon, because if she could see their reflection, they just might be able to see hers. Another calming breath and she moved smoothly to a crouch and rested her pistol on the cabinet.

That was when it went wrong.

Something inside the cabinet started pounding and then shouting.

"Is anyone out there? Anyone? I'm locked inside and can't get out."

It was just loud enough that the men started. They were in motion toward the sound and they saw her instantly.

Sveta began firing.

The first man went down with a headshot. She took out the second the same way. Couldn't risk a body shot in case they were wearing protective armor.

She clipped the third man's ear. He screamed and reached for the side of his head. Sveta was up and running toward him. His AK swung crazily at his side while he tried to staunch the blood.

His eyes widened when he saw her, and he pulled his hands away from his head reaching for his weapon.

Her next bullet caught him in the side of the throat and he dropped, but still writhed on the floor. He'd rolled over and was on his stomach squirming; now pressing his hand to the side of his neck.

Sveta moved to his side and finished him off with a shot to the back of his head. Blood pooled out beneath him and she took a deep breath.

That son of a bitch in the cabinet. His fault the way it went down. And she thought she knew the voice.

After snapping another magazine into her pistol, she went back to the cabinet and kicked it so hard she felt shock all the way up to her hip.

"Hey, Mishka, is that you in there?" she yelled.

"Who...who...Sveta, is that you?"

"It's me."

"Get me out of here. I locked myself in. There's no latch in here to open it from the inside."

"Are you sure you can't get out?" she said.

"Yes I'm sure. Do you think I'd still be here if I could get out?"

"Is air getting inside?"

"Maybe. I don't know," he said. "I'm still alive so I guess there is. But I've been knocked out since that monster shoved this thing over. I hit my head and I think it's bleeding."

"I can hear you so that means there must be some air getting through. Can't you find any way at all to get out, cousin?"

"No, I told you I'm completely sealed in."

"Good," she said, and started walking back toward the stairs.

Then the breath exploded out of her lungs as someone slammed into her back and flattened her. Her face hit the bricks and she saw lights. She felt her nose flatten and fill with blood.

She heard someone scream, "Bitch," and felt a pair of knees press against her back.

Something hard pushed against her skull and then the weight fell away from her. Confused, she tried to clear her head, but her body reacted first, her hands reached under her chest and pressed upward to get her to her knees.

A severed head rolled in front of her and she blinked.

"He was right," she heard a gravelly voice say. "It's a pretty good sword. I like it."

CHAPTER THIRTY-TWO

Sveta wiped blood away from her nose with the back of her hand and got to her feet.

She saw two men, both dressed in black like field operatives, one tall and good looking with dark hair and a hard, careful face and the other a short, extraordinarily muscled older man with smooth skin and deep set eyes.

"Who are you?" she asked.

Her eyes looked for the pistol she had dropped as she spoke and she took a step toward where it fell.

"Uh-uh," said the older man with a smile, and, with a quick movement he used the tip of his sword to slide the pistol to his feet.

"Hauck sent us," said the taller man.

Her face went dark.

"To save you," said the man quickly.

"You lie," said Sveta. "I turned on him. Hauck wants me dead."

The taller man looked uncomfortable.

"If he wanted you dead, you'd already be dead," he said. "The fact that you're alive says we were here to help."

"Shove your finger up right under your nose and push," said the shorter man. "It'll stop the bleeding."

Sveta stared at him incredulously.

"Do what he says," said the other. "He knows what he's talking about."

"Yeah, what he said unless you want to keep bleeding."

She did as she was told and before long, the red flow stopped. She wiped away the excess blood with her sleeve.

"You still look like shit, but you ain't bleeding no more," said the shorter man.

"Who are you?" she asked Hauck.

"I'm ... Anatoly."

"Bullshit. I've never heard of you. And you," she asked the other.

"I'm Prince Charming," said the short man with a grin. "But I left my white horse back on the farm."

"Where's Zoe?" said the tall man.

"Dead."

He looked away, something in his eyes that he did not want her to see.

"Listen, can we just get out of here and talk about this later?" said the other man.

"If Hauck really isn't going to kill me, let me have my gun."

"I don't think so, girlie," said the short man.

"Let her have it."

"Your funeral," said the other.

He reached down, picked up the pistol, and gave it to her, barrel first. He moved closer to her, waiting for her next move, but Sveta turned it around and looked at the tall man.

"Okay for now. How'd you get in?"

"Same way as that creature. I don't suggest we go back that way."

"What about the explosion?"

"Later. Where do these stairs go?"

"Up to street level. I don't know how many men are still left out there."

"Not enough," said the Instructor. "Let's go."

"After you," Sveta said to the tall man.

"Hey, you hear that?"

"What?" said the tall man.

"It sounds like somebody yelling in a tin can."

"It's nothing," Sveta said. "Somebody left a radio on. You don't hear anything."

The short man said, "I like her, you think she's too young for me?"

And they went up. The tall man in the lead, Sveta in the middle, and the short, muscular man taking up the rear position. No one spoke on the way.

When they made it to the last platform right before the metal door that Mishka's men had blown wide open, the tall man leaned back to her and spoke.

"Keep it low, keep it soft," he said, and turned to climb the last few stairs.

Sveta moved as quickly as she'd ever moved, snaking an arm around his neck, spinning him around so that he was between her and the short man while pressing her pistol to the side of his neck.

"Hello, Hauck," she whispered in his ear.

*****

"Sveta," he began.

"Shut up," she said, "and drop your pistol nice and slowly."

"We ain't got time for reunions," said the short man quietly.

"I can explain."

"You don't need to explain. Lies and more lies. Zoe's dead. How many others because of you?"

"There are always risks in what we do, you know that."

"Don't give me that shit. You kept me in the dark every step of the way on this. You keep everyone in the dark so you can play your spy games. Drogol was right. You have no heart. You don't care who dies as long as you get what you want."

The short man took a small step forward.

"I'll kill him," she said.

"Honey, if you were going to kill him, you'd have already done it."

She got a tight grip on Hauck's throat and aimed the pistol at the other man.

"Now if you don't put that away, I'm going to have to take it away from you and hurt you."

Sveta had enough. She lowered the pistol and shot at his legs.

Except he wasn't there anymore.

He was suddenly right beside her with his hand clamped on her wrist. Incredible pain shot through her forearm as he twisted it and grabbed hold of her neck. She almost screamed in agony as he yanked her head to the side and she could no longer feel anything but her spine compressing in on itself. Her pistol dropped to the floor as she fell to her knees completely unable to move. She no longer had control of her body.

The Instructor leaned over and kissed her on the cheek.

"Honey, you're good, but I'm a hell of a lot better," he said.

*****

"Let her go," said Hauck, massaging his neck.

"You crazy? She just tried to shoot me in the leg."

"My fault. I should have told her who I was."

"You don't know nothing about women. You told her who you was and she would have shot you right then."

Hauck squatted down in front of Sveta and looked her straight in the eye.

"Sveta, please trust me on this. I never knew that things would get this far out of control. Believe me. I was trying to do it the best way I knew how. I was wrong. But you can shoot me later if you want, after I've told you everything."

He waited for an answer.

"She can't talk, Bozo," said the Instructor. "She's kind of paralyzed right now."

"Let her go. If she shoots me I probably deserve it."

The Instructor looked down at Sveta and smiled.

"Ain't love grand?" he said.

*****

They encountered no one on the rest of the way to the building. The Instructor checked around while Hauck dismantled the GPS in the SUV. Neither he nor Sveta spoke a word to each other as he did so. Sirens blared in the distance as though there were a major fire somewhere in the direction of downtown.

"Lot of bodies outside," said the Instructor when he returned.

"Evgeny had it under surveillance."

"Evgeny had shit to do with it. They're pretty well ripped to pieces and chewed up."

Hauck started the SUV. Sveta got in the front passenger seat and the Instructor got in the back.

"Let's roll," he said.

They backed out onto the street, and then Hauck sped away without so much as a backward glance at the bodies. He could feel Sveta staring at him as he reattached his throat mic.

"Yuri," he said.

"Where the fuck have you been? All hell has broken loose everywhere. Evgeny's dead and your monster has gone public."

"Evgeny is dead?"

Sveta turned away and stared out into the night.

"What happened? Tell me everything."

So Yuri did.

"Fucking thing is on national television now. It's running through the streets of Detroit nailing everything in its path. Cops everywhere. Helicopters. They're shooting up the place like it's a war zone."

That would explain the sirens, he thought.

"Son of a bitch just threw a police car into the GM Building," shouted Yuri.

'What's going on?" asked the Instructor.

Hauck told him.

Sveta listened with her mouth open.

"Threw a police car into them big towers?" said the Instructor. "Man, I wish I was there to see that."

"Homeland Security's all over this," said Yuri. "They're going nuts. Chatter on the official wires is screaming hot. They're sending everything they've got after it. I think they're bringing the military into action."

"Time to disappear," said Hauck. "This is totally out of control."

"Anna Kazakova is dead," added Yuri. "I picked it up a while ago before this went crazy. Heart attack. Hold on, shit, the damned thing just downed a helicopter. You ought to see this shit. It's on every channel."

"Listen to me, Yuri. Listen hard. Close everything down. We're coming to the firehouse and from there we'll wind things up. Do you understand? We have to move quickly."

"I've got you boss, but they just fired a missile at it, but it moved out of the way and the Joe Louis Arena exploded."

"We're on our way."

"So what's going on?" said the Instructor. "Give me the juicy."

Hauck told them both.

Sveta stared coldly at Hauck.

"See what you've done?" she said. "All this because of your obsession."

"A fucking helicopter?" said the Instructor. "I'm telling you, we're missing out on all the good stuff."

*****

The beast was invincible.

Power flowed through it, supercharging its body with such bursts of resonant energy the pavement shook beneath it. Blinding helicopter floodlights targeted it. Round after round of bullets pounded into its body, but each impact seemed only to make it stronger as the Tesla resonance energy absorbed and multiplied it back outward.

And it exulted in this sensation.

In the beast, power and destruction existed as one.

Traffic was a confusion of crushed cars and bleeding people. Police personnel bullhorning commands to the stampeding crowds were drowned out by the sounds of sirens, gunshots, explosions and the roaring of the monster.

Behind it, a shattered Joe Louis Arena burned. Fire trucks couldn't find their way through the tangle of upside down, crushed vehicles. Water shot out and up into an arcing spray from broken fireplugs.

The corner of West Jefferson and Woodward was like an opening night riot. Painfully bright halogens strobed the streets arcing crazily as helicopters swooped in and out. The creature changed direction so fast it was all they could to avoid mid-air collisions. Street lights shattered and sparked as bullets strafed the scene. The beast leaped to the side of the old Ponchartrain Hotel and began scrambling up its side, smashing windows with clawed hands and feet and using ledges for purchase. Jets screeched through the night sky.

A police helicopter moved too close and the creature thrust back from its position two thirds up the side of the Ponchartrain Hotel, arcing back with extended claws and jaws opened wide. In a blind rage it grabbed the landing skids and swung back and forth. The helicopter rocked from the impact, canting and swinging wildly. The beast reached one clawed hand up and smashed through the cockpit windshield. It yanked the pilot with such force it broke him free from his seatbelt With an angry roar the monster threw him out into the night.

A cabin door slid open and a policewoman decked in full riot gear leaned out with a long barreled rifle. She aimed directly at the top of the creature's wire-haired head and pulled the trigger. She fired until her weapon was empty and then struggled to keep her balance long enough to slap a new ammunition clip into place.

The helicopter rocked wildly to one side. Dangling from her safety strap, she looked straight down into the yellow eyes and slavering maw of the monster and began to scream. The swirl of malevolent yellow eyes fixed on her horror as it slashed viciously upward at her. Its sharp claws cut through her and she burst open like a sack of blood.

The creature released its grip on the helicopter skid and dropped straight down. The sensation of free fall lit its nerves with pleasure.

Impact.

It landed on a SRT personnel van with a sound like a tin can being stomped flat. Broken fragments of safety glass flew outward, spraying a man and woman clutching to each other as they pressed against the side of a building. A jagged shard sliced into the woman's eye and she screamed. Gasoline poured from the ruptured fuel tank.

"Stay inside, stay inside. All citizens must stay inside for your own safety," blared an electronic bullhorn as the beast tore off down the street.

Seconds later, the helicopter came crashing onto the flattened SRT. An exploding fireball shot straight upward with a blast so powerful, windows shattered down West Jefferson, spraying the night with deadly glass projectiles.

Across the river, Canadians lined their side of the riverbank, watching the chaos through binoculars and telescopes. The Windsor Tunnel was blocked by collisions and pileups. Terrified people abandoned their cars and tried to make it on foot. Shots were fired and a mobilized Border Patrol locked down the Canadian tunnel entrance.

High above the water, the Ambassador Bridge was a mass of stalled and abandoned cars. It was a giant parking lot of honking horns, fist fights and shootings. A bus lay on its side crumpled and smoking after a head on collision with a tractor-trailer. It was impossible to pass either way in the panic. Within half an hour of the beast's entrance onto Detroit's center stage, the bridge that carried one fourth of the commerce between the United States and Canada became a battleground of people so terrified they would maim or kill their neighbors to escape.

The Detroit River itself was a scramble of Coast Guard vessels herding ships like cattle to safer pastures. Military assets from both the United States and Canada turned the river into a barrier the beast could not cross.

But it was now headed for I-75, with an entourage of police vehicles, helicopters and fighter jets keeping up with it almost as well as the television news crews.

CHAPTER THIRTY-THREE

The monster bounded on four legs like a giant wolf tearing through a rusted steel forest. Twenty feet tall and growing. A blur of wire-brush hair, teeth and claws.

It threw cars over the edge of the freeway overpass in a sparking shower of shrieking metal and exploding plastic. The immense power of Tesla's resonance waves shot through its body with each chaotic act. Sirens blared their warning across the night. The constant noise created more confusion as panic spread.

Rain mixed with 50 caliber rounds poured from the sky like an angry judgment. The beast's heart pumped rage and power. It exulted in the chaos and destruction.

Up ahead lay a sprawling production refinery with lighted towers and distillation columns surrounded by acres of gigantic storage vessels. Thick, gray clouds of steam billowed up from its operations and wrapped its machinery in a somber cloak.

After a quick, defiant upward glance at its enemies, the monster reared back its head, fixed its eyes on the pale red moon and roared. Before the echoes had died away, it was bounding toward the refinery, pulled toward it by an image of flashing red atop one of the towers.

Its pursuers blasted away with no effect. The city of Detroit was a war zone, but the beast moved so quickly and erratically that most of the rounds and ordinance tore up empty ground. Nothing in their planning had prepared the security forces for an enemy that moved with such blinding speed and lashed out with such destructive power.

The night lit suddenly with a terrifying yellow-orange radiance when a plane tore through high-voltage power wires. Live wires ripped through the air and snapped against the ground like manic spider legs.

When the beast reached the refinery, frantic commands were issued to security personnel to cease firing, to pull back. But as the monster clawed up the side of a storage vessel painted up like a giant basketball in honor of the Detroit Pistons basketball team, bullets strafed after him. Suddenly an angry explosion erupted into the night skies the likes of which no one had ever seen.

*****

"Fuck, would you look at that," said the Instructor.

They were at the firehouse, which Yuri, following Hauck's instructions, had cleared of all other personnel for the meeting. Curtains were drawn and only a single solitary desk lamp lit the room. They were assembled around banks of monitors that Yuri had hooked into the national and local news stations which showed endless loops of video and still footage of the refinery explosion. In the heat of combat, where one mistake leads to another, flying pieces of metal ripped open other storage vessels that exploded like fireworks strung on a line. A running tally of dead refinery workers was displayed on the screens while reporters interviewed families of those who had died.

"They tried to put a lid on news coverage soon as this started, but there was no way. No way at all. It was too late. YouTube took it viral and I think Facebook is overloaded with everybody in the country talking about it. The government started shutting down websites and Twitter feeds, but there was no way for them to keep up. The Feds are used to control and this thing just can't be controlled."

Sveta watched with the rest of them. She tried to keep a grip on her emotions, but the awe and terror she saw played out on the screens was too much. Hauck paced the room, unable to sit down for a moment. The Instructor slid a chair next to Yuri's to get a front row seat. Yuri alternated between watching the destruction and stealing glances at Hauck. He'd never really thought he would ever see the man's face.

"If we would have just left him alone," said Sveta, "none of this would have happened. None of this."

Hauck raised his hands in frustration.

"Left him alone? He's a monster. Look at what he's capable of. And it's not we who have caused this destruction, it is Drogol himself."

"They're not reporting any sign of him," said Yuri. "Consensus is that he was destroyed in the explosion."

The Instructor looked over at Hauck, who looked away.

"We must debrief before we separate," said Hauck. "I need to know everything that means something before we disappear."

"Debrief," said Sveta. "What are you, a machine? How about we mourn for our dead first?"

"Sveta," began Hauck.

"Have you no heart at all? Zoe is dead. Evgeny is dead. Crue is dead. I could have been killed. All of those people who died when the beast ran loose tonight, have you no thought for them?"

"Of course I feel them. But I also feel for those of us left alive. We didn't kill those people."

"You may not have pulled the trigger, but you killed them" said Sveta coldly.

"Get hold of yourself. You are a field operative. I have to hear what you learned from Drogol so that I know what to do to protect us."

Sveta stood, knocking over her chair, which hit the floor with a loud bang.

"Could you two keep it down," said the Instructor. "I'm trying to listen to television."

"And who—and don't lie to me anymore—who is this evil little man?"

"Evil little man? I like that," said the Instructor.

"We have to stay on point, Sveta. We have so little time. What happened to you in that underground complex?"

She walked up to him, and, only a foot away, propped her fists on her hips.

"Did you know that since the moment I went to work for you, I wondered what you were like? I fantasized meeting you someday. And now that I've met you, do you know what I want most?"

"This ought to be good," the Instructor leaned over and whispered to Yuri.

"No, I do not, and now is not the time."

Sveta made a slight pivot as though to turn away, but turned back in a smooth motion and drove her fist forward and up into Hauck's chin. He flew back, taken completely by surprise, and crashed to the floor.

"What'd I tell you?" said the Instructor.

But she wasn't through. She was on him, her knees pinning down his biceps, and she started swinging. He twisted and turned his head to avoid the blows. He arched and tried to throw her off to the side, but she was too practiced a fighter. Blood flowed from a split lip and he was only saved when she missed his head with a straight-on punch and hit the hardwood floor instead.

As she drew her hand back in pain, he reached up and grabbed her sweater, gathering it in his fasts. With a quick roll he sent her flying.

"Enough of that shit. Can we get down to business?" said the Instructor.

Sveta sat up and held her injured hand.

"I should kill you," she said.

"I'm bleeding," he said in disbelief.

Hauck's high shirt collar had popped open, revealing an ugly, congealed scar at the base of his neck. When he saw Sveta looking at it, he hurriedly buttoned it.

"Yeah, well push your finger in that spot under your nose like I showed her so you don't mess up the floor."

The old man was out of his chair and walked over to stand in front of them.

"You," he said to Sveta, "have got talent. You, Hauck, you should have seen that coming."

She got to her feet and confronted the Instructor, looking down at him.

"You tell me since he won't. Who are you?"

The Instructor looked over at Hauck and raised an eyebrow. Hauck nodded and got to his feet, heading toward a roll of paper towels to soak up the blood and put ice on his jaw.

"Me? You want to know who I am, girlie?"

"Don't call me that."

The Instructor laughed.

"I'm the boogeyman, *girlie*. I'm the bad man that people with money call when they want something done nobody else can do."

"Is that so?" said Sveta contemptuously.

"That's the way it is. Hauck said you were GRU. Is that right?"

"Go on."

"I did work for them. Did work for the CIA and the rest of them, too. I don't care what side I'm on. I just do the job. I kill people, I rescue people and it's all the same to me."

"You're like him," she said, pointing at Hauck.

"Him? You think so? I trained him, but me and him are different. He's good, I give him that. He's a smart bastard, except he don't know when to duck, ain't that right, Hauck?"

Hauck was too busy putting an ice pack on his jaw to answer.

"The way it is, Hauck's got a conscience, and that gets in the way. All he would talk about before we came after you was how he wasn't going to let you and that other chick die."

A look of confusion crossed Sveta's face, but she did not turn to look at Hauck.

"Zoe," she said. "Her name was Zoe."

"Whatever. Point is, he wasn't going to let you die. Me, all I wanted was to whack that thing. That's what I was getting paid for. If you or Zoe got in the way, well that would have been too bad."

Sveta finally turned to look at Hauck.

From his chair at the computer bank, Yuri watched, hanging on every word.

"Is this true?" she asked.

"What's the difference?" he said.

"Is it true?"

"Yes, it's true, all right. I'm not a monster."

"Then why didn't you tell me what Drogol was in the first place?"

"Because I thought it was a safe situation. He is eighty years old for God's sake and Zoe had him convinced you were the reincarnation of Alexandra."

"And Crue?

"Crue knew everything going in. Drogol killed my brother and Crue's father at Ryazan. He was supposed to take out Drogol. Chenko thought he was there to collect a tranquilized beast and return it to Russia for Anna Kazakova. We were going to send him back with a picture of Drogol's dead body. Do you think I really believed they would take the price off my head?"

"You couldn't have told me this?"

"I told you what I thought you needed to know. How was I supposed to know that he would turn into the beast before you arrived?"

"That's the point," she shouted back at him. "I was on your team and you sent me in blind to a situation where you didn't have enough controls in place."

"Hauck," said Yuri, "there's something you have to know. With all this going on I forgot to tell you."

"Know what? Tell me."

Hauck was glad for the distraction.

So Yuri brought up the two images, side by side as before. Sveta, Hauck, and the Instructor closed about him in a tight semicircle to see.

"Uh-oh," said the Instructor.

"What is this, Yuri?" said Hauck.

"Two different beasts," said Sveta.

"Like she said. The one picture is from Evgeny's remote camera, taken after it … after it killed him. The other is taken from the night we raided Drogol's house."

Hauck steepled his fingers and stared, the confusion on his face evident. Moments passed in silence as he took in the implications.

"Is this our problem?" asked the Instructor.

Another pause.

"No," said Hauck. "There's nothing we can do. Homeland Security is involved and every police and emergency force in the area. We have to clear out by tomorrow or eventually we'll be caught in the net."

"I can't believe this," said Sveta. "There's another monster running around out there killing people and you're just going to run?"

"He'll let them know," said Yuri, "but by an anonymous, untraceable tip."

"Thank you, Yuri," said Hauck. "I can speak for myself. And, yes, that's what we will do. They are better equipped to handle this than we are."

"What will you tell them?"

"I'll have to think about that, Sveta. If this second thing is like Drogol, how exactly will I tell them that there is a man who sometimes turns into a monster? Don't answer. I'll come up with a way."

"Two of them, huh? But this one here looks like a baby version," said the Instructor.

"I did extrapolations," said Yuri. "It's about six and a half feet tall— best estimate."

"Am I still bleeding?" said Hauck.

"Okay, *Sveta*," said the Instructor, drawing out her name, "your turn. What have you got? What did you find out down there?"

"Yuri," said Hauck. "Get her a drink. Get us all a drink."

"Didn't I teach you not to drink on the job?" said the Instructor.

"Make mine a double, no ice," said Hauck.

Five minutes later, Sveta told them everything that occurred in the underground complex.

*****

Throughout her entire retelling of the events, Hauck betrayed no emotions and asked no questions. Sveta was an experienced operative and left nothing of consequence out. At the recounting of Zoe's death, however, his face tightened and he looked down at the floor as though in silent prayer.

When she was finished, Yuri whistled.

"So you're saying Drogol brought Zoe, back from the dead once, healed her again and you, too?"

Sveta finished her drink.

"I know how it sounds, but I was there."

"That's not possible," said Yuri.

"Neither is him turning into a monster," she said.

"I get your point."

She looked at Hauck, and saw him exchange a glance with the Instructor.

"You say," he said, "that he believed cutting off his head was the only way to kill him?"

"Not counting an exploding oil refinery," said Yuri.

"Please, Yuri. Is that what he told you?"

"Yes, it was."

"So we know how they can kill this other one?" said the Instructor.

"That's what I was thinking."

"You knew nothing about this second creature?" asked Sveta.

"No, believe me," said Hauck. "I had no intelligence whatsoever about its existence. Although considering the werewolf legends, I should have had a suspicion. But Drogol's case is so different than all of the lore. That is, if he indeed was hit by a blast of energy as he was bit by another werewolf that would explain why he was unique. You know, I thought all along that he was deranged, thinking he was Rasputin, but after seeing for myself the underground complex and hearing your story, I'm not so sure."

"Who cares?" said the Instructor. "Are we done here? The big bad wolf blew himself up and the Feds will take care of the little one. Because if we are done, I'd like to get out of here and go home."

Hauck looked at them each in turn, rubbing his jaw as he did so.

"Yes, we're done. Yuri will wire money to your account, Sveta, plus a substantive bonus."

"What about me?" said the Instructor.

"I'll take care of you," said Hauck. "Any other questions, anyone?"

"No," said Yuri.

"I'm going to bed," said the Instructor.

"Why are you lying to me again?" said Sveta.

"What are you talking about?"

Sveta got back in his face.

"You don't think Drogol is dead, do you? I saw the way you looked at the old man. For once in your life, just come out and tell me the truth."

"It's not our problem, Sveta. If he's alive, and I am saying *if*, we don't even know where he is."

Sveta turned to the Instructor.

"He's lying again, isn't he?"

"Pretty good bet."

"Where do we find him, Hauck?"

Hauck looked as miserable as he felt. His jaw was swelling in spite of the earlier ice treatment; his lip was cracked again and began to bleed.

"Tell me, Hauck," she said, "or I'm going to hit you again."

Finally he broke.

"He'll return to the underground complex."

"And how do you know he's not dead?"

"Because he's fucking fireproof," said the Instructor. "You should have seen him burning down in the sewers. Son of a bitch kept on running after I nuked him with a shoulder-fired rocket."

"So what do we do?" asked Yuri.

"I think we're going to have to cut his head off," said the Instructor.

Sveta suddenly remembered something.

"Hauck, did you choose me because I looked like the Tsarista Alexandra?"

He hesitated.

"I should hit you again," said Sveta.

CHAPTER THIRTY-FOUR

Yuri, to his relief, was told to stay behind.

And despite Hauck's forceful objections, Sveta was going anyway.

"I started this with you, and I'm going to finish it with you," she said. "And besides, I believe that he trusts me."

Hauck sent a team to dispose of the bodies outside of the building where the other beast had killed Mishka's men. What was left of Evgeny was collected to be given a proper, if anonymous, burial. Hauck and the Instructor retrieved Zoe's body, to be given the same treatment as Evgeny.

After that was in order, they finished preparations.

The Instructor went armed only with his newly favorite sword, Hauck took a machete and Sveta, contrary to her wishes, ended up with another machete. They also went armed with rifles and plenty of ammunition."

"For the wolves," said Hauck.

But when it came to loading their vehicle with explosives, Sveta demanded to know why.

"Because," he said, "if we can't kill it I'm going to bury it by blowing that place up. It might not kill it, but it may contain it."

He reached out then in a sudden, unexpected gesture and took her hands. It startled her so that she stepped back, but he held firm.

"Listen to me, Sveta. If it comes to that, if there's nothing else we can do, then I want you and the Instructor to get out. Get out as fast as you can. I'll detonate the explosives."

"You're crazy. I'm not going to leave you down there to die. Detonate them by remote."

His face was emotionless and his voice was calm, as though he were discussing the weather.

"I can't take that chance. We lost contact with the surface for a while down there, so I can't be sure that it would work."

"But Zoe contacted you to let you know where we were."

"We never received a transmission from Zoe. The only way we knew where to find you was because Anna's men tracked your vehicle's GPS and we intercepted their communications. You see, there's really no other way to be sure that the explosives detonate."

"I warned him about getting a conscience," said the Instructor.

*****

Although they took sufficient provisions, it was the third night before Drogol appeared.

They saw no wolves the entire time that they were there, as though they had never been there in the first place. The smell of death and decay began to permeate the air. The bodies of Mishka's men lay where they had fallen. Golden light from the remaining globes still gave them light enough to see, but to Sveta they were no longer magic.

The first night they spent placing explosive charges throughout the complex. It was difficult work considering the size of the place, but with Hauck and the Instructor's expertise, they were able to place them. The idea was to take out enough key wall and structural support to bring the ceiling down. Hauck wasn't worried about risk to anyone overhead because, as he said, it was a vacant area of the city. He kept the radio activated detonator in his pocket.

While Sveta and Hauck took turns sleeping in the same small building where Drogol had healed Sveta and Zoe after they were attacked, the Instructor roamed the complex seeming to need no sleep at all.

On the second night, he told them he'd come across a recess in one of the walls filled with human bone fragments.

"Bones?" asked Sveta.

"Yep."

"How many?" asked Hauck.

The Instructor looked at him as though he'd lost his mind.

"You think I counted them? Shit, must be thirty or forty people, but it's hard to tell. They've been chewed on pretty bad. Want to see them?"

Sveta and Hauck both declined.

While they waited, the two of them talked off and on. Hauck told her in detail about the killings at the prison that changed his life. He told her how his brother had been a guard there. He told her about his life on the run since that night.

She asked him about Zoe and he told her what he knew.

They talked about the mystery of Drogol and his transformations, of werewolves and curses.

"Do you think that it's possible," she asked. "that what he said about Tunguska and the Tesla ray actually happened?"

"I don't know," he said.

"Do you think that he is responsible for what he's done?"

"Who else?"

"But he didn't choose to become a monster. And he spent his life trying to cure the disease."

"I'm a spy, Sveta, not a philosopher. And he should have killed himself if he knew what he'd become."

"How?" she asked. "We weren't able to kill him."

"Stuck his head in a guillotine and pulled the cord. I don't know. I have to sleep. You stand guard."

On the third night, while he was dreaming of his brother for the first time in years, Sveta came in to the building, sat on the edge of his cot and shook his shoulder gently. His eyes snapped open.

"What?" he asked.

"He's here," she said simply.

Hauck reached for his machete.

*****

Drogol stood on the Tesla tube platform, wearing the same black priest's robes he wore when Sveta first saw him. He was looking out across the complex, a distant, sad smile on his face.

She and Hauck went slowly up the steps to meet him. Hauck's agitation was evident to Sveta, though he tried to hide it. The machete dangled from his right hand. Sveta's hung from her belt in a canvas sheathe. As they ascended the steps, Drogol turned to look at them.

"So," he said in a soft voice. "You come to end my wretched days. I knew you would not fail me, Tsarista."

This time, Sveta did not correct him. She had come to see Drogol in a different light. Despite his violent other self, she had come to pity him.

"And you, you are much older, Hauck. That is your name, isn't it? Who else would the Tsarista bring to my execution than the man with no heart?"

"You killed my brother," said Hauck. "I won't have tears for you and his soul will finally rest in peace."

Drogol flared, and the sudden anger in his face made both Sveta and Hauck take a step back. For a moment, he seemed about to burst into rage, but then, slowly, his fury subsided.

"The beast that comes through me killed your brother," he said. "As you see me now, I have never taken another's life. I have been poisoned and stabbed and shot and thrown into a freezing river to die, but I have never done the same to another."

The two men stood looking at each other. Hauck's fingers tightened on the handle of his machete, while Drogol removed a cross and thin chain from a hidden pocket and put it around his neck.

"I am ready to die tonight, and I see you have come prepared to execute me. The Tsarista has heard my confession, so what else is for me to do but kneel and be set free. I cannot live with myself. I cannot be both beast and man, and I would rather die as a man than live as a beast."

Simple, so simple, thought Sveta and she felt tears forming but blinked them away. He offers no defense, no excuses. *It was not me, he was saying, it was the beast but I am the beast.* Sveta had no idea what to think anymore.

"You have created another creature," said Hauck. "Now it, too, runs the streets killing innocents."

"Another? Yes, it is this wretched curse. The wolf-beast bites and who lives to see another day will turn at the next full moon. That is the legend."

"Is it true?" asked Sveta.

And it hit her at that moment. Here, in the underground complex, they were talking to the being who days before had been on a killing rampage, leaving hundreds of dead behind as evidence of his monstrosity. Was this what the judges at Nuremberg felt like when they talked to Nazi war criminals?

"It is true," he said. "Some legends are true and some are imaginings, but this one is true. Some do not turn, though, ever in their lives. No one has ever known why. But if they have children after having been bitten, old, very old legends tell us that their children will transform. Not at once, but on a special night of alignment when the full moon burns pale red in the sky, that night the curse overtakes them. Each full moon from then on, they will be under the curse and will … become a monstrosity."

He turned to Hauck and said, "Remember well what I have told you. You must sever that one's head to destroy it. There is no other way."

Hauck seemed to go rigid.

"Now, I will kneel and pray, then you must do as I told you," Drogol told Sveta.

"I can't," she said.

"Do not let me die at the hand of a man with no heart," he replied.

And then he knelt and began to pray.

"Father," he began, "I have confessed my sins to you and now accept the blade of justice which will restore me to a true man again by freeing me from this curse. I—"

Hauck kicked him square in the side of the head, knocking Drogol onto his side.

"What did you say?" Hauck spat.

He kicked him again in the face.

"Tell me, you bastard. Tell me again, what did you say?"

Sveta grabbed his arm to pull him away.

"What are you doing?" she shouted. "Get hold of yourself."

But Hauck was like a wild man. He threw her off and went to kick Drogol again, but Drogol was up and on his feet. His face was contorted with a terrifying look of rage.

"You dare kick me, a holy man, while I pray for my release and salvation? I will kill you with my own hands."

Drogol rushed forward and grabbed Hauck by the neck, lifting him into the air and shaking him. Hauck's machete dropped to the platform and he began beating at Drogol's arms.

"Stop," screamed Sveta. "Stop it, both of you."

She pulled out her pistol and aimed it between them.

"You stop or I swear I'll shoot both of you."

Drogol, at that moment, his face flush with hatred, began to change. She saw the dark shimmering she had seen before. With a sudden, growing sense of horror she threw away her pistol and pulled her machete out from its sheath. She stepped toward the two men but could not find a way to swing at Drogol without killing Hauck. Drogol was walking around the stage still shaking his enemy. Hauck was turning color. He'd scrunched down his neck to stop from being strangled, but Drogol's grip was too powerful for that to work for long.

Sveta's mind burned through scenarios but couldn't come up with anything. With each passing second, the twisting darkness spread further over Drogol. Soon it would be too late. She would have to risk killing Hauck.

But before she stepped forward she saw a flash of movement onto the stage followed by a glint of polished metal. There was the little man with his sword. Drogol's head dropped to the platform and rolled away before his lifeless hands let go of Hauck. Drogol's body stood for a few seconds more before falling over.

*****

Sveta pulled Hauck into a sitting position. She lifted his chin to examine his throat and saw Drogol's fingerprints. Hauck coughed and gagged and crawled away to throw up.

"You see why they pay me the big bucks," said the Instructor.

Sveta stared at him. He was the craziest man she had ever met.

"I think so," she said.

"Another couple seconds and Hauck would have been dead, too. I cut it kind of close," he admitted.

Nothing can ever be more surreal than this moment, Sveta thought.

Drogol's head lay there, blood seeping onto the platform from the neck. His body lay fallen with his arms outstretched and his legs together like a horrifying religious symbol.

"You want I should throw that head over the side?" asked the Instructor.

Sveta sat down, exhausted. She laid her machete next to her.

"Machete's good, but you got to know how to use it," he said. "You okay, Hauck?"

"I'm going to live, I think. I'll be off of solid foods for a while," he said, massaging his throat, "but I'll make it."

"That's good, that's real good, now what do you say we get

out of here? We can still blow it up on the way out if you want."

The Instructor walked over and kicked Drogol's head off the platform like it was a football.

Sveta recoiled in horror.

"Can't forget the body," said the Instructor.

Sveta turned and crawled toward Hauck to avoid seeing the old man throw it over the side. She took a rag out of her pocket as an offering.

"Thank you."

"Now tell me what the hell that was all about? You almost got us all killed."

Hauck leaned forward and covered his face with his hands and sat there, saying nothing.

"What's the matter with him? He sick?"

Sveta waved the Instructor off.

"What happened, Hauck, why did you go off like that?"

After a few moments more of silence, Hauck got to his feet with Sveta's help.

"I have a son," he said finally.

"You got a kid?" said the Instructor. "Congratulations but so what?"

With trembling fingers, Hauck opened his high collar and pulled his shirt open, revealing the scar Sveta had seen earlier.

"In the prison, when we were attacked, Drogol bit me."

"But—"

"I have a son," he repeated. "And he was brought here by Anna Kazakova. He was our child."

She looked at him in horror.

"You and Anna Kazakova?"

"Before the disease took her, when she was younger, she was a very beautiful and powerful woman. She was older than me, and she was my superior, but she was—"

"No shit," said the Instructor.

"She raised him. Time passed and there was no way for me ever to have contact with him. I was not a part of his life. But she brought him here days ago to find Drogol. The night that the second beast killed Evgeny, there was a red moon, just as he said. He caused my son to have his curse, too. I hated him more at that second than I thought I could hate anything or anyone. If I could bring him back to life again I would do it just so we could kill him again."

They stood together on the platform for a long time before leaving.

On the way to the stairs, the Instructor said to Sveta, "I heard some more scratching from that cabinet lying on its side and I was going to stick my sword through it and poke around, but I didn't."

"Good," said Sveta.

At the door that Mishka's men had blown apart, Hauck removed the detonator from his pocket.

"When we leave here, it's over," she said to him, laying a hand on his arm.

He shook his head.

"No, he's my son. I can't ignore what I know. I can't call the authorities anymore. I have to find him. There must be some way to stop him, some way to help him. I abandoned him once. I can't do it again."

"Let it go, Hauck," said the Instructor.

"I can't," he said simply. "This is for me to do alone."

"The missus is going to hate you for this, you know that? She already hates you. I stay here looking for your kid and she's going to blow a gasket."

"You don't owe me anything. I would be dead back there without you. Sveta and I both would be dead without you."

"You hear that, girlie? What do you think of that?"

Sveta laid a hand over Hauck's, carefully choosing the hand without the detonator. She looked at him for a long time before saying, "I told you I started this with you and I'm going to finish it with you. And if you hold off on pushing that button, Yuri might be able to find something down here to help save your son. Drogol must have left notes. He said he found something in alchemical literature that had to do with colloidal gold and for years it kept his transformations in check."

"Perhaps," he said thoughtfully.

"But Hauck," she said.

"Yes?"

"If you lie to me again or hide something from me, I'm going to shoot you."

Hauck smiled for the first time since she'd met him. He looked out over the complex and then said, "It could make a good base of operations, you know. We would have to rebuild it, but it could work."

He put the detonator back in his pocket and they entered the hallway.

"I'm going to have to go home every now and then to get laid," said the Instructor as they walked. "I'm just saying."

About the Author

Ferrel Moore is a Michigan writer specializing in dark fiction. His stories have appeared over the years in anthologies from Elder Signs Press and Sams Dot Publishing. A lifelong passion for the martial arts and esoteric pursuits frequently find their way into his writing.

His new novel *The Ghost Box* will be out in 2012. Currently, he is working on the sequel to *Tainted Blood*, which is tentatively titled *The White Death*.

You can contact him via his blog at
thewriterandthewhitecat.blogspot.com

www.ingramcontent.com/pod-product-compliance
Lightning Source LLC
Chambersburg PA
CBHW071138260626
47162CB00003B/835